A DANGEROUS LOVE

"Sam," she moaned his name, and he knew then that he could not let her go. He would never let Zora go.

She pulled away from him, her breath coming in fast, hard gasps. Then, she said, "Do you still think that I want to beg Milton to take me back?"

He shook his head. "I think you've effectively dispelled that notion."

He watched as her lips curved into a smile. By God, he wanted to kiss her again.

"I'm glad that's settled," she replied. "Are you still going to send me away?"

"No," said Sam, "God help me, I'm not sending you away. We started this journey together, and we're going to finish it."

He couldn't let her go. His good sense had flown out of his head with one kiss. Lord, help me, he thought as he looked at the woman he'd fallen in love with.

Zora smiled at him and any hope he had of sticking to his guns and sending her home was lost.

"Well," said Zora, "what are we waiting for? Let's go catch ourselves an art thief."

PORTRAIT OF DECEPTION

JANETTE McCARTHY LOUARD

KENSINGTON PUBLISHING CORP.
http://www.kensingtonbooks.com

For Cecille,
who will forever be in that
beautiful island in the sun

DAFINA BOOKS are published by

Kensington Publishing Corp.
850 Third Avenue
New York, NY 10022

All Kensington titles, imprints and distributed lines are
available at special quantity discounts for bulk purchases for
sales promotion, premiums, fund-raising, educational or in-
stitutional use.

Special book excerpts or customized printings can also be
created to fit specific needs. For details, write or phone the
office of the Kensington Special Sales Manager: Kensington
Publishing Corp., 850 Third Avenue, New York, NY 10022.
Attn. Special Sales Department. Phone: 1-800-221-2647.

Dafina and the Dafina logo Reg. U.S. Pat. & TM Off.

First Printing: December 2004
10 9 8 7 6 5 4 3 2 1

Printed in the United States of America

PROLOGUE

The end was coming. Ma Louise could feel it, even as her eyes grew dark and her breath came in slow, labored gasps. At least the pain had finally stopped. She didn't know whether the drugs were doing their job, or whether she was at a point where pain no longer mattered or affected her. She wasn't sorry. She had lived a full and wonderful life. There had been hard times; but the good times, the times that mattered, far outweighed the difficulties. She'd known love, and she'd known more joy than sorrow. She couldn't complain about the hand that the fates had dealt her. There was only one thing left to do, and Ma Louise prayed that she would have the strength to do it.

Ma Louise was grateful that her family had finally given in to her wishes that she die in her own bed, and in her own home. Her daughters had been against it, thinking that perhaps there was a chance medical science could stop the inevitable, but she knew better. The rest of the family had insisted that she should be placed in the hospital or in a nursing home, but there was one voice that had adhered to her wishes, her grandson, Sam. He'd refused to be bullied and he'd refused to be made to feel guilty for his acceptance of her decision that she wanted to leave this earth in the same house where she was born. In the end, the family had listened to her and to Sam. It seemed that in death, just as in life, she and Sam were a formidable pair.

Ma Louise had sent the rest of her family out of her room. They had all gathered at her house for what she knew was a death vigil. She'd said good-bye to all of them, and it had been difficult. Ma Louise had known for a long time that this day was coming, but it didn't make the good-byes any easier. She forced her thoughts away from the family that she had loved, protected, and, even now, worried about. They would survive, just as she had survived the loss of her parents. They would hurt, but her blood ran in their veins—she knew that they would overcome their grief. Turning her attention to Sam, she hesitated, trying to find the right words to say to him.

She'd always been the head of the family, and now that she was going she knew that it was Sam who would take her place. The responsibility of keeping the Trahan family together now fell squarely on his shoulders. She prayed that those shoulders would be strong enough to handle taking care of that tempestuous brood. Even now, the family was torn apart, although she knew that in deference to her, there was a halt to the hostility, but she also knew that was temporary. Ma Louise was certain that underneath it all, they loved each other. Still, she'd failed to teach them the lesson of the importance of unity. Now the responsibility for keeping the Trahan clan together was passed to Sam.

Her eyes rested on her grandson and, once again, she felt a curious mixture of pride, love and worry, feelings she got often when she regarded him. He was her favorite, and although she tried to hide it, the bond between her grandson and her was unmistakable. He was the one in the family that was most like her. He was ambitious, smart, overly confident and stubborn. A man who believed that the word "no" did not apply to him, just as many years before, she'd refused to let the fact that she was African American and a woman stop her from achieving exactly what she intended to achieve—life on her own terms. Sam's hand grasped hers, and she fought back tears. Lord, she was going to miss him. Unlike Ma Louise, her grandson had never known love, not the kind of love she had known for over forty years with her Samuel, her deceased husband, the man for whom her grandson was named. This saddened her. She had told him on many occasions that with all the success he had achieved, it was time to find someone special to share his life with. She'd hoped one day to watch him walk down the aisle, and raise beautiful brown children who had his dark eyes and wide smile. But that was one dream she'd never live to see.

Still, one of the things about dying, Ma Louise thought as she lay in her bed surrounded by her favorite things, is that there was no time for regrets. Whatever time she had left she was not going to waste on what ifs and why nots. There was something very important to be said to her grandson, and there was no time like the present.

"Sam," it took more effort than she had anticipated to talk, but she continued. She knew that her time was drawing to a close and she needed to talk to Sam about this last matter.

Samuel Trahan leaned his face close to his grandmother's, and he squeezed her hand again as if to reassure her.

"I'm right here, Gram."

She smiled at him. Her Sam. She knew that her daughter-in-law, Carmel, was jealous of their closeness, and for that, she was truly sorry, but her love affair with her grandson was immediate, from the first minute he fought his way into the world with his mother's umbilical cord wrapped around his neck. He was a survivor, just like her.

"You must—" her breath was coming even slower now. It was time to say good-bye. She prayed for the strength to say what she needed to say. "You must find the Black Madonna—it's our birthright—it belongs to—this family."

The portrait of her great grandmother, Antoinette Millefleurs, a Creole slave from Louisiana had come to be known as The Black Madonna. The artist, her great grandfather, Zachariah Sangster, a freed slave, had painted the portrait on their wedding day, shortly before his murder. Zachariah's paintings were now famous, and hung in various museums around the world—although his ancestors never financially benefited from Zachariah's fame. After his death, Antoinette had bought her freedom with Zachariah's paintings. She'd kept one painting, the

Black Madonna, and that portrait had remained in their family for generations, until it was—one month ago—stolen from Sam's office where it had hung for years.

There had been dissension among the family members because Ma Louise had allowed Sam to take the painting from her home to his office. But Ma Louise had been firm in her decision. She was certain that as a former slave, Antoinette would have been proud to have her portrait in her descendant's business, a business that he built and owned. Ma Louise knew that Sam wrestled with the guilt that the painting was taken on his watch. She'd tried to absolve him of whatever guilt he felt. Guilt was a useless emotion as far as Ma Louise was concerned. Still, she knew that Sam would not rest until he had reclaimed what was rightfully theirs. Over the years many art dealers had tried to buy the painting from them. It was now worth millions. Still, the family had resisted the lure of money. This was all they had of Antoinette and Zachariah. In order for Sam to have any peace he would have to get the painting back. She was certain of this fact.

"Gram, I'll get it back. You have my word."

She could tell from Sam's voice that he was not ready to say good-bye. It was too soon. It would always be too soon.

There was still one more thing she needed to say to him. "You need to find someone to love, Sam," she said, thanking God that she was getting the words out. "Don't forget, Sam. It belongs to us."

He did not respond to her words; instead Ma Louise watched as the tears fell freely down his face. She looked at her grandson one last time, and said a prayer that one day he would know love; that was all she wanted for him. She would miss him. She would miss all her family, but in her heart, she knew that they would be all right. Looking at Sam she knew that she'd left them in good hands. A feeling of peace washed over her. She'd done all she could do. It was time to let go.

She said, "I love you, Sam."

Then, she said no more.

1

New York City

Sam Trahan remained calm as he repeated the question which no one in the room seemed prepared to answer.

"What do you mean you can't find him?"

Sam watched as one very well paid private detective and the even better paid Vice President of Operations of his company shifted uncomfortably in their seats. He'd spent a lot of time and money furnishing this office. The West African antique mahogany desk, the Persian rugs, his Romare Bearden original prints that graced the walls, the bookcase filled with rare first edition books all spoke of understated and sophisticated elegance. Sam wasn't a man who shrank from spending too much money on his comfort or his surroundings. Therefore, Sam was absolutely certain that the chairs on which these two unhappy men were sitting were not the cause of their obvious discomfort.

"Gentlemen," said Sam as he stood up and walked over to the window and looked out at the scene unfolding twenty stories below. It was six o'clock in the evening and people were hurrying to their homes or to various other appointments. Sam envied them. They were on their way somewhere other than work, but he had at least four more hours to put in at the office before his day was through. Still, he knew that this was the choice he'd made to ensure that North Star Technologies was a success, and if he had his life to live over again he would not have made any other choices than to be where he was, president and owner of his computer company, North Star Technologies.

Turning his attention to more immediate matters, Sam spoke to the two men sitting in his office. "I'm waiting for the answer to my question."

The private detective spoke first. "We know that he's back home in Jamaica, but we're not certain about his exact location."

"You're not certain," repeated Sam slowly. He raised one eyebrow, which those who knew him well recognized was a bad sign. "I'm paying quite a bit of money to ensure your certainty on this particular subject."

The detective cleared his throat nervously before he began speaking again. "We'd hope that his girlfriend could give us some information, but it seems as if they've parted ways."

"The state of Milton Alexander's love life doesn't interest me," said Sam, trying to keep his voice, and his emotions under control. "What does concern me, however, is that after two months we're no closer to finding Milton than we were the day that I hired your firm."

The private detective wisely chose to remain silent.

Sam then turned his attention to Harold Meade. As his Vice President of Operations for North Star, Harold was his right-hand man. He'd worked for the company for the past seven years and until the day he'd urged Sam to hire Milton Alexander, he'd never made a mistake in judgment. "What next, Harold?" Sam asked.

Harold refused to meet Sam's eyes. "I don't know, Sam. We've tried everything. Relatives. Friends. No one seems to know where Milton is. He's been seen in Jamaica—as recently as two weeks ago, but that's all we know."

"That's not good enough, Harold," said Sam.

"Yes," he said unhappily. "I understand."

"No, Harold," Sam's voice was soft again, "I don't think you understand the situation at all, so I am going to explain it for you. Milton Alexander, a man whom I hired based solely upon your glowing recommendation, has disappeared along with a painting which not only has tremendous senti-mental value to my family, but which is worth a lot of money—three million dollars. The painting has belonged to my family for generations. I want it back. Two months ago, when Milton left, you as-sured me that with the assistance of the detective agency, which once again you recommended, both Milton and the painting would be located. This hasn't happened. Two months is a long time, Harold. A lifetime. We don't know if Milton still has the painting, or if he's already sold it. We don't know anything. This angers me, Harold."

"I'm sorry, Sam," said Harold, his eyes fixed firmly on a point just beyond his shoes.

"Your being sorry doesn't change things," Sam replied. "You're my right hand, Harold. I asked you to handle this for me, and you've failed."

Harold looked at Sam with undisguised fear in his eyes. He had a second wife with expensive tastes and a first wife who had already gotten her hands on a large part of his assets. He couldn't afford to lose this job. Sam was generous with his employees and Harold knew that he would never find another job with a salary as high as the one he had at North Star Technologies, and with a more loyal employer, even if he wasn't easy to work for.

"Are you firing me, Sam?" Harold asked.

"No," said Sam, "I'm not firing you."

"Mr. Trahan—" the private detective spoke up quickly. "I've got a few leads—"

Sam had heard enough. His patience had been tested enough for one day. Another second with this man and he was going to lose it completely. Sam had always prided himself on being a man who wasn't ruled by emotion. He'd learned early not to waste time and sentiments. It was time to move on, time to do what he should have done two months ago.

"Send the bill to my assistant," Sam turned to the private detective. "She'll pay you promptly. Your services are no longer required."

For a moment, the detective looked as if he wanted to challenge Sam, then he apparently thought better of it.

He stood up, and Harold stood with him. They both seemed anxious to leave Sam's office.

"I'm sorry this didn't work out as we had planned," said the private detective.

"Not half as sorry as I am," said Sam as he nodded in the direction of his office door.

Sam watched as the two men walked out of his office. They'd failed him, but worse, he'd failed his grandmother by leaving this whole mess in their hands. He knew what he had to do. He'd known it from the minute Milton disappeared, but he let Harold talk him into having someone else take care of business. Harold had cautioned that Sam should be discreet. North Star Technologies had recently gone public and any hint of scandal like this could affect their stock. Sam's attention had been focused on his company, but he'd made a promise to his grandmother and it was time to fulfill that promise, even if it meant that his business for once would not be his first, and only, priority. It was time to find the Black Madonna. He was still grieving the loss of his grandmother. She'd been the rock he'd leaned on all his life and even now he wished he had her words of wisdom. She would have been able to advise him as she always had done before. During the past two months, his attention had been rightfully focused on his grandmother's illness and impending death. Now that she was gone, he was determined to honor her request to find the painting. He prayed that he wasn't too late.

Sam knew he had no other choice. He was going after Milton and he knew that he had at least one weapon in the war against Milton, and Sam thought grimly, this was war. There was one person that he

suspected could lead him to Milton. Sam opened
the file that the detective had prepared and took
out a picture of a laughing, brown-skinned woman,
Milton's ex-girlfriend, Zora Redwood. Her dark
hair was cut short and her tight curls framed her
oval face. A small pert nose competed with full
ruby colored lips. Large, expressive eyes fringed
with long eyelashes stared directly into the camera. He was caught by her eyes—they were an unusual color of light brown. In another life or at
another time, Sam would have admired the beauty
of this woman because, unless the picture lied, she
was unmistakably beautiful. But Sam had no time
for beauty or admiration. Time was of the essence.
Thus far, the painting hadn't surfaced, but who knew
whether Milton had already sold The Black Madonna. Sam pushed those thoughts away. They
hinted of defeat, and Sam wasn't defeated. If there
was a chance, even a slim chance that Milton still
had the painting, then Sam was going to be the one
to get back what rightfully belonged to his family.

He didn't know a lot about Zora Redwood. He
knew that, like Milton, she was Jamaican, and that
she taught in a neighborhood nursery school in
Brooklyn. Judging from the file, she didn't seem to
have much of a social life. The only social activities
recorded by the detective were church, volunteer
work with a homeless shelter, and dinners and
movies with her girlfriends. There wasn't much to
go on, except his hunch that she would be the key
to finding Milton. The fact that they were no
longer romantically involved threw a wrinkle in
things. It would be harder to find Milton, but Sam

was convinced that this woman would know how to get to Milton and Sam had just been given the ammunition that would make her talk to him. Sam was a man who believed in hunches. He'd built his company and staked his business on hunches, and he'd yet to be disappointed.

Zora Redwood was certain that the man in the dark blue suit was following her. He'd walked at a discreet distance from her and had tried to blend into the crowded streets of Brooklyn, but no matter where she walked this Saturday morning he was never far behind. She'd first noticed him when she walked to Miss Chen's bagel shop. Then she noticed him when she went to the Korean deli to buy her fresh-squeezed orange juice. When she walked over to the dry cleaners, he was there also.

She had no doubt that Milton was somehow wrapped up in all of this. Two months ago, he had walked out of her life without explanation. One day, they were engaged, a couple planning to spend the rest of their lives together. The next day he was gone. He'd cleaned out his apartment overnight and disappeared. At first Zora had been frantic, fearing the worst, that her fiancé had been a victim of foul play. But a visit from a private detective two days after he disappeared, and then a visit from another detective, this one a member of the New York Police Department, provided the explanation for Milton's disappearing act. He had stolen a very expensive painting.

At first she'd been stunned. The Milton she knew

had never even gotten a traffic ticket, now he was accused of grand theft; however when the detectives told her that he was under suspicion for the theft of a valuable painting, the Black Madonna, she knew then that they spoke the truth. The man that she had planned to marry was a thief. She'd seen the painting, a beautiful rendition of an African woman, in a long, white dress, standing barefoot in the grass with her hands clasped in front of her, as if she were in prayer. It was a simple painting, but Zora had been struck by the elegance and the power of the woman that stared back at her from the portrait. There was a look of pride, defiance and also, sensuality about the portrait. Milton had told her that the painting had been done by the woman's husband who had been murdered shortly after the painting was finished.

Perhaps it was the story, which Zora now suspected was another of Milton's fanciful tales, but according to Milton, the artist had been murdered in his sleep, and a cache of diamonds which he intended to give to his beloved as a wedding present had disappeared. The story had touched her, just as the love that was painted in those dark eyes of the subject of the painting had moved her. This was clearly a depiction of a woman in love. At the time, she'd wondered if the love she felt for Milton was as deep as the love reflected in the woman's eyes. Milton had disappeared before she could discern the answer to that question.

Shortly before he'd disappeared, Milton had asked her to keep the portrait for him. He was holding it for a friend, he said, but he had concerns that his apartment wasn't safe enough for something so valuable. She asked him why he didn't leave the painting in a bank vault or some other place where folks kept their valuables, but Milton replied that there was no one he trusted more than her, and Zora had accepted his explanation, even though she hadn't entirely believed him. This story did not make sense. Still, she'd never in her wildest imagination thought that Milton had stolen the painting.

She'd kept the portrait in her bedroom closet. Milton had warned her that he did not want anyone to see the portrait because of its value. He did not want to "tempt fate," as he told her. She'd responded that no one who came to her apartment would ever steal from her, but Milton had been adamant. He'd even told her not to talk to her friends or to her family about the painting. Looking back, she had viewed his trust in her as a good sign, a sign that they were compatible. On more than one occasion Milton's moods had caused her to question their compatibility. Now, in the clear light of day, knowing what Milton had done, she realized that he had used her and she had been an unknowing, trusting, and ultimately, foolish participant in his schemes.

On the night before he disappeared, the last time she saw him, he'd been distant and moody. He told her that he was returning the portrait to his friend. When she questioned him about his friend, he'd lectured her about trying to get into his business. She'd been offended; after all, she'd carefully looked after the portrait and now he was acting as if she were an inquisitive nuisance. They'd had words, but by the time he left her house, he was again whispering sweet promises about their

future together. The next day, he walked out of
her life.

She didn't tell the detectives about her role in
Milton's deception. Instead, she informed them
that he was probably in Jamaica, the place where
he was born, the place where they had met, and
the place where Milton went when he needed to
return to his refuge, as he called the green hills of
the island. Since then, she had lived in fear that
the police would discover her role, however inad-
vertent, in the theft of the Black Madonna.

On the day she discovered that Milton was not
only a thief, but someone who had placed her directly in the line of trouble, she had stopped loving him. Still, until things were resolved she was
inextricably linked with his crime. She believed the
correct legal term was "accessory after the fact."

"Miss Redwood, may I have a word with you?"
Zora felt someone lightly grasp her arm, and she
turned around and saw the face of the man who
was following her. All thoughts about Milton left
immediately as she found herself staring into a
pair of angry dark eyes.

She recognized him instantly. Looking into the
face of a man whom she'd seen on numerous occasions, in the society pages of the *New York Times*,
the *Daily News* and the *Amsterdam News* and most
recently in a television interview on *CNN Business
News*, she wondered how she hadn't recognized him
before. Sam Trahan was not an easy man to forget.
There were not many African American men who
had reached the pinnacle of success that Sam
Trahan had, and his rise had provided plenty of
copy for the New York newspapers and the media.

Tall, dark, with looks more interesting than handsome, Zora could see firsthand what all the eligible women in New York were making such a fuss about. He had well defined features, large dark eyes, high cheekbones that jutted from his face as if someone had carved them out of ebony, and a nose that could only be described as patrician with nostrils that flared over full lips that were now in a tight line.

"What do you want, Mr. Trahan?" Zora said coolly, although she had a good idea what, or who Sam Trahan was seeking. She'd learned from the detectives that The Black Madonna belonged to the Trahan family.

"I'd like a word with you, Miss Redwood," he said. His grasp on her arm was light, yet deliberate.

"I've already talked to your detective, and to the police," said Zora, moving quickly to extricate herself from his hold. "I'm sorry about what Milton did to you, but I've nothing more to add."

"That may be true," replied Sam. "However, I still need to talk to you."

"I'm sorry, Mr. Trahan, I don't have anything else to add to what I've already said. I'm quite busy, so if you don't mind, I need to be on my way."

"Either you talk to me now, Miss Redwood, or we can do this at the police station where you'll explain why you lied to them about your role in the theft of my property." Sam's words were quiet, but his anger was unmistakable.

Zora straightened up, all five foot three of her, and forced herself to be in as calm a manner as she could muster under the circumstances, although her heart was hammering in her chest. She didn't care how rich he was. She didn't care about his business acumen. She was sorry that Milton had stolen from him, but she did not have to put up with that tone of voice from him. She was not about to be bullied by him. She didn't steal his painting. True, she had played an unwitting role in the theft, but certainly there'd been no intent on her part to steal the painting. Besides, she'd already told the police and the private investigators everything she knew about Milton's possible whereabouts. He had no right to treat her as if she were a recent subject on the *America's Most Wanted* television show.

"There's a very good diner about two blocks from here. Maybe we could have some coffee and talk about our mutual predicament," he said.

"What mutual predicament?" asked Zora, not certain how much information Sam Trahan knew about her involvement in this fiasco.

"I believe his name is Milton Alexander," Sam said smoothly. "It seems that he's disappeared from both our lives."

"From where I stand, Mr. Trahan," said Zora, not bothering to hide her exasperation with Milton and his latest mess, "that doesn't seem to be much of a predicament for me."

"Oh, but I think it is, Miss Redwood," said Sam, his eyes never leaving Zora's face for a moment. "Once again, let me ask you—would you rather talk to me or would you rather talk to the police?"

Zora felt the blood drain away from her face. Stay calm, she told herself, even as she saw a clear picture of a prison cell in her future.

"I'm listening, Mr. Trahan."

Sam took a step forward and stood directly in front of her. His closeness unnerved her and Zora felt a sudden and inexplicable urge to back away from him, but she stood her ground.

"Miss Redwood, we have a witness who is willing to testify in a court of law that you assisted Milton Alexander with the theft of my property."

"I didn't know that the painting was stolen. Milton said that he was keeping it for a friend."

"Milton's secretary is ready to testify that he gave you the painting. She's also prepared to testify that you knew that the painting was stolen."

"Milton's secretary? Why would Felice say something like that? How in the world did Felice know that Milton gave me the painting?"

"They've been romantically involved for months. He told her everything."

Zora remained impassive. She knew that pride was a sin, but her pride wouldn't let her give this arrogant stranger the satisfaction of seeing that his words had their intended effect—to catch her off guard. She'd closed her heart to Milton. Once he'd left her, she no longer wanted him. The words of one of her father's Jamaican sayings came back to her "one hand can't clap." She wasn't one to pine for unrequited love. It wasn't in her nature. Perhaps it was that stubborn pride that her parents had often accused her of having. Still, the thought that once again she was learning things about Milton which showed that not only had she given her love unwisely, she was also unaware of who Milton was and although she didn't think it was possible, Milton had hurt her once more.

"It seems," continued Sam, "that Milton had convinced her that he would get rich, dump you, and marry her, in that order. He disappeared from her life and you know the rest. Hell hath no fury . . ."

"I did not help Milton in any scheme," said Zora.

"So you've already said," replied Sam. "But the fact remains that either you and I talk or we go to the police. The choice is yours."

"That sounds like blackmail, Mr. Trahan," said Zora, her calm voice at odds with her blazing light brown eyes.

"Call it what you like, Miss Redwood. But you and I need to talk."

Zora knew when she was defeated, but she refused to concede graciously. It was simply not her nature.

"You have fifteen minutes, Mr. Trahan."

"That's all I need, Miss Redwood," said Sam.

"How did you know about the diner in this neighborhood? We're a long way from Park Avenue. I wasn't aware that multimillionaire owners of computer companies were familiar with neighborhoods like these."

"You underestimate me, Miss Redwood," said Sam, "I grew up around these parts. Not too far from where we are right now."

"Going back to your roots?" Zora could not resist this jab.

"Miss Redwood," he replied, "I never left."

Zora could have sworn that she heard a low chuckle come from his direction, but when she looked at Sam Trahan, his expression remained inscrutable.

* * *

Zora Redwood was nothing at all like Sam expected her to be. He'd thought that she was going to be some empty-headed beauty who would fall apart quickly after learning about Milton's betrayal. True, she was beautiful. Her picture, though flattering, had not done her justice. It did not capture the smooth brown skin, the way her light brown eyes sparkled when they glared at him. It didn't capture the delicate nose and her full, generous lips that came straight from some undoubtedly equally beautiful ancestor in Africa. It didn't capture her spirit.

She hadn't dissolved into tears as he had expected her to do when she learned about Milton's dalliance with his secretary. He'd found out more from his hour-long visit with Felice than his detectives had learned in the past two months. Felice had been much more forthcoming with him. Alternately flirting with him, and, he was sure, lying to him, Sam had been able to find out about Zora Redwood and the part she had played in this whole mess. He had no doubt that Felice had played a part in this also, but his instinct told him that Felice didn't know Milton's whereabouts. Sam was convinced that the lovely Miss Redwood would lead him directly to Milton. A man did not walk away from someone like Zora Redwood. Milton was sure to get in touch with her somehow. Sam was certain of it, and in the meantime, he would use Miss Redwood to help him find Milton and the Black Madonna.

Their walk to the diner had been instructive. He learned that Zora Redwood was popular. As they walked, Zora had called out greetings to several people, from grocers who knew her by name, to children playing kick ball on the sidewalk, to an old homeless man, who she stopped briefly to ask whether he had seen the doctor at the homeless mission. The man had sheepishly refused to look at her eyes when he admitted that no, he had not gone to see the doctor, but he would be doing that in the near future. She'd gently chided him, given him a few dollars, and told him in that charming West Indian lilt of hers that if he didn't go to see the doctor soon, she would personally haul him over to the mission. She seemed to Sam a little too good to be true, but if this was an act, she was giving an Academy Award performance.

Sam saw the way that people stared at her, as if they wanted to protect her. They'd stared at him speculatively, but Zora had refused to acknowledge his presence. Sam couldn't blame her hostility towards him. He was the enemy and even though Zora had to put up with his presence, her cold silence as they walked towards the diner told him as explicitly as if she'd used her own words, that she didn't have to be happy about it.

When they reached the diner, Zora turned to him. "I don't see how I can help you, Mr. Trahan. I've told your detectives everything I know about Milton and your painting. I think he's in Jamaica and that's what I told your detectives, but I really don't know anything else. I haven't heard from Milton in two months."

"You should give yourself more credit," Sam replied. "No man would walk away from you without trying to get back in touch with you."

Zora gave him a tight little laugh. "I hate to disappoint you but that's exactly what Milton did."

A waitress materialized as if on cue and led them to a table in the corner of the diner. Sam was aware that people stared at them, but he focused on the task at hand. He was used to having people stare. Despite his aversion to being in the limelight, the nature of his business kept him in the public eye and although he was sure that most people didn't know who he was, they had a vague sense that they'd seen his face before.

Sam waited until Zora took her seat and then he sat down across from her.

"What can I get you folks?" the waitress asked with a good-natured smile.

"Nothing for me," Zora quickly replied.

"I'll have a coffee," said Sam. "Black, no sugar."

The waitress left with a quick smile. The diner was full this Saturday morning and Sam had no doubt that she was going to be busy all morning.

Sam turned his attention to Zora as she stared out the window. He found it more difficult than he imagined to keep his mind on the matter at hand, finding Milton. Instead, for the moment he was more interested in studying this beautiful woman's profile. What on earth was wrong with him.

Clearing his throat to get her attention, he asked, "Where is Milton?"

She turned and looked directly in his eyes. "I told you that I don't know."

"That's a problem," said Sam coolly. "That's a very big problem."

"So you've mentioned."

She looked out of the window again and studied the scene unfolding before her on the Brooklyn street. An ambulance drove by, its lights flashing and its siren giving a signal to all on the roads to stand clear. After the ambulance went its way she turned and looked at him directly, her eyes never leaving his.

"I didn't steal anything," said Zora. "Felice is lying."

"But your boyfriend did," said Sam.

"Ex-boyfriend," replied Zora emphatically.

"The status of your love life doesn't concern me. I need to find Milton and frankly, I'm running out of patience. I have information that you're involved in this mess and even if the case isn't strong enough to get a criminal indictment against you, I'm going to sue you for every cent you have if you don't help me find him."

If he'd expected some sort of reaction to that comment, he didn't get one. Instead, she stared at him and said, "Corporate giant sues nursery school teacher?"

"Something like that," said Sam. "I can make your life a living hell."

Zora laughed, but her laughter didn't reach her eyes. "Stand in line, Mr, Trahan. There are quite a few folks that have actually already had the pleasure."

"I assure you," said Sam, who found her laughter disconcerting, "this is no laughing matter. How would your nursery school like to find its star teacher on the evening news charged with being an accomplice to theft? I know that your school depends on the kindness of several wealthy benefactors. I don't think that they would take too kindly to hearing that the school's teacher is mixed up with something this—shall we say, distasteful, and although I can't confirm this firsthand, I've heard that prison is a particularly unpleasant place."

Sam watched with satisfaction as her face grew serious.

"I'll do whatever it takes to stop Milton from taking what belongs to me and to my family," said Sam.

"Apparently," Zora replied. "What do you want from me?"

He'd clearly gotten her attention, and more importantly, her cooperation. Perhaps now it was time to dangle the carrot to ensure that her cooperation would not be short-lived.

"I need you to help me find him," said Sam. "If you do, as far as I'm concerned, your involvement with this incident will not be at issue."

"Let me get this straight," said Zora, "if I help you find Milton, then I'm off the hook?"

"I couldn't have put it any better myself," said Sam.

"What about Milton? What happens to him?"

"I can't make any promises, but after I retrieve my property from him, it's my guess that he'll be on his way to jail," replied Sam. "You'll help me find him?"

Zora hesitated a moment before she responded. She didn't want to be a party to Milton's downfall, but his own actions had dragged her into this mess. "Yes, Mr. Trahan. I'll help you find him. I'm sure he's in Jamaica. Have you got a passport?"

"I've got a passport and two first-class tickets to Jamaica. Air Jamaica Flight 057. It leaves for Montego Bay tomorrow morning. I assume you have your passport in order."

Zora looked at him with an expression that was a cross between admiration and amusement. "Yes, I do possess a valid passport."

"Good," Sam Trahan replied.

Zora nodded her head. "I'm sure that he's on the island, but it won't be easy tracking his whereabouts. Milton is a very smart man."

"I'm smarter."

Sam placed a twenty-dollar bill on the table and said, as he stood up, "Tell the waitress to keep the change."

He turned to Zora and said, "The flight leaves at 8:00 tomorrow morning. My car service will pick you up at your home at five-thirty."

"You know my address?" Zora asked.

"Yes, Miss Redwood, I do," Sam replied. "I've made it my business to know everything I can about you."

He left before she could respond.

Later that day, Quentin Brooks sat in Mama Joy's restaurant and savored the smell of fresh peach cobbler. It was one of his favorite desserts and Quentin knew that peach cobbler was also a particular weakness of his best friend, Sam Trahan. But the peach cobbler, as delicious as it smelled, sat in front of Sam, cold and untouched. True, Sam had his share of problems recently. His grandmother's death had taken its toll on him, and Quentin knew that Sam blamed himself for the theft of the painting his family put so much stock in, but from the faraway look in his friend's eyes and the uncharacteristic lack of appetite Sam displayed, Quentin decided that there was something else, not entirely un-pleasant, that was occupying Sam's thoughts.

After he finished his peach cobbler, Quentin decided that he'd waited long enough for Sam to vol-unteer the information about the lady whom Quentin thought just might be the real reason for Sam's lack of appetite. He knew from experience that only a woman could account for that look of complete bewilderment on a man's face.

"What's Milton's girlfriend like?" Quentin asked.

Quentin Brooks was more than a friend to Sam. He was more like a brother than Sam's own brother had ever been. Quentin and Sam had been room-mates at business school and from a rocky begin-ning, a friendship had formed that Sam had not ever shared before or since his meeting with Quentin. They had disliked each other instantly. Quentin, with his movie star good looks and easygoing nature, had nothing in common with Sam.

There were folks who said that Sam Trahan in-vented the word "intense." When Quentin met him, he was intense and disagreeable, but somehow, they'd managed to form a bond which grew into friendship. Sam had asked Quentin several times to join his business, but Sam knew Quentin had his sights on a career in politics.

Quentin repeated his question to his distracted friend.

"What's Milton's girlfriend like?"

"Who?" asked Sam as he stirred his coffee ab-sently.

Sam had asked Quentin to meet him in one of their favorite hangouts, Mama Joy's, a soul food restaurant in Harlem. They had discovered Mama

Joy's while at business school, and like most of Mama's customers, they had remained loyal all these years.

The restaurant didn't look like much from the outside, but once you stepped inside it was like being in a different world. Sam had once compared the restaurant to an image he had of a bordello. Quentin thought Mama Joy's looked more like a speakeasy. The walls were painted red with streaks of gold. On the walls hung pictures, originals Mama Joy would proudly announce, of famous jazz singers and musicians. Dizzy Gillespie, Billie Holliday, Ella Fitzgerald, Thelonious Monk, and various other famous people whose names Quentin did not know vied for space on the crowded wall. The chairs were a garish red velvet and the tablecloths were either red or gold. In the corner was a jukebox which only played jazz and there was a small bar in an adjoining room where smoking was permitted. Garish decor notwithstanding, Mama Joy served the best soul food in Harlem.

"Milton's girlfriend," repeated Quentin once more. "What's she like?"

"Not like I expected," Sam replied.

"Uh oh," laughed Quentin, "this woman seems to have left quite an impression on you."

"I'd say that's pretty accurate," said Sam slowly, his thoughts clearly someplace other than Mama Joy's restaurant. "She has made quite an impression. However, her ex-boyfriend has left a greater impression on me, unfortunately."

Ex-boyfriend thought Quentin. Now this was going to get interesting.

"She's the key to helping me find Milton," said Sam. "She's got to be. I can't let Gram down. She's depending on me." Sam still couldn't refer to her in the past tense.

Quentin knew how important it was to Sam to fulfill his grandmother's wishes. He also knew what very few people other than those with the last name Trahan knew just how important the Black Madonna was to the family. They had been described as "clannish" and Quentin was inclined to agree with that assessment. There always seemed to be some friction between family members but they banded together whenever anyone outside of the family tried to pick a fight with a Trahan. Now that Ma Louise had gone to the great hereafter, Sam was the head of the clan, although there were some Trahans, particularly Sam's younger brother, Justin Trahan, who were not happy about Sam's new position of power within the family.

Justin was unhappy about some other things as well. Sam had told him that the fighting had begun about his grandmother's will. She'd left everything she owned, including her two-hundred acre farm in South Carolina to Sam, with instructions that he dispose of her assets fairly. Justin was outspoken in his blame of Sam for the theft of the Black Madonna and, according to Sam, the family was now divided into two factions: those clearly behind Justin, and those who supported Sam. For Sam, the key to getting his family back together was the return of the Black Madonna. He was convinced that the portrait was some sort of talisman, a symbol of unity. Personally, Quentin did not think that it would be that easy to reunite the feuding Trahans, but he supported his friend.

"Tell me what you need me to do," said Quentin.

Sam looked over at his friend. He seemed tired, yet Quentin could see that the fight was still in Sam's eyes. He hadn't given up. "I know I'm going to need you at some point, Quentin, but right now I think the only person that can help me is Zora Redwood."

"Do you trust her?" asked Quentin.

"No," said Sam with a quick shake of his head, "but right now I don't have a choice. I need her help."

"What do your instincts tell you about her?" asked Quentin. "You usually have a pretty good read on people."

"That's just the thing," said Sam, "I don't know. She's nothing like I expected. I can't imagine what the hell she was doing with a man like Milton. She's just—just—"

Sam struggled for the right word.

"Different?" Quentin volunteered.

"Yeah, different. That's a perfect word for it. I've never met anyone else like her. It's clear that she hates my guts because I've forced her to help me in this mess, but she didn't fall apart. Even when I told her about Milton's dalliance, she remained calm. And she knows everyone in her neighborhood by name. What's more, she volunteers in a home-less mission and teaches nursery school, but she's no shrinking violet. She gave as good as she got, even though she knew that I had her at a disadvantage. Worse, she makes me feel like *I'm* doing some-thing wrong—trying to get my property back."

"Most folks don't like to be forced to do things, even attractive folks."

"Did I say she was attractive?" asked Sam, surprised. "Actually, she's beautiful."

"She sounds intriguing," Quentin said, trying hard not to smile.

Sam proceeded without responding to Quentin's last comment. "She's not impressed with me. Not in the least," said Sam as if he found this fact not only perplexing but distasteful as well. "In fact, I think it's quite the opposite. Most folks who meet me are either impressed or afraid. She's neither."

"Hmm."

"I've never met anyone like her," said Sam.

Quentin struggled to suppress a smile, but it was a losing battle. He covered his smile behind the brightly painted menu. In all the years he'd known Sam, he'd never known him to be confused about anything, let alone a woman he just met. This could prove very interesting indeed.

"Well, buddy," said Quentin, "you know you can call on me anytime you need help."

Sam stood up quickly. "Thanks, you need a ride anywhere? I've got some things to take care of."

Quentin shook his head. "No, I think I'm going to stay here awhile longer and enjoy some more of Mama Joy's peach cobbler."

"I'll give you a call once I'm down in Jamaica," said Sam.

"I'll be waiting," said Quentin, "and Sam—take care of yourself."

Quentin watched as his friend walked away and then started laughing. He had a suspicion that this nursery school teacher was going to turn his friend's life in a very unexpected direction. God help him.

Mama Joy, the proprietor of the restaurant, walked over to him.

"What's so funny?" she asked.

"I think," said Quentin, once his laughter finally subsided, "our friend Sam may have finally met his match."

"Amen to that," said Mama Joy. "It's about time!"

Terrence Phillips stood in line patiently. No one could guess that beneath his ordinary, placid exterior, he was in a place between anger and retribution. If one had chosen to look in his direction, one would merely have seen a man in a wool suit that was completely inappropriate for the warm climate to which he was heading. After he got the information that Milton was in Jamaica, he'd booked passage within the hour and was now waiting to get on an airplane heading to Montego Bay. He still didn't know exactly where in Jamaica Milton was hiding, but he was certain that this information would soon be forthcoming. After all, Terrence had ways, some pleasant and some very unpleasant, to make folks become quite talkative. It was just a matter of time before Milton would be found.

The line was beginning to move. Honeymooners, college students, and people returning home with suitcases laden with the fruits of what appeared to be ardent shopping waited with seeming patience and good will while the line waiting to board Caribbean Air moved slowly to the airline gate. Life was full of ironies, one of which was his desire to visit Jamaica. The island had always seemed like a place of mystery and beauty to him, two attributes which were intriguing. His business had kept him busy these past few years, and vacations to any destination had proved to be impossible. Now, he was on his way to Jamaica, but this trip was not a vacation. This trip was for the sole purpose of taking care of someone who'd betrayed him, and who'd cost him a lot of money. He was going to take care of Milton. He was going to teach him the folly of his actions. Terrence smiled now. The hunt was on, and he, the hunter, was planning to win this particular game. Unlike some of his other jobs, this one was personal, and that would make it all the more sweet.

2

Milton walked to the veranda and looked below him at the hillside which sloped gracefully towards the wide expanse of sky-blue sea. He watched as the sun seemed to melt into the sea, signifying that evening was near. He'd been all over the world but in his opinion there were few places which rivaled the island of Jamaica for its sheer dramatic beauty. He sat down on one of the several white wicker chairs that graced the veranda and contemplated his next move. For a moment his left hand began trembling and he thought with a wry smile that if his aunt were with him, she would have told him that this was not a good sign. His aunt, although deeply religious, like many of her generation believed in the supernatural. Pay attention to the signs boy, she would tell him often. But Milton had no respect for superstition and dismissed his aunt's warnings as the ravings of an ignorant country woman. His hands trembled because he was nervous. He'd every reason to be nervous. He knew that they were coming after him.

With great effort he forced himself to remain calm. He wanted a drink. He needed a drink. The bar was well supplied. The caretaker of the property had seen to this before she left for her week-long vacation with her relatives in Kingston. She'd done her job well. The house was immaculate, the kitchen was stocked with food, and the extra money he paid her had ensured that his privacy would not be violated. Not that it mattered, thought Milton. She never knew his real name. All she knew was that he was Nathaniel Porter, a businessman from Foreign, as the local people called the United States.

He'd bought this house two years ago, when the plan to take the Black Madonna was first formulated. No one knew about this house, not even Zora. She would have disapproved of his choice of lodging. It was too grand, too ostentatious and worse, too isolated for her. She craved neighbors and company. Zora, like his superstitious aunt, would never have been comfortable staying in a villa surrounded by nothing or no one for miles except a solitary dirt road from which Milton could see whomever was approaching his house, and an occasional herd of wild mountain goats.

The house had belonged to an Englishman who was believed to be either a reclusive author, a wealthy and allegedly titled member of the aristocracy, or a drug dealer, depending on whose opinion was being given in the closest town, Highgate, where the Englishman would go once a month to get his supplies. He lived alone, except for his dog and the caretaker, until the lure of England proved to be irresistible, twenty years after he had last set foot on English shores.

Milton first learned of the house's existence through the real estate section of the *Weekly Gleaner*, the Jamaican newspaper. The advertisement caught his attention immediately. The house fit his needs perfectly. It was secluded, in a remote area of the island, with a caretaker and relatively inexpensive. The sale of the house was completed three weeks after Milton first spotted the ad.

He would visit the house during his periodic trips to Jamaica. He never brought anyone to the house with him, not even the various women who invariably kept him company during his stay in Jamaica. He would spend a day or two at the house, relishing the seclusion. It was here in this house that he finalized the plans that were going to make him a very wealthy man.

His left hand began to shake uncontrollably and he gripped the handrest of his chair in order to stop the shaking. After a moment, it subsided to occasional tremors. Once again, he thought about the fully stocked bar but decided against the drink that he knew from experience would calm him down. He needed to keep his wits about him. The stakes were high and he couldn't afford to make any mistakes. He closed his eyes against the haze of the setting sun.

Night had fallen in New York City and Carmel Trahan stared out at the lights of New York, praying once again that the good Lord would knock some sense into her two oldest children—Sam and

Justin. Carmel Trahan watched both her sons with growing concern. Sam and Justin were born eleven months apart, but they'd never gotten along. Carmel had hoped that one day they would understand the importance of their shared blood. The importance of family. Her recently departed mother-in-law, God rest her soul, had tried, without success, to get Justin and Sam to understand that a house divided would not stand. Her other two children, her daughter Celia and Zachary, her youngest son, had not caused her any worries. Celia was self-sufficient, disciplined, and eminently reasonable, and Zachary, at twelve years old, was simply too young at this point to cause his mother any real trouble—although the teenage years promised to be interesting, if his brothers were any indication. But her two oldest sons were quite a different matter.

The Trahan family was a house divided. As she thought of Ma Louise, Carmel grew sad. She could use some of her tough, wise counsel right now. When Carmel married Ma Louise's son, Ezekiel, Ma Louise had not only given the union her blessing, she'd given Carmel her love.

Carmel thought, as she often did, that she was glad that her Ezekiel didn't live to see his sons at war. He had been a gentle man, so unlike his two oldest sons. They'd inherited her turbulent spirit and, apparently, some of their paternal grandmother's stubborn nature. Carmel had asked her daughter, whose reasonable voice and ways could sometimes reach her brothers, to talk to them this evening. Carmel had known that the conversation today wouldn't be pleasant. Justin blamed Sam for the loss of the Black Madonna, and Carmel well knew that Sam did not take kindly to criticism, particularly from his brother. Carmel hoped that the presence of their sister, whom both loved, respected and trusted, would keep the conversation from degenerating into a free-for-all.

Celia was the only person who was able to talk to Justin and Sam, other than Ma Louise who was now in Heaven, probably shaking her head at the antics of her grandsons. Although Celia was only twenty-four years old, she had been born with a gift of maturity, a gift of being able to make hard choices, without making enemies, and her brothers loved her without reservation. Carmel turned her attention back to her sons and let her gaze drift from their angry faces, and the concerned face of her daughter, and stared at her surroundings. This was her favorite room, the living room, filled with antiques, pictures of her family, plants, and her prized possession, her white piano. The piano had been a wedding gift from her Ezekiel. At the time, she hadn't known how to play the piano, but with the encouragement from her husband, a long-held dream to surround herself in music was realized. Ezekiel had been an accomplished pianist and sometimes she thought if she listened with her heart and not her ears, she could hear some of the melodies he used to play for her, long ago.

Celia cleared her throat. She sat on the windowsill, and her slender form was framed by the sunlight which streamed into the living room from the floor-to-ceiling French windows. She was a beautiful woman, Carmel thought with pride. She'd inherited her father's dark skin and height. Her delicate features came from Carmel. Still, beauty was fleeting and, as Carmel knew, it could bring as much pleasure as it could pain. Carmel was far more proud of Celia's intellect, she was studying at Columbia University to be a doctor, and of her compassion. Somehow she had failed in raising her first two children, but with Celia and Zachary, she had done something right.

"I think that Sam is right," said Celia, her deep, husky voice more at home with a blues singer than the tall slender female who was speaking. "He's got to go after Milton, and this Zora Redwood will probably give Sam the best chance he has to find Milton quickly. Before he sells the Black Madonna."

"I'm sure he's sold it already." The anger in Justin Trahan's face and in his voice was unmistakable. Carmel looked at her second child. Like all of her children, he was blessed with good looks, but there was something wild about Justin, a sense that just below the surface lay something untamed and unharnessed. He wasn't like anyone else in the family. He often put himself in danger, paragliding, rock climbing, traveling to exotic places usually on the State Department's list of places to avoid; Justin went out of his way to court disaster. That he was still alive, and healthy, and in one piece, although he broke his leg in a skiing accident last year, his mother attributed solely to her daily prayers to the Lord to protect her foolish and headstrong son.

"Whether he's sold the painting or not," said Sam, not bothering to hide his growing loss of patience, "he has to pay for what he did."

"How can you trust this woman, Sam?" Carmel asked, once again bringing her attention back to

Sam's discussion of Zora Redwood and the role she would play in the return of the painting.

"I don't trust her," said Justin. "For all we know she's working with Milton."

"She's the best lead I have at the moment," said Sam, leveling his gaze on his brother, "but if you have a better suggestion, I'm open to hearing it."

He had thrown down the gauntlet and deliberately challenged his brother. Everyone in the room knew it, and Justin knew it. Carmel watched as Justin's mouth hardened. He looked as if he could easily tear his brother's limbs from his body and derive great pleasure from that task. Justin had no suggestions. He had already tried to use his connections in the art world to help locate Milton or the Black Madonna.

Sam was standing in the corner, at the furthest distance he could be from his brother and still be in the same room. His arms were folded across his chest, and one mocking black eyebrow was raised. Carmel noted that even though Sam wore an expensive and very well tailored dark blue suit, to her eyes, he still looked like the little boy who'd refused to say "I'm sorry" to his brother. He had the same defiant look in his eyes that he had as a three-year-old, when, unrepentant, he went to bed without dinner for punching his brother, after Justin had broken his favorite toy.

"I'm not the one whom Ma Louise trusted with the Black Madonna, and I'm not the one who had it stolen on my watch," Justin replied. "I only suggest that you proceed with more caution than you exhibited when the painting was in your possession, and then maybe you'd have a better chance at getting it back."

Justin walked over and sat on the couch beside his mother. He was as different from Sam as night from day. He had inherited Carmel's light skin, and sandy brown hair, which he wore in thin dreadlocks, pulled back from his face. He was tall and wiry, with the lean looks of a runner, and was dressed in his usual uniform of blue jeans, T-shirt, and ratty blue blazer, that had seen too many washes, judging from its faded appearance. Unlike Sam and Celia, who'd both excelled in school, Justin had dropped out of college. He was always an indifferent student on all subjects, except for art. His small art gallery in the East Village of New York City was a moderate success, but Carmel knew that his dream was to sell his own art.

"Go to hell, Justin," Sam said, his voice quiet, his black eyes blazing with anger.

Celia stepped in quickly before the inevitable argument began.

"Stop it," she said. "You're both acting like spoiled children."

Well said, thought Carmel although she remained silent.

"This has been a difficult time for all of us," Celia continued. "After Ma Louise died, it seemed as if nothing would be normal for this family, and God knows that I miss her more today than the day she died, but this family has to pull together. That painting meant a lot to us, and it meant more than we would ever know to Ma Louise. We've got to get it back. Justin, blaming Sam for the theft of the portrait is not only irresponsible, it's plain old stupid. Sam, you're wasting time getting mad at Justin."

Both brothers glared at their sister, but neither dared contradict her. Carmel said a silent prayer of thanks that she had asked Celia to be present for the conversation.

"Justin, even if Sam doesn't find the Black Madonna, it's worth it to the family, to Ma Louise's memory, to at least try," said Carmel. She had no illusions that they might never find the painting, and she did not want the feeling of guilt that she was certain her son felt to become a permanent state of mind. She wanted him to understand that as much as that picture meant to the family, as valuable as it was, he was more valuable.

"I'll find it," said Sam. "Trust me, I won't fail."

"Everybody fails at something, brother," Justin replied without missing a beat, "even you."

"That's where you're wrong," Sam shot back.

Carmel sighed and suppressed the urge to raise her hands to Heaven. Here we go again.

Celia stood up. "I won't be a part of this. I've got more valuable things to do with my time than to watch my two brothers attack each other."

Celia kissed her mother good-bye and strode out of the house without giving either of her brothers a second look. They had the good sense, thought Carmel, to look ashamed. They loved their sister, and her disapproval of their actions hurt.

After Celia left, Carmel spoke.

"Sam, if you're leaving tomorrow, you need to get things in order."

Sam walked over and kissed his mother on the cheek.

Justin looked over at his brother and said, "Even though you don't think you need my help, if you do, just let me know."

"Thanks," Sam replied, his voice tight. He wasn't one to accept olive branches gracefully.

Carmel stifled a sigh. What was she going to do with her two sons?

Zora didn't like being dishonest. She'd stammered when she left the phone message on the principal's answering machine. Family emergency, she told the principal, apologizing profusely for any inconvenience. "Tell the children that I'll be back soon and I'll bring them all presents from the island." The phone call to the Homeless Mission had been equally difficult. It didn't help that she was lying to a man of the cloth, her friend and pastor, Father Scott.

Father Scott had asked her twice to explain her reasons for going to Jamaica. First, she told him that she had a family emergency, then she told him that she had business to take care of. It wasn't until she hung up the telephone that she realized the discrepancy in her stories. She knew that Father Scott had noticed the discrepancy also; very few things escaped his notice, but he had not pressed her for further clarification. The only comment he made to her was "I hope that Milton isn't involved in this."

Zora wasn't surprised that Father Scott had accurately determined that if there was trouble in her life, Milton was usually involved. He was not a fan of Milton's, but Father Scott felt that with enough prayer, even Milton could change his ways.

Still, he had been unable to suppress his delight when Zora told him two months ago that Milton was out of her life.

"Everything happens for a reason," said Father Scott. "There's someone special out there for you, you just have to believe." But Zora didn't want to meet any new men. It would be a long time before she jumped back into dating. She'd no desire to rush into another relationship, only to end up with nothing to show but her disillusion. Frankly, she'd rather read a good book or see a good movie.

As Zora packed her suitcase, she thought about the place to which she was returning, Jamaica. She was born on the island, and had grown up there. Back then, she'd thought that she would never leave the safety and the familiarity of her home in Jamaica, but college, and now her career had kept her from the island. Unlike Milton, Zora had not gone home often. She'd always had good intentions, but she never could seem to find the time to go home. Father Scott thought that she was running away from something—or someone—and, once again, he was absolutely correct in his assumption. She'd left home determined to be a success in her parents' eyes.

They'd wanted her to become a doctor. That was their dream for her, and she had thought that was also her own dream. But one year of biology, physics, and chemistry was enough to teach Zora that she would never become a physician. Her dream was to teach children. For her parents, teaching was an honest profession, but not a spectacular one. They wanted spectacular for their only child. They hadn't taken her decision not to apply to medical school well. Zora had grown up in a house of overachievers. Her father was a physician, a noted Caribbean orthopedic surgeon who taught at the University of the West Indies. Her mother, who'd met, fallen in love with her father, and married him at medical school, was a pediatrician. It was always assumed that their only child would follow in their footsteps. Zora was academically gifted, and her parents were certain that their little prodigy would be the next Doctor Redwood, but it was not meant to be.

If you want to teach, why not teach at the University level? Her mother had wailed. Zora stood her ground. She wanted to teach children. That was her dream, and although her choice of a career caused a rift in her relations with her family, she refused to give in to her parents' wishes. She avoided them whenever possible. She knew that in their eyes she was a failure, someone who chose not to use her talents. She could only imagine what they would say when they discovered that in addition to being a failure she possibly was a criminal as well. The fine distinction that she didn't know that she was engaging in criminal behavior when she broke the law would, undoubtedly, be lost on them.

She was grateful that her parents wouldn't be on the island when she returned. She didn't want to face their inevitable questions about her sudden appearance in a place she had refused to come back to despite their entreaties. Although it was quite possible to go to the island without seeing her parents, she did not want to take the chance that she'd run into one of her parents' friends or her friends who would quickly inform them of their daughter's presence in Jamaica. There would also be questions about Milton. She hadn't told them of her broken engagement. They'd never particularly liked Milton. Her father found him to be "frivolous, with no real sense of professional direction" and her mother had declared that any woman who married a man as good-looking and flirtatious as Milton was begging for trouble. They were both right, but she wasn't ready to hear "I told you so" yet. There was time enough for that.

Her parents had called last week to tell her of their planned trip to the Far East. Her mother had given her an itinerary, and if her parents followed the carefully laid plans of their travel agent, they were somewhere in Singapore. However, knowing her parents, they'd veered off the beaten and well-planned path to do their own thing. She had no idea where they were, but she was just grateful that they weren't home in Jamaica.

As she'd done several times in the short time she had known him, she cursed Sam Trahan again for bullying her into doing something she was not ready to do. Although she hadn't known him long, she could tell that he was arrogant, insufferable, opinionated, stubborn, and just plain annoying— qualities that she did not admire in anyone, let alone someone who was blackmailing her. She just hoped that they would find Milton quickly, so she would be able to put the experience behind her as quickly as possible and return to a life she had grown comfortable, if not completely happy, with.

* * *

Sam closed his suitcase. Everything was packed, he was ready to go. The conversation with Justin had bothered him, unnecessarily so he thought, for he knew his brother's sole purpose, other than wasting his inheritance, was to annoy him. Justin had raised annoying him to a fine art. He excelled in it. It pained Sam to admit that after all this time, Justin still got under his skin. He was a pro, thought Sam. He'd been doing it for a lifetime.

There was, however, a small, nagging feeling that was beginning to take shape in Sam's mind—the idea that maybe, just maybe, Justin had a point that he was to blame for the whole Black Madonna fiasco. After all, the painting, a family heirloom, had been taken on his watch. His grandmother had entrusted the painting to him and it had been stolen. Hubris, he thought. He'd displayed the portrait prominently in his office for all the world to see. He was proud of his ancestor Antoinette Millefleurs, proud that as her descendant, a descendant of a slave, he now owned his own company. Displaying the painting had been his way of not only paying homage to her, but also of reminding himself of how far the Trahan clan had come.

He'd felt that the painting was secure. There was an expensive alarm system which should have alerted security if anyone even touched the portrait. Instead, Milton had walked away with it, under the noses of security, and everyone else in his company, including himself. The thought galled him, but it did not humble him. There was a lesson to be learned in all of this, and Sam intended to learn it. He also felt, without any other reason than his instinct, that finding the Black Madonna would play an important part in his future, and the future of his family—and he was going to do whatever he could to ensure that the picture was returned. He lifted his suitcase in one fluid, decisive motion. It was time to go and do what he should have done two months ago. It was time to get back the Black Madonna.

3

The next morning, Sam sat in his first class cabin seat of Air Jamaica and watched his beautiful companion grip the armrests of her seat as the plane dipped from side to side. Zora Redwood was a mystery to him. This woman hadn't bat an eyelash when he told her about Milton's affair with his secretary, not to mention the serious trouble that both she and her boyfriend were currently facing, yet here she was sitting beside him with her eyes squeezed shut, holding on to her armrests like a baby holding on to her mother's hand.

"You must be a nervous flyer," said Sam, his voice betraying little of his amusement.

"You might say that," said Zora. Her eyes remained closed and her hands did not let go of the armrest.

"These things are safer than cars," Sam commented. On the drive to Kennedy Airport earlier that morning she'd barely acknowledged his presence. Instead, she'd stared determinedly out of the window. He hadn't attempted to make small talk with her. He had a goal to accomplish and that was the only reason she was there. Still, her complete disregard of his presence struck him as curious. It was a long time since he had met a female who wasn't at the very least intrigued by him.

Keep your mind on the business at hand, said the voice inside him that always stressed caution. Sam knew that this voice had never failed him and he could not afford to lose his focus.

"If you don't mind," said Zora, "I'd rather not discuss the safety of airplanes with you at this particular moment."

"I'm sure that you'd rather not discuss anything with me at this particular moment—or any other, for that matter," responded Sam.

"You're right about that," said Zora through clenched teeth.

"Is there anything wrong?" the voice of one of the stewardess interrupted their conversation.

The stewardess spoke to Zora, but her eyes did not leave Sam's for a second. Those eyes held an invitation. "Is your wife all right?"

"I'm not his wife," said Zora quickly.

"Oh," purred the stewardess happily, "is there anything I can help either of you with—"

"A drink would be nice," replied Zora. "The stronger, the better."

"Certainly," said the stewardess with a quick smile in Sam's direction, "would the gentleman like a drink?"

Sam shook his head. "No thanks," he said, "never touch the stuff."

"A light refreshment perhaps?" The stewardess did not give up easily.

"No, thank you," said Sam smoothly, "I'm perfectly fine, but if that should change, I'll be sure to get your attention."

"Oh please," said Zora, exasperated, "the man doesn't want a drink! I am the one about to pass out here!"

The stewardess turned her attention back to Zora and stared at her blankly as if she had no idea what Zora was taking about.

"My drink?" commented Zora as if she were refreshing the woman's recollection.

"Oh yes, your drink," replied the stewardess, who bestowed one last smile on Sam before she turned and left them.

"Friendly woman," Sam commented, keeping his eyes on his reluctant traveling companion. "You know, since we're stuck in this together, at least until we find your fiancé—"

"Ex-fiancé."

"We might try getting along," said Sam, ignoring Zora's last comment. "It might make this trip a little easier."

"I'm not usually that chummy with folks who are blackmailing me."

Sam admired her. With everything that was facing her, she still had spirit. She might be down, as the saying went, but she was definitely not out. His grandmother would have liked her.

"Perhaps another time . . ." Sam let the sentence dangle for a moment. He was flirting with her and damned if he couldn't help it. Sam was not one to act inappropriately and flirting with the ex-fiancé of the man who had stolen from him was, at the very least, inappropriate. His apparent lack of control where Miss Redwood was concerned should have bothered him more than it did. Before he saw her today, his mood had been dark; thoughts of his failure to protect his family's prize possession figured dominantly in his mind, but when his car pulled into her block and he saw her waiting there—with her ridiculous yellow sundress and white sweater draped around her shoulders, her wide-brimmed straw hat, and holding a small floral suitcase in her hand like a shield—his spirits had soared. He waited for her reply to his not-so-veiled proposition.

It came quickly.

"Never," said Zora as she stared directly into his eyes. "There will never be a time when I would have anything to do with you or your kind."

"My kind?"

"Yes," she said, her voice as firm as her convictions, "your kind. People who feel that their position in life entitles them to rule the world and the people in it."

Sam chuckled, "Rarely has someone looked so deeply into my soul and found the truth."

He was mocking her and she knew it. This only seemed to make her angrier.

"When this whole ordeal is over," she said, "I sincerely hope to never see that smirk of yours again."

"Never is a long time, Miss Redwood."

He watched as she leaned back in the seat and closed her eyes, effectively dismissing him. "Not long enough, Mr. Trahan. Not long enough."

* * *

"Ladies and gentlemen, we have begun our final descent into Donald Sangster Airport. In just a few minutes we will be landing in Montego Bay . . ."

Zora felt a sense of excitement as she looked out of the window at the rolling green hills, their pastel colored villas and more modest houses adorning them like ornaments. Below her, a sea of blue and green with patches of turquoise in some places glistened in the sunlight. She watched the small boats carrying what she knew were local fishermen competing with huge white ocean liners laden with tourists.

The leaves of the palm trees seemed to wave a welcome home salute to her. As the airplane made its way across the north coast of the island, she could see familiar landmarks, lighthouses that were there when she was growing up, the Rose Hall Mansion where it was rumored a witch lived with her slaves, Tryall golf course, where her father regularly played golf, the winding hillside roads surrounding Montego Bay, where her mother drove her Aston Martin at speeds in excess of any legal speed limit. It was hard to remember that there was a time when her parents had been the sun, moon, and the stars to her. Those were some very happy times.

"Beautiful."

Sam's voice interrupted her reverie.

Zora looked over to find him staring in her direction. For a moment she wasn't sure if he was referring to her or to the scene just outside the window.

He clarified his statement. "Your country is quite lovely. Under other circumstances, I'm sure that I would have enjoyed coming here."

Other circumstances. The reason for her return to the island reared its ugly head. How was she going to find Milton? There were many places to hide on the island. She thought of the Maroons, African slaves, who'd hidden in the mountains from the British for centuries. Milton was no Maroon, but he was cunning. Like a chameleon, he could blend into his surroundings so perfectly he could appear to be invisible. Everything had happened so suddenly. Yesterday, she was a nursery school teacher planning her lessons for the next week. Today, she was in search of a thief, who she'd just a short time ago pledged to love forever.

She looked down at her bare left hand. Even after she found out about Milton's deception, it had taken her a long time to take the ring off. Even after her feelings for Milton ended, she'd worn his ring. Looking back, she realized that it wasn't sentimentality that kept her holding on to his ring after she had ceased holding on to him. It was difficult to let go of the dream of what Milton represented: love, family, future—the dream of what could be. She'd grown up with parents whose passion for each other had never waned. Her father still brought her mother hand-picked flowers. Zora had hoped that lightning would strike twice, and that she would find someone who would make her heart sing. However, it was not to be. Last week, she had finally let go and had taken off the ring. She'd placed it in a box and put it away in her desk drawer. Her thoughts returned to finding Milton. She knew

that there was one person on the island who would
help her, and that was the first place she would
start in this hunt for Milton. It wasn't too long ago
that she had prayed never to see Milton again,
after she learned about his true character. Now,
she was praying that she would find him.

"Now that the plane is landing," said Sam, interrupting her reverie, "perhaps this would be a
good time to discuss your plan to locate Milton."

"I haven't formulated a plan just yet," Zora
replied honestly.

"Well, may I suggest that there is no time like
the present," said Sam.

"I'm working on it," said Zora.

Zora marveled at the sights and sounds around
her. She was home. The taxi stand where she stood
waiting with Sam Trahan was filled with taxi drivers
calling out towns to which they were going. "Negril!
Negril, here!" "Fastest and safest ride to MoBay!"
"Ocho Rios!" "Discovery Bay!" Zora drank it all in.
She was back home and, despite the circumstances,
her spirits rose. There was no place like the land
where she was born. She drank in the smell of the
sea which followed you no matter where you were
on the island and she drank in the lush scenery,
the green foliage, the bright-colored flowers, the
vendors hawking their wares, the palm tree leaves
that swayed gracefully in the wind.

"Okay," said Sam, as they stood outside by the
taxi port, "How're we doing on that plan of yours?"

Zora turned and looked at him. She'd thought
that with his business tycoon air that clung to him

like perfume, he would look out of place in Jamaica, a place where being casual and unhurried was a way of life. Instead, he looked as if he belonged here, as if he'd lived in the tropics all his life. He looked, she thought, searching for the right word, comfortable.

"We're going to Goshen," said Zora, "that's where Milton is from. It's also where I'm from. If Milton is on the island, someone in Goshen would know about it. I'm sure that his aunt would be able to at least give us some information, or a way to find him."

"Why didn't you give this information to the detectives?" Sam asked, his voice clearly showing that he was at the very least, annoyed, and at the worst . . . well, Zora didn't want to think about that.

"They didn't ask me," Zora replied. She hadn't wanted Milton's aunt to be dragged into his mess. Aunt Essie was innocent and Zora hadn't wanted her to get hurt, as she had, by Milton's deceit.

"Do you think his aunt will help us?" asked Sam.

"I'm sure of it," replied Zora. "Aunt Essie is close to me."

"What're you going to tell her?" asked Sam.

"The truth," replied Zora. "With Aunt Essie, there is no other way."

"All right," he said slowly as if he debated the wisdom of every word. "I'm giving you two days to find your fiancé. If you can't do it by then, we'll have to follow some other course of action."

Zora's patience was wearing thin. Sam Trahan had completely disrupted her life in the space of less than forty-eight hours. He'd demanded that she help find Milton and now that she was helping him accomplish this, he seemed to doubt that she would be able to do what he requested. If he had so many doubts why did he pull her into this scheme?

"What other course of action could you possibly be thinking of? You're in a foreign country where, with the exception of yours truly, you don't know a soul," said Zora, certain that although she was stating the obvious, the words needed to be said.

"That may be so," replied Sam, unwilling to concede, "but I'm a desperate man, Miss Redwood, and as the saying goes, desperate men often employ desperate measures."

Zora looked at Sam again. "I know that the painting is worth a lot of money, but it seems that you're going to a lot of trouble to find it."

"It belongs to my family and I want it back," said Sam, as if that one statement explained everything. "It's not about the money."

She debated whether to ask him more. She wanted to understand what it was about this painting that had propelled him to travel to another country, not to mention blackmail her, just to find it. She knew that it was worth a great deal of money, but she was certain that it was insured. He did not strike her as someone who was obsessed with art, but then, she knew very little about the man, Zora chided herself. Now was not the time to lose herself wondering about other people's business. She needed to focus on more immediate matters, finding Milton.

She raised her hand and signaled for a taxi. Almost instantaneously a yellow taxi cab appeared.

The driver rolled down his window and asked Zora, "Where to, boss lady?"

"We're going to Goshen," she replied, "and we're in a hurry."

"You don' have to say not another word," said the taxi driver as he opened the door and stepped into the hot Caribbean sunshine. "Jus' give me your bags and settle yourselves in my cab. I'll get you to Goshen so fast you'll think that you just took another airplane ride."

The taxi driver was many things, including a lousy driver, but he wasn't a liar. Sam couldn't have imagined traveling any faster by airplane. The taxi had careened through the streets of Montego Bay and then through the surrounding countryside at speeds well in excess of common sense. They drove along a winding road that seemed to hug the coast.

About two hours after the start of the journey, the taxi veered away toward the hills and they began a sharp and precipitous drive up the hills. This was slower going; at times the roads were unpaved. Sam had to admit that the view below of the green countryside, sloping hills, and the sea—which was now a brilliant blue that stretched out joining the horizon—was spectacular.

His companion was silent for most of the ride. She stared out of the window, lost in her own private thoughts.

"So what brings you to Jamaica, mon?" asked the driver, as the taxi slowed down to a halt to let some pedestrians cross the road. "Business or pleasure?"

"A little bit of both," Sam replied.

Zora remained silent, continuing to look out of the window. An air of sadness had descended on her as the taxi made its way up the winding hillside road. Sam wondered if she was thinking about Milton. He knew that she was from these parts, and these surroundings undoubtedly carried many memories with them. There was a lot troubling her, and Sam knew that he played a part in that. It was not his intention to cause Zora Redwood the pain that was now reflected in those faraway eyes. When this was all over, he would do everything in his power to see that she didn't get caught in the same net as Milton. Anyone could see that she was no thief. But, for now, he needed her help and the only way to ensure that she continued helping him was to let her think that she was in as much trouble as Milton.

"Your wife is very quiet," remarked the cab driver.

This was the second time today that someone had mistaken them for a married couple—first, the stewardess, and now, the friendly cab driver.

Sam did nothing to correct the man's mistake. Instead, he changed the subject.

"What part of the island are we in?" he asked.

"We're in St. Ann's Parish," replied the cab driver. "God's country, mon. Nothing like it. These are my people, mon. I grew up around these parts an' I still come here often."

The cab driver and Sam continued talking for the remainder of the ride. By the time they reached Goshen, he had told Sam about the history of St. Ann and the history of his family.

Zora gave the driver the directions to the home

of Milton's aunt. The sadness that had enveloped her during the ride seemed to evaporate into the steamy, tropical air. She once again became the prim, businesslike nursery school teacher that he'd met yesterday on a Brooklyn street, giving directions like a drill sergeant.

"We're going to twenty-four Hibiscus Road. Make a left here, and then go up two more blocks, then you make another left, and it's just up the road from the Anglican Church."

"I know the place," commented the taxi driver. "I used to be a good Anglican before I married my wife. Then I became a good Baptist."

The telephone rang seventeen times before Milton picked up the receiver. He'd counted each ring as his heart pounded with the fear that surrounded him. No one knew his telephone number. The telephone was to be used only if there was an emergency. He'd never called anyone using this phone. He knew that the people who were soon going to make him a very, very wealthy man were also dangerous. He didn't want to take the chance that they would trace his call back to his sanctuary.

Perhaps it was a wrong number. Still, the telephone continued ringing. I won't answer it, he thought, as he stood by the phone, watching as it continued to ring. Whoever it is will soon hang up. On the fifteenth ring he reached for the telephone, but he did not pick it up. On the seventeenth ring he'd grabbed the phone for fear that he'd go out of his mind.

He picked up the receiver and waited.

"Milton, I know that you're there. Answer me."

It was Felice. How the hell did she find him? He'd been certain to cover his tracks, particularly where that bloodhound Felice was concerned.

"How did you find me?"

He heard the sound of her laughter. "Don't worry about how I found you."

Milton felt his heart hammering in his chest. He'd been so careful and still he had been discovered. If an amateur like Felice could find him, then his business associates most certainly would do the same. He was going to have to leave this place and quickly.

"What do you want, Felice?" he asked, but he already knew the answer to his question.

"I want my money, Milton. You double-crossing . . ."

"I was just laying low," said Milton. "I was going to get back in touch with you."

"This wasn't the plan, Milton. Not at all. Sam Trahan paid me a visit, and do you know what he wanted, Milton? He wants you. I strongly suspect that Sam Trahan always gets what he wants, which usually is of no concern to me, but if he gets you, then that road will lead right back to me, then I have a problem."

"Don't worry about Sam Trahan," said Milton. "I can take care of him. He hasn't found me in two months, I don't think he'll find me now."

"Don't be a fool," said Felice. "I found you. It's only a matter of time before Sam finds you."

Her point was undeniable. From the time he had left New York, he had kept moving. He knew that the first place that anyone would look for him would be Jamaica, so he had gone first to Canada, then to the Cayman Islands where he had friends who didn't ask questions. He'd stayed there until last week when he came home to Jamaica. This was the place that the actual business transaction was supposed to occur. It was the only place where he had complete control over his environment. Once he got his money, he planned to leave the island and not return for a long time. His immediate destination had not yet been determined, perhaps someplace in South America. He could lose himself there very easily. But now, he had to be careful, very careful. Felice had tracked him down, and she was right, Sam Trahan was no fool. He was going to have to leave his hideaway and find another place on the island to become invisible until he contacted his buyers.

" I want my money now, Milton."

"You know that's not possible yet," replied Milton. "And why're you contacting me now? You know that the sale's not for another week. Once I sell the painting, then you'll get your share."

"This may come as a surprise to you, Milton," said Felice, "but I don't trust you. I'm coming to Jamaica, and I want my money."

Milton placed the telephone back in its cradle without responding. Then he took the phone off the hook. He did not want any more phone calls from Felice.

4

Although it had been years since Zora last saw
Miss Essie, and months since she'd spoken to her
on the telephone, she didn't look particularly surprised to see Zora standing on her doorstep.
Milton had always said that his aunt had a sixth
sense about things. She could tell trouble was coming long before its actual arrival. Many people in
Goshen would consult Miss Essie about their problems. She was good at giving advice, but she
stopped short of predicting the future. Only God
can do that, she would say, but she would warn
folks to walk with care because hard times were
coming, or she would tell folks that it was time to
get out their dancing shoes because something
good was on the way.

"Come on in, Zora," she said simply, "I've been
expecting you."

No "hello, how are you." No "what are you doing on the island?" No "who's that strange man standing behind you?"

Zora and Sam followed Miss Essie through the various rooms in her split-level house until they reached the back porch, which was set off from the kitchen. Zora had been to this house many times. Before she and Milton became an item, they were friends. Most of the neighborhood children had been afraid of Miss Essie. They called her a witch behind her back, but Zora had been fascinated by Miss Essie. For Zora, the tall, thin woman, the color of wheat after it had been in the sun awhile, who would drink rum, smoke cigars, and carry on each Friday and Saturday but who always faithfully made it to church on Sunday, was one of her earliest friends. Even as a young child Zora recognized that Miss Essie didn't care what folks said about her, and Zora who grew up caring about people's opinions, admired her.

One day on the way home from school, Zora had accepted Miss Essie's invitation to ride home in her car. From that point, they became good friends. Miss Essie let her be herself. When Zora was with her parents, she always felt as if she had to perform for them. They were constantly quizzing her on the latest political debate, scientific theories, her views about literature. It didn't seem to matter when she got things right, they would just continue drilling in the importance of being absolutely and unequivocally perfect in everything she did.

At Miss Essie's house, Zora could run barefoot in the yard with mango juice rolling down her chin and no one would yell at her. She could read the dime-store detective novels that her mother denounced as "rubbish" and "a waste of brain matter." She could talk about her dreams and not have anyone challenge them and, more importantly, she could be whoever it was that she wanted to be on that particular day. The only rule in Miss Essie's house was that children should never, ever be rude. They could be inquisitive. They could be loud. They could be messy. She did not, however, tolerate rudeness.

Milton had been a sickly child, aloof, handsome, and condescending. He would watch her playing in the yard without making much comment. He lived with his aunt after his mother died, but he had never become particularly close to her. Miss Essie, for her part, loved the strange, quiet boy, but she never grew to understand him. Years later, when Milton and Zora started dating, when they were both in New York, Miss Essie had not hidden her disappointment or her disapproval.

"Milton is blood to me, but this union will bring water to your eyes," declared Miss Essie.

Zora knew that Milton wasn't perfect. Still, she'd let her common sense take wings and fly away when Milton's friendship turned to a romantic direction. Looking back, she realized that her loneliness had driven her straight into his arms. In time, she'd convinced herself that she was in love with him. After all, he was smart, handsome, ambitious, and Jamaican. For Zora, that was a winning combination, until the truth revealed itself. It hurt that everyone had been right about Milton's shortcomings. She wondered how she alone could have been so blind.

"Sit down, Zora," said Miss Essie, "and your friend, too."

Zora sat on one of the four identical white wood chairs with their multi-colored cushions, and Sam sat in the chair next to her. Miss Essie sat across from them, her hands folded in her lap.

Esmene Viola Bogle was known to most people in Goshen as Miss Essie. To strangers she was Miss Bogle. As was her habit she was dressed completely in white, from her white cotton dress to her white sandals with heels so high that Zora wondered how she walked in them. A tall, thin woman, Miss Essie stood just over six feet barefoot and with the heels Miss Essie usually wore, she towered over most people. The fact that she had seen her seventieth birthday five years ago did nothing to diminish the quiet power that seemed to be as much a part of her person as the small, black mole on her chin. Her hair was completely white and she wore it in two braids wrapped around her head as if they were a white crown. Her eyes, which were staring directly at Zora, were gray.

"Perhaps you should introduce me to your gentleman friend, Zora," said Miss Essie, clearing her throat.

Sam introduced himself. "My name is Sam Trahan, ma'am."

Recognition lit Miss Essie's gray eyes.

"My nephew worked for you," she said. "He spoke of you and your accomplishments often. I would say that it is a pleasure to meet you, but I suspect the present circumstances of our meeting is going to be anything but pleasurable."

"I'm afraid that you're right about that, ma'am,"

said Sam. "I would've preferred meeting you under different circumstances."

Miss Essie turned her attention to Zora.

"You might as well tell me why you're here, Zora," she said. "What has my nephew done now?"

"He's stolen something that belongs to me," Sam replied, without waiting for Zora's response.

Zora flashed him a look of anger—and exasperation. She'd wanted to tell Miss Essie in her own way. She knew that although Miss Essie knew the true nature of her nephew, this information was just going to hurt her. She took everything Milton did, from leaving Zora to his other acts of casual malice, personally.

"Is this true, Zora?" she asked.

Zora nodded her head. "Yes, Miss Essie, it's true."

Miss Essie looked directly at Zora. "Are you mixed up in this, Zora?"

Again, Zora nodded her head. "Yes, I am. Milton told me that he was holding a painting for a friend, and he asked me to keep it for him. I did. I never knew that the painting was stolen until after Milton left, and the police paid me a visit."

"The painting belongs to you, then?" Miss Essie asked, turning to Sam.

"It belongs to my family, but it was taken from me."

Miss Essie shook her head. "Every time I think that Milton can do nothing more to surprise a very old woman, he proves me wrong."

"I'm sorry," said Zora, and she meant it. Miss Essie had always done right by Milton. She had taken him in, when the rest of his family had turned their collective back on him. She had treated him as if he were her own child, yet, almost from the beginning, Milton had given her trouble.

"There's nothing for you to be sorry about, Zora," replied Miss Essie. "It's me who should be sorry for ever letting you get mixed up with Milton."

"I made my own choices," said Zora. "I knew what I was getting into with Milton."

"No, you didn't, child," replied Miss Essie, gently patting Zora's hand. "You didn't know."

Miss Essie turned her attention back to Sam. "So, you need to find my nephew, and you want my help, is that so?"

"Yes," replied Sam, nodding his head.

"If I help you, will you leave Zora out of this?" asked Miss Essie.

"I'll do what I can," replied Sam.

"Not good enough," said Miss Essie, her gray eyes turning to steel. "I need your assurance that Zora will not get involved in this mess."

"You have my word that I will do everything in my power to clear Zora's name once we find Milton. That's the best that I can do."

"Are you a man of your word, Sam Trahan?" asked Miss Essie.

"I live and die by my word," Sam replied without hesitation.

"If you have any information, please tell him," said Zora. "That's the only way that my name will be cleared."

"He's definitely here in Jamaica," said Miss Essie. "One of my friends from church saw him in Montego Bay airport two days ago. He didn't see her, but my friend called me the same day. You know her, Zora. Alva, Preacher Rose's sister."

"Do you know where he is?" asked Zora, feeling something close to hope that this ordeal would soon be over. Once they found Milton, she'd be free. She could put this experience behind her and she could have her life back again.

Miss Essie shook her head, "I don't know where he is, but I have a good idea who can help you find him."

"Who?" asked Zora.

"There's a woman in Runaway Bay, by the name of Shelly Wong. He's been keeping company with her for years. I'm sorry, Zora—I always planned to tell you but I didn't work up the nerve. Milton kept telling me that he would end the relationship with her and I was afraid to hurt you. You've had more than enough hurt, even as young as you are—I'm sorry."

Zora felt her hands go cold. It wasn't that Milton's betrayal hurt her—she now knew what he was capable of—it was Miss Essie's silence that stung. Miss Essie had always been the one person Zora thought she could trust. She would have trusted Miss Essie with her life, but all along Miss Essie knew that Milton had another woman, and she had remained silent.

"After Milton left, I thought that there was no need to tell you about his woman in Runaway Bay." She stared at her hands. "I should have said something—forgive me . . ."

Zora forced herself to speak. She kept her voice under control, even as her heart hammered in her chest. "Don't trouble yourself, Miss Essie, he had a woman in New York, also."

Miss Essie didn't look surprised. She just repeated the words "I'm sorry."

"How far is Runaway Bay?"asked Sam.

"It's about two hours away," replied Zora, forcing herself to remain composed. She hoped that the humiliation she felt wasn't evident. Of all the people in this world, Sam Trahan was the last person she wanted to witness this. Why she should care about Sam Trahan's opinions of her remained a mystery to her, but she did care.

"Where can we find this Shelly Wong?" asked Sam.

"She owns a small hotel there, really its more of an inn. It's called 'Runnings,' and it's right off the main highway. near Porto Seco beach. Zora will know where it is."

"We need a car," said Sam. "Is there anywhere we can rent one here in Goshen?"

Miss Essie said, "You can take my car. I don't have much use for it anyhow."

"That's not necessary," replied Zora, not wanting to take any more favors from Miss Essie. She knew that she was being petulant, and foolish as well, but the thought of being the beneficiary of Miss Essie's kindness, after what she had just learned about her, didn't seem right.

"We can rent a car in Montego Bay," said Zora.

"Don't be foolish," replied Miss Essie, in a tone of voice that showed that she would not tolerate any foolishness. "Take my car. I don't need it."

"You're absolutely right," said Sam, "and we appreciate your generosity."

"Then that's settled," replied Miss Essie.

Zora stood up, eager to be as far away from Miss Essie's porch as modern machinery could take her.

"Forgive me, child." Miss Essie's voice rang out in the quiet of the late afternoon. The sun was beginning its descent, and Zora could see that its rays had started to drape the tops of the hills in the distance.

"There's nothing to forgive," said Zora, keeping her attention focused on the hills which flanked Goshen in the distance. She didn't look at Miss Essie.

Miss Essie turned to Sam and said, "I wonder if you could give us a few moments alone?"

"Certainly," said Sam. "I'll be waiting outside."

After Sam left the porch, Miss Essie got up and walked over to where Zora was standing. "I know that you're hurt, and I know that you're angry, but I want you to know that I'm sorry, child, for any part that I played in your pain."

Zora shook her head, not trusting herself to talk. She'd never been disrespectful to Miss Essie and she didn't want to start now, but the anger that had grabbed hold of her might make her tongue say things that she would regret later. Miss Essie had known about what Milton was doing, and she'd remained silent. As far as Zora was concerned, Miss Essie was a part of Milton's lies. There was no other way to look at it.

"I love you like my own child, Zora," Miss Essie continued. "I thought that Milton would come to his senses one day and see you for the jewel that you are. I thought that once that day came he would stop playing the fool. I made a bargain with myself that I would tell you one day, but that day didn't come Zora. I'm sorry."

"I'm going to be fine," said Zora in a voice which

was stronger than what she was feeling. "Don't worry about me."

"I know that you'll be fine," said Miss Essie. "But that doesn't make up for what I've done, Zora. I know that forgiveness is too much to ask, but I pray that one day you'll understand that it was just an old woman's desire not to hurt you that caused me to keep silent."

Zora was angry but she knew that her anger, like all other bad feelings, would pass in time. Miss Essie had wiped many tears from Zora's eyes when she was a child and she could not forget that.

"Don't worry, Miss Essie," said Zora. "I know you didn't want to hurt me."

The words sounded hollow to her own ears, but they had to be said. Zora didn't want to hurt Miss Essie, any more than Miss Essie wanted to hurt her.

"I understand, child."

Zora kissed Miss Essie and turned to leave. As she walked to the door leading back to the main dining room, she heard Miss Essie say, "Don't let Milton close your heart, Zora. Don't let him make you look happiness in the face and not recognize it."

"What are you talking about?" asked Zora, turning back to face Miss Essie.

"I'm saying that there's a good man on his way to you. Open your eyes or you won't recognize him."

Miss Essie was talking in riddles once again, but this time Zora didn't have the energy, or the inclination to try to understand the message that she was giving her. As far as Zora was concerned, meeting a man—good or otherwise—was not anything she wanted to spend any time on. She wasn't interested. She wasn't ready to join a nunnery yet, but she was close.

"Take care, Miss Essie," said Zora, and she left the flower-filled porch.

"This is Miss Essie's car?" Sam stood in front of the open garage door adjacent to Miss Essie's house and stared at the bright red convertible Porsche two-seater.

He watched as Zora walked around to the driver's seat and opened the door. "I'm driving," she said as if she expected Sam to challenge her.

She needn't have worried about that, thought Sam, he'd seen enough crazy driving on the island. Besides, he thought as he put their luggage in the trunk, these folk drive on the wrong side of the road.

Zora slid into the seat, shut the door and turned on the ignition.

"Are you getting in or am I taking this part of the trip on my own?" she asked him.

Sam closed the trunk and walked over to the front of the car. After opening the passenger door, he got in the car beside her. "Not on your life, sweetheart. You're stuck with me until we find Milton."

He slammed the door shut as if to emphasize the point. At the mention of Milton's name, Sam saw a shadow cross Zora's eyes. A momentary flicker of pain which disappeared so quickly, Sam wondered if he had imagined it. What kind of fool would let a woman like this go, he thought for the second time in as many days.

Sam buckled his seat belt and settled into his seat.

"What's the matter?" asked Zora. "Don't you trust my driving?"

"No offense," replied Sam, "but what little I've seen of the way folks drive around here has convinced me that I'm safer with a seat belt."

"True," conceded Zora. "We Jamaicans drive without fear."

"Oh, is that how you describe it?" Sam said, keeping his tone mild. "Sweetheart, I would've described the way I've seen folks drive here a little bit differently."

Zora shifted gears into reverse and they pulled out of the driveway quickly. As they drove away, Sam could see Miss Essie standing by a second floor window. She'd reminded him of his own grandmother—domineering, loyal, feisty. He'd also seen the closeness that Miss Essie and Zora shared. It was evident from the moment they laid eyes on each other. But now that closeness had been poisoned by Milton's actions. He knew that the latest news that Miss Essie had hidden the truth from her had been a blow to Zora.

He glanced over at her and felt an unfamiliar feeling of protectiveness towards her. Where on earth did that come from, he wondered. He should be worrying about finding Milton before he did any more damage to the Black Madonna, not worrying about some woman who was foolhardy enough to trust Milton. The fact that he, too, had been foolhardy in trusting Milton didn't escape him.

Still, Zora was holding up under pressure. In spite of everything, she was keeping her head up. That only made him want to protect her all the more from Milton. It was obvious that behind that tough, cool exterior, there was a woman who was hurting. She could never be a good poker player, not with those eyes which, if one looked closely, and Sam always did, betrayed her feelings.

"Mr. Trahan," said Zora, keeping her eyes on the road, "don't feel sorry for me."

"I don't," Sam said honestly. Pity was the last emotion that came to his mind where Zora Redwood was concerned. Grudging admiration, yes. Growing attraction, perhaps. But pity, that never entered into the equation at all.

Zora pressed her foot down on the gas pedal, and they hurtled forward.

"One more thing," she said, taking a steep curve in the road like a seasoned race car driver.

"Yes?" Sam asked.

"Don't call me sweetheart."

5

They reached Runaway Bay just as night fell.
The seaside town was familiar to Zora. The narrow
road on which they were driving cut almost
straight through the center of the town and was
flanked by pastel-colored houses, newly built hotels, shops and several churches. Zora drank in the
scene around her—market women balancing baskets full of fruit on their heads, children running
along the side of the road, Rastafarians with their
dreadlocks hanging down their backs driving by
on mopeds, prosperous-looking folk dressed in suits,
old women walking together intent on their conversation, adventurous tourists looking both bewildered and beleaguered wandering around and
others still dressed in their Sunday Church dresses.
Her mother was from the area, and as a child growing up, Zora had spent many weekends visiting her
relatives in the Runaway Bay area. Her relatives had
moved from the area long ago. Most had migrated

to the United States or to England, but there were a few that remained in Kingston, the capital, where, like her parents, they prospered.

She was tired. She was hungry, and she was depressed. She felt as if she were running a race where there was no prize at the finish line. She thought of Milton and the role he played in bringing her back to the land where she was born. He had always vowed that he would get her to return to Jamaica, and in this, as in many other things, Milton got his way. Once again, she cursed the day she'd allowed Milton access to her heart.

"How far are we from Runnings Inn?" asked Sam, interrupting her thoughts

"Miss Essie said it's on the main road just past the market, so we should be there in the next five minutes or so."

"Are you familiar with every part of Jamaica?" asked Sam. "You seem to know your way around these parts pretty well."

"Not every part," conceded Zora, with a smile; it was the first compliment she'd gotten from him. "But I know the north coast pretty well. We spent summers here when I was growing up."

"It sounds like heaven," said Sam. "My summers were spent working on my grandmother's farm in South Carolina. My grandmother believed in hard work."

"I'd say that your grandmother's work ethic paid off handsomely for you."

Sam laughed, "She would've appreciated hearing that. She constantly gave herself credit for everything I ever achieved, not that I disagree with her, of course."

"It must be nice to have family that appreciates what you do," Zora commented. "Mine are hoping that one day I'll grow up and get a real job."

Zora didn't know why she told him this. She'd never talked much about her family, even to Milton. Her parents' disapproval was a painful subject; one she tried to avoid whenever possible.

"How could they not be proud of you?" asked Sam. He sounded so surprised that Zora knew his statement was genuine and not merely spoken to soothe her feelings—not that Sam Trahan appeared to be a person who cared about the feelings of others, particularly hers.

"You've never met my parents," replied Zora.

"Perhaps one day I will," said Sam, mildly.

Zora thought about that statement as she drove towards Shelly Wong's hotel. The chances of Sam Trahan meeting her parents were as remote as her winning the New York State Lottery.

They drove the rest of the way in silence until Zora saw the sign for Runnings Inn. She turned into the driveway of the inn, and drove the short distance to the front entrance. The inn was built in a Spanish hacienda style with a white stucco exterior and maroon shutters. There was a garden in front of the hotel in which tropical flowers and various species of green foliage gave the inn an exotic air. There were white lights strung throughout the branches of the tree in front. From the outside, the hotel looked charming. It looked like a place for honeymooners, for lovers. Zora turned off the engine and sat silently, trying to wrestle with her thoughts. An unwanted fear gripped her. Even though she knew about Milton's inability to be faithful to her, it still hurt. There was a part of her that wanted to run away. She didn't want to meet the other woman. Seeing her would make her existence real, and the inevitable hurt that would follow wasn't something that Zora wanted to deal with. What was so wrong with me, Milton, she wanted to ask. Why wasn't I good enough for you?

Sam cleared his throat and said, "Maybe I should handle Miss Wong. Your presence might, well, complicate things."

Zora raised her left eyebrow. "Complicate things?"

She knew that she was being unreasonable. Sam had just handed her an escape route. He was offering to deal with Shelly Wong on his own. She didn't have to see this woman. She could turn tail and hide. Still, she didn't want Sam to think that she was weak. Not that his opinion of her should matter, but on this subject it did. She didn't want his pity and she didn't want him to take care of her. She could handle Shelly Wong.

"I'm sure that a meeting with this woman is bound to be awkward for you—"

"Don't be so sure of that, Mr. Trahan. I'm a strong woman. I think I can handle seeing Milton's . . . friend . . . without falling apart on you."

Although Zora knew that Sam was right, it would be hard to face Shelley Wong, but she refused to let him see her fear. Maybe it was pride, or maybe she was just her mother's child. Zora could not abide other people's pity.

"I didn't mean to insinuate—"

"Yes, you did," Zora cut him off. "I'm now as

much a part of this situation as Milton. I'll be damned if I let Milton drag my name through the dirt with his. I'm going in there with you and just you try and stop me. The quicker I find him, then the quicker I can get my name out of this mess, and the quicker I get away from you."

"You mean you don't enjoy my company." Sam Trahan had the nerve to grin at her.

"Let me put it this way," Zora replied. "I'd rather be at the dentist's office, getting a root canal without the benefit of novocaine."

What happened next came so swiftly that Zora didn't see it coming. Sam Trahan leaned forward and kissed her lightly on the mouth. Zora instinctively moved to pull away, but he put one hand behind her head and the kiss grew deeper, more intimate. For one treacherous moment, Zora felt herself respond to the kiss and she wrapped her arms around him, drawing him closer. He tasted like honey with spice. She tightened her embrace and she felt his hands caress the side of her face, then reality came flooding back. She pulled away from him, breathless.

What on earth was wrong with her? She was kissing a man who was blackmailing her, and what was infinitely worse, she'd enjoyed it! Shaking her head, she tried to rid herself of the part of her that wanted to throw herself back into his arms. She'd never, never been kissed like that before. Other kisses had been pleasant, this kiss had been . . . she struggled to find the right words to describe Sam Trahan's kisses . . . toe curling, mind blowing, hallelujah hand clapping downright delicious . . .

Nerves, she thought. She'd been through a lot these past few weeks. She wasn't herself—that was all, but she couldn't deny that she had enjoyed kissing Sam Trahan.

Sam cleared his throat and she focused on his face. He looked as stunned as she felt. He didn't look any happier about the kiss than she did.

"Maybe you should wait here for me," he said, his voice hoarse.

Zora stared into Sam's eyes and said, "If you think that one kiss is going to stop me from doing things the way I see fit, then you're dead wrong, Mr. Trahan."

She watched with disbelief as his mouth curved into a smile. "I think that after what just happened Zora, surely we've moved on to a first name basis."

She took a deep breath and forced herself to remain calm. This was exactly what he wanted to do, thought Zora. Throw her off balance, so it would be easier for him to make her do his bidding. Well, he had already forced her into helping him find Milton. She would not let him get hold of her emotions. She just had to focus on the task at hand. Once her goal was accomplished, she need never see Sam Trahan again.

"Mr. Trahan," replied Zora, keeping her voice calm, "may I suggest that instead of sitting there grinning at me, you use your charm somewhere it might actually work, on Shelly Wong."

"So you think I have charm?" asked Sam, grinning.

Zora rolled her eyes in exasperation, "Let's go,

Mr. Trahan. I don't have time to sit here chatting with you. This woman is the only link that I have to clearing my name and you have to finding your painting."

Her voice was calm and steady, but when Zora opened the car door, her hands were shaking.

6

After leaving the car, they'd walked to the hotel in silence. Sam knew that Zora was angry with him about the kiss. not that he blamed her, He was angry with himself for showing such lack of control. It wasn't his style, although he was sure that she'd never believe him. Ever since he met her, he had been acting like a schoolboy with his first crush. Instead of focusing on the serious problem at hand, he'd found himself fantasizing about what her lips would feel like. He hadn't intended to kiss her. One minute, he was his sane, rational self; the next minute he was ravishing her as if they were out on a hot date. He needed to keep his mind on the task at hand. She was becoming a distraction, and there was a part of him—the level-headed part—that told him that perhaps he should undertake the rest of this journey without Zora. But he knew that he couldn't find Milton without her. He couldn't explain it, but he had been sure, almost from the first time he met her, that she would be the key to finding Milton. Well, he would just have to try harder to keep his emotions in check when he was around her.

Pushing all thoughts of his growing attraction to the delectable Zora Redwood out of his mind, Sam walked into the reception area of Runnings Inn with Zora following him. The décor of the inn was similar to several other Caribbean hotels he'd been to—complete with tan rattan chairs, white ceiling fans, bright-colored pictures of tropical birds and flowers. Still, the place had a certain charm to it which was heightened by the steel band music coming from just outside the open windows. There were a few people sitting around on the chairs, but the reception area was remarkably low key for a hotel. The receptionist was reading a novel. Sam walked over to where she sat and Zora followed him. The receptionist continued reading even as they waited by her desk.

Sam cleared his throat twice before she finally looked up at him with an apologetic smile.

"Welcome to Runnings Inn, do you have a reservation?"

Zora spoke up. "We're looking for Shelly Wong."

"Ah," said the receptionist. "Ms. Wong is on the patio with the guests—"

"Which one is Ms. Wong?" asked Sam.

"She won't be difficult to spot," she replied with a smile. "She'll be the prettiest woman out there."

Sam looked at Zora to see how she was taking this comment, but her expression remained inscrutable.

"Beauty is a very subjective thing," Sam commented.

The receptionist laughed. "That's very true. Ms. Wong is wearing a red dress."

They found Shelly Wong standing by an oval-shaped pool. The patio was filled with several guests, most of whom were either dancing to the music of a live steel band, or drinking at the bar by the pool. Sam saw that the receptionist was correct: Shelly Wong was pretty and she was wearing a red dress. Even for Sam, a man who was used to seeing beautiful women, Shelly's beauty was extraordinary. Her skin was a flawless color of mahogany and everything about her seemed magnified—from her large brown eyes, to her exotic cheekbones, to her long brown hair which cascaded around her shoulders and hung almost to her waist. Her lips were full and painted a bright red, which gave a vivid contrast to her brown skin. The red-and-white cotton dress she wore clung to her curvaceous frame as if it were a second skin. Long, brown legs and high heeled white strap sandals completed the picture. She seemed, in a word, perfect—perhaps too perfect. She looked like a store mannequin that had somehow come to life.

Sam held out his hand in greeting, "Miss Wong?" he asked.

"Who wants to know?" Shelly replied. Her voice was deep, as if it could have belonged to a man, but there was a softness to it. Her handshake was firm.

"James Brown," replied Sam. It was the first name that popped into his head, and he went with it.

"Not *the* James Brown," Shelly replied with an easy smile.

"If you mean the singer, no, I'm not that James Brown," Sam said, smiling back at her. "That James Brown is a little older than I am, and while he can carry a tune. I, on the other hand, am practically tone deaf. When I sing, dogs howl."

Shelly Wong laughed at his bad joke, and Sam started breathing a little easier. He was still working on finding a way to get Shelly's cooperation, but at least she was pleasant. This would make his task easier.

"I'm from New York," said Sam. "I'm a friend of Milton. He told me about you, and about this place. I'm on vacation here in Jamaica, and I thought that I'd pay a visit to your establishment."

"He told you about me?" asked Shelly, genuinely pleased. "That's sweet. It's funny, he never mentioned you, Mr. Brown."

"Oh you know how Milton is," Sam continued smoothly, "he likes to keep things close to his vest. Maybe he was worried that you'd meet me and fall madly in love with me and leave him."

Shelly laughed, while Zora remained stone-faced at Sam's side. A quick look into her eyes showed that she was definitely not pleased, although Sam didn't know whether it was he or Shelly Wong who was the subject of her displeasure.

"As charming as you are, Mr. Brown," said Shelly Wong, "there's no other man in this world for me besides my Milton."

Once again Sam regretted allowing Zora to come with him to meet Shelly Wong. Even if she were a glutton for punishment, there was no reason for him to be a willing participant with yet another person who would hurt her. Why was she so stubborn? She could've waited patiently in the car, but instead, she was here with her ex-fiancé's gorgeous lover. This went way beyond rubbing salt into an open wound.

"And who is this?" asked Shelly, including Zora in her smile. "Mrs. Brown?"

"No," said Zora.

"Yes," said Sam.

"I'm confused," said Shelly. "Is this Mrs. Brown, or isn't it?"

"She's my fiancée, Rachel," Sam lied smoothly. "We're on vacation."

"Oh, how lovely! Pleased to meet you, Rachel," replied Shelly. "Where are you folks staying?"

"Well, we thought we had a reservation at a hotel in Montego Bay, but that fell through. So, we're actually looking around for a place to stay—" said Sam, hoping that Shelly would invite them to stay at her inn.

Shelly took the bait effortlessly. "You two must stay here! In the honeymoon suite! It's perfectly lovely. Best room in the house!"

"Oh no, we couldn't!" Zora said quickly. "We're actually on our way to Ocho Rios."

"At this time of night?" asked Shelly. "It's going to be hard to find a place to stay tonight. You must stay here. I insist! It's not often I get to meet friends of Milton."

"Well, that is very hospitable of you," said Sam.

Shelly clapped her hands, and called, "Herbert, come here quick!"

A small, dark man who could have been anywhere

between forty years old and seventy appeared as if he materialized out of the night. "Yes, Miss Shelly?"

"Please show these folks to the honeymoon room. They're spending the night. They're friends of Milton."

Herbert looked at them suspiciously as if he had a hard time believing that Milton had friends, but he kept silent.

"You can check in later," said Shelly. "After you folks freshen up. Dinner is served at eight in the dining room. Our cook is superb. She's well known in the island for her expertise in Jamaican cuisine. Other hotels serve bland food, designed for the palate of the timid. Here at Runnings, we believe that if you're going to come to Jamaica, we're going to give you the privilege of eating like a Jamaican!"

"We look forward to it," replied Sam. "Don't we, darling?"

Sam pulled Zora to his side and he could feel her stiffen. He knew that there'd be hell to pay later, but right now he was rather enjoying himself.

He watched as Zora forced a smile. "It's very kind of you, Miss Wong."

"Not at all," replied Shelly, looking at Zora. "By the way, have we met? You look very familiar!"

Zora shook her head quickly. "No, I don't think we've met. I would have remembered meeting such a beautiful woman."

Shelly laughed, "I see that you're just as free with the compliments as your fiancé. By the way, where are your bags?"

"In the car," said Sam.

"After I get you folks settled," said Herbert, "I'll get your bags for you."

"Thank you," said Sam. "We appreciate it."

"Well, I'll see you folks at eight sharp!" said Shelly. "Don't be late. Dinner is four courses, and believe me, you don't want to miss even one course!"

Zora waited until Herbert left the honeymoon room before she exploded. "Are you completely crazy?!"

In two swift strides, Sam covered the distance between where he was standing to where Zora stood fuming by the door. He pulled her close and clamped one hand over her mouth and hissed, "Shhh!"

Zora struggled to pull away from his hold, but Sam only tightened his grip. He lowered his mouth to her ear and whispered, "For God's sake, keep your voice down and stop your struggling. Do you want everyone in the hotel, including Shelly, to know that we're not a couple?"

Zora relaxed her body instantly. He was right. They were supposed to be lovers on a holiday. Although she didn't want to admit it, his ruse was a pretty good one. It was not unusual for lovers to come to Jamaica, and Shelly had bought the story.

"If I remove my hand from your mouth, will you keep your voice down?" Sam asked her.

Zora nodded her head and Sam removed his hand.

"I'm sorry," he said. "But I didn't want Herbert to hear the happy honeymooners arguing. I'm not sure he's quite as trusting as Shelly Wong."

Zora moved away from Sam. His closeness was unnerving. Unbidden, the recent memory of his kiss surfaced. She felt her face flush as she wondered

if Sam could tell how nervous she was around him.
She wanted him to kiss her again. There had to be
something wrong with her to allow her mind to go
down this path. She was just tired, that was all, she
told herself. Once she'd a chance to rest, she could
think more clearly and, more importantly, she would
act as if she had some sense, instead of acting like
a foolish, heartsick groupie.

Zora walked over to a chair in the corner of the
room and sat down. Looking around, she was dis-
mayed that this room was made for romance.
There was a king-size bed; mosquito netting descended from a hook on the ceiling and draped
the bed. There were candelabras with white candles placed strategically around the room. The furniture was almost uniformly wicker—wicker chairs
with brightly colored floral cushions, wicker end
tables on which were placed two brass lamps, and a
bureau made of wicker placed adjacent to the window. There were French doors to the right of the
bed which opened on to a balcony. The doors
were open and Zora could hear the sound of the
ocean, as well as laughter and conversation. The
steel band was still playing. It was beyond romantic, Zora thought unhappily.

"What do you think of Shelly?" Sam's question
cut through Zora's thoughts.

"I don't know," she admitted.

Zora hadn't expected Shelly to be as open and
friendly as she apparently was. She'd envisioned a
coldhearted home-wrecker. Instead, she'd found a
beautiful, hospitable woman with an easy smile.
Still, there was something about her that Zora didn't

trust. She wasn't sure whether this distrust was based on her relationship with Milton. It was hard to view the woman Milton chose over her with fair eyes. Thank God, there was no jealousy. Zora didn't want Milton back, but it was still difficult for her to meet the woman who'd been her rival; all her insecurities came rushing back.

It was obvious from the way Shelly's eyes shined when she spoke of Milton that whatever relationship she shared with him was more than a mere dalliance. That hurt, but Zora supposed the signs were there for her to read and she'd chosen to be blind. The frequent trips to Jamaica. The long periods where she would not hear from Milton. Work was a convenient excuse; Milton had always told her how busy he was. Even with his time in Jamaica, he'd claimed that he was working, when in reality he'd been enjoying a fine romance with a beautiful woman.

"Well, I hope she can lead us to Milton," said Sam.

Zora watched as Sam walked over and lay on the bed. She looked around for a couch where she could sleep, but apart from the floor where she was certain that Sam Trahan would not be sleeping, there would be no other place to lie down.

"We can't stay here tonight," said Zora. "We have to find another hotel. I'm sure that there are other hotels around here."

"I hate to disappoint you," replied Sam, "but this is where I plan to stay the night, and since you're stuck with me until I find Milton or my painting, then this is where you will be staying also."

"Well, we need another room," replied Zora. There had to be rooms with two beds in this hotel.

"Whatever for?" asked Sam, his expression as bland as his voice.

"I know that I am pointing out the obvious, but there's only one bed in this room."

"What's your point?"

Zora took a deep breath, "We can't sleep in a room where there's only one bed, unless you plan on sleeping on the floor."

Sam stretched out on the bed, and put his hands behind his head. "I certainly don't plan to sleep on the floor tonight, do you?"

"Well, no . . ." replied Zora, "but if you were a gentleman, you'd take the floor and let me take the bed."

"I never said I was a gentleman, Zora." Sam grinned at her and once again her heart did that funny twisting thing.

"Well, at least we agree on something."

"Good, then it's settled. We'll stay the night right here in this room."

"What about asking for another room?" Zora wasn't ready to give up. "One with two beds in it."

Sam sounded as if he were talking to a petulant child. "Zora, remember we're supposed to be in love. Why would we want a room with two beds? I'm sure that Shelly Wong would wonder the same thing."

Once again, he had a point. A very good point.

"What's the matter, Zora—afraid that I'll ravish you in your sleep?" Sam stared directly into her eyes.

Zora's response was quick. "Don't flatter your-self. It's just not proper."

"Not proper?" he repeated the words slowly, as if he were trying to understand them.

"Yes," replied Zora firmly, "it's not proper."

"O.K.," said Sam. "Then I'm not a gentleman and I'm not proper. Look Zora, this is a very com-fortable bed, and I intend to spend the night in it. Whether or not you want to share it with me is en-tirely your decision. As you point out, there is the floor . . ."

Zora shook her head. "I don't know why I ex-pected you to behave differently. I should have known."

"Perhaps you should have," was his bland reply.

Zora suppressed an irritated sigh. The thought of sleeping on the floor tonight wasn't appealing, but it was infinitely more appealing that sharing a bed with Sam Trahan.

"Listen, Zora," said Sam. "You're perfectly safe with me. I won't ravish you, not until you ask me to, that is."

He was insufferable. Arrogant. Conceited. Delu-sional. A few other choice words came to mind, but Zora pushed them away. "That day, Mr. Trahan, will never come."

"Never is a very long time."

"So you keep telling me," said Zora.

Sam glanced at his watch. "We've got about an hour and a half before dinner, I suggest you take a nap. You seem tired."

"Are you leaving the bed?" asked Zora.

"Not on your life," replied Sam.

"Then I'm staying right here."

"Suit yourself," said Sam, as he pulled a light blanket over himself. "I intend to get myself a nice little nap before dinner."

Sam awoke to the sight of Zora sleeping in the wicker chair. He glanced at his watch and saw that he had been sleeping for just under an hour. How she could sleep sitting in that uncomfortable-looking chair, with her head nestled on the cushion on the back of the chair, was a mystery to him.

Stubborn woman, he thought, feeling mildly annoyed that she'd rather sleep in an uncomfortable chair than share the bed with him. She was being ridiculous, but Sam didn't doubt that the backache that she would certainly have from sleeping in the chair would remind her for the next few days of just how silly she had been in refusing to sleep in the bed.

In sleep, with her features relaxed, she looked peaceful, like someone who didn't have any cares. Sam had often marveled at people who could sleep in places other than a bed. His friend Quentin was like that. He'd seen Quentin fall asleep on the subway, only to awaken automatically at his destination.

As he stared at the beautiful woman sleeping in the chair, he felt something stirring within him. He didn't want to admit it, but he was attracted to Zora. It was there, undeniable, irresistible, and ever growing. Sam had always believed in keeping the line between business and pleasure firmly delineated. The two, quite simply, did not mix. He'd never had trouble following this basic principle, but the more time he spent with Zora Redwood, the harder it was to focus on seeing her merely as a tool to get Milton and, ultimately, the Black Madonna. She tugged at him in a place that Sam hadn't known existed. Unlike Quentin, who seemed to fall in love with a woman every five minutes, Sam hadn't had a serious relationship in the last five years, since Lena left him.

He thought of Lena. With her good looks, her thriving real estate business, and her entree into New York society, she would have made a perfect wife, and she had. She was now married to a federal court judge who had family money and good connections. Sam doubted whether Lena loved her judge, but for Lena, love was not a necessary prerequisite to a successful marriage. She'd said this often enough to Sam. Lena didn't love him and he didn't love her. Still, they had been compatible on all levels, and regularly graced the society pages of the New York City papers. But Sam had been bored out of his mind and it was a relief to him when Lena finally left him. As Sam lay there contemplating the profile of the sleeping Zora, he was quite sure that as long as he knew Zora Redwood, he would never be bored. He might be frustrated, enraged, upset, and a good many other things, but he knew that Zora Redwood would never bore him.

Her eyes opened, and for a moment, she seemed bewildered by her surroundings. Then, as recognition swept over her, her mouth turned down into a distinct pout.

"I was having a wonderful dream," she said, her

voice hoarse from sleep. "I dreamt I was back in New York, taking my kids to the park, and you were nowhere around."

"Sounds like a nightmare to me." Sam replied.

Zora sat up in the chair, stretching.

"Did you sleep well?" asked Sam, deliberately trying to goad her.

"Yes," replied Zora.

They both knew that she was lying, but Sam chose to remain silent. She'd already been punished enough for being stubborn by having to sleep in the chair. Sam suspected that her body would be stiff for some time.

Zora stood up.

"I'm going to take a quick shower before we meet Shelly for dinner," she said.

A vivid image of Zora in the shower came close to shattering whatever self-control Sam still possessed. He wanted this woman. He wanted to hold her. He wanted to kiss her. He wanted to devour her. What was it about this prim nursery school teacher that got to him? Oh hell, he thought as he watched her walk to the bathroom, I'm in trouble here. Deep, deep trouble.

7

Love the one you're with. That was Felice's motto in life. It had saved her skin on numerous occasions, and she was betting that this philosophy would save her now. Felice lay on the bed in her hotel and tried to figure out her next move. There was one thing that was certain, her next move didn't involve that double-crossing Milton.

It was hot as hell in the hotel room. How could it be this hot at nighttime? The air-conditioning was broken, and all the ceiling fan did was push hot air around. Her clothes, which she had just changed an hour ago, clung to her sweat-drenched body. In the room next to her, she could hear the sounds of a couple arguing. The argument had gone on for at least half an hour, and showed no sign of abating in the near future. She had shouted at them, telling them to be quiet, but it was clear that they didn't hear her, or they simply didn't care.

It was supposed to be different. She and Milton were supposed to be waiting in style at a villa he was to rent for them. Instead, she was in this low-budget hotel, bathed in her sweat, trying to salvage her hard work. She was the one who'd first introduced the idea of taking the painting from North Star. She knew that it was valuable and she also knew the folks that would have no problem spending big money on it. Personally, Felice wondered what the fuss was about. She'd seen stuff hanging in garage sales that looked better. Her taste in art ran towards sunsets and watercolors. A picture of a strange-looking African woman didn't interest her. But there were people who wanted this Black Madonna. They'd told Milton that the buyer would kill for it, and Felice hoped that they weren't speaking literally. Milton had double-crossed the people who they were supposed to meet here in Jamaica, just as he had double-crossed her. But Felice knew where he was and she could lead them directly to him and to the painting. Once they had the painting, she'd get her money.

The plan had been for Milton and Felice to meet in Jamaica and then hand over the portrait to the buyer. They didn't know much about him, other than the obvious: he was an art lover, and he was very wealthy. He'd agreed to wait the two months that Milton insisted on. Milton felt that it would take a good two months for him to disappear, or at least get beyond the reach of Sam Trahan. At the time it seemed like a good idea, but Felice now suspected that Milton wanted to use that time to set his own plan firmly in place—and to distance himself from her.

He'd refused to tell her where he would be once he left New York. The less you know right now, the better, he'd said, and Felice had agreed with him. The police had questioned her several times, and although it would take more than a seasoned member of New York's Finest to get her to talk about what she knew about the missing painting, it was much easier to look a policeman in the face and say that she didn't know where Milton was. It was the truth.

Milton would contact her every few days, just to see what was going on. Felice suspected that he secretly enjoyed being the subject of a manhunt, even more than he enjoyed stealing something from Sam Trahan, a man he disliked simply because he was everything Milton aspired to be, namely wealthy. Without her assistance, he would still be an underling, doing the bidding of his superiors. Felice had placed the idea in his head and, once it took root, the rest came rather easily. A life of crime seemed to suit Milton. He flourished in it. Together, they planned and executed a successful million-dollar theft. Milton's goal of becoming a rich man was now in his grasp, but it seemed as if Milton was trying to cut her out of the deal.

Milton was supposed to sell the painting next week for the agreed upon price, but instead, he'd sent Felice a telegram telling her that there had been a change in plans. That was all. She heard from the buyer later that day. Milton had called him to tell him that he was asking for another million, and thereafter, he would decide when and where the exchange would take place, but first the money had to be wired into an account in the Cayman Islands.

Felice knew that the painting was worth at least
three million, which is what they'd asked for originally. Now Milton was asking for four million, and
worse, he seemed to be cutting her out of the deal.

He was a fool. Plain and simple. The buyer told
her explicitly that unless he got the painting on the
date and for the price originally agreed to, there
would be repercussions. She got the message when
she returned home to an apartment that looked as
if a hurricane, or some other destructive force had
just paid a visit. They had searched her apartment,
broken her furniture and left a note with a telephone number on it. Felice called the number.
She knew it well. It was the telephone number of
the buyer. At that point, Felice switched allegiances.
She gave her word that she would help him find
Milton and the buyer assured her this was a good
decision as he couldn't guarantee a healthy or otherwise long life for her without her cooperation.

She'd flown down to Jamaica earlier that afternoon on her way to find Milton and the painting.
Once that was accomplished, she could disappear
with the money that the buyer promised her. Things
could have been different. They could have taken
that money and together built a very comfortable
life somewhere far away. But she knew now that in
love and in business, Milton couldn't be trusted.
Soon she would have three million dollars. After
Milton's betrayal, she'd decided to cut him out of
the deal, as he was planning to do to her. She
could go many places with that money, and she intended to do so. Still, there was just one more hur-
dle to cross before she became a wealthy woman.

8

Sam stared at the woman who emerged from the bathroom. Zora had changed into a pale gold silk dress which hung just above her knees. Two thin straps held the dress in place, but as Zora moved across the room towards him, one of the straps fell to her arm, giving him an unencumbered view of a smooth brown shoulder. Her legs were bare and she wore gold sandals exposing the sexiest toes he'd ever had the pleasure of encountering—toes exposing bright red polish. The prim nursery school teacher that he'd come to know was gone. Instead, a sexy, and very annoyed, woman stared back at him.

Her short curls framed her face and in her ears two small hoop earrings dangled, catching the light as she walked to the other side of the room by the window, as if she didn't want to get too close to him.

"Stop looking at me like that," she said, as she placed her loose strap back on her shoulder.

"How am I looking at you?" asked Sam, when he had regained his voice and his composure.

"I don't know," she replied. "But I don't like it, and I'd appreciate it if you'd stop."

He knew that he was standing there looking foolish; it was all he could do to keep from puckering up right there and then and sounding a low whistle, but he was certain that Zora wouldn't be amused. She was beautiful, but he had seen other beautiful women. What struck him about Zora Redwood was that she seemed completely oblivious to her looks and the effect those looks had on men. He was used to women who wielded their looks as a Samurai used a sword. There was an innocence about her that he found intriguing and irresistable

"I see you've also changed," she said, staring back at Sam.

While Zora was in the bathroom, he had changed into his casual attire of choice: khaki pants, white oxford shirt, and loafers. Looking at Zora, he felt underdressed. He hadn't brought anything fancy with him; after all, this wasn't a holiday but a mission to retrieve the Black Madonna. It was going to be damned difficult to remember that tonight.

"I hope my outfit meets your approval," said Sam.

"Whether I approve of your outfit doesn't matter—but if it's any consolation, I'm sure that Shelly Wong will approve. She seemed to be quite fond of you."

Was she jealous, Sam wondered, quickly dismissing the thought as soon as it came to him.

"Ah yes, Miss Wong, we can't keep her waiting now, can we?"

They walked out of the room together, and the

thought crossed Sam's mind that this must be what
it felt like to be part of a couple. It had been a long
time since he'd had anything but his work to keep
him company. Although he went on a few dates
since Lena left, mostly blind dates that his well-
meaning friends would fix him up with, none of them
had turned into anything but casual evenings out.
He'd long since decided that he was not the type
of man who should enter into a relationship. His
job was his relationship. Whatever he had to give,
he gave to his career, to building his business. There
was no woman who could compete with that—or
was there? It didn't matter what he thought, it was
clear that Zora had no interest in being in his company any longer than was absolutely necessary—
not that he blamed her. He didn't suppose that too
many women found their blackmailers attractive.
Still, he wondered if they had met under any other
circumstances, whether Zora Redwood would be
quite so firm in her dislike of him.

The restaurant at Runnings Inn was just off the
main lobby. There was not much to the place, really, just a few tables with white tablecloths, and
white chairs, votive candles on the tables, and dim
lights. Still, the whole effect came together to add
an air of romance to the restaurant. Shelly had
placed several candelabras around the room, filled
with long, white candles which were all lit. There
were windows at the far side of the wall which were
open. Sam watched as the flames from the candles
flickered in the light breeze and let the aroma of
good, spicy food arouse his senses.

Shelly Wong was sitting alone at the table farthest from the entrance. She waved as soon as she saw Sam and Zora. Sam waved back. He took Zora's hand as they walked across the restaurant to Shelly's table. Sam felt Zora try to pull her hand away. He turned to smile down at her, then he tightened his grip.

"We're a couple, Zora," said Sam softly. "Couples hold hands."

He noted with some satisfaction that her struggles ceased. At least she was listening to reason. The last thing he wanted to worry about was raising the suspicion of Shelly Wong. Besides, her hand felt good in his, like it belonged just where it was.

"Don't you two look darling!" Shelly's husky voice greeted them.

"You look pretty darling yourself," replied Sam. Shelly was dressed in a long black dress, which, like the red-and-white one she had on earlier, clung to her in all the strategic places. Her long brown hair was a riot of curls which she had clipped back with two rhinestone barrettes. Once again, she had on her dark red lipstick. She was also a beautiful woman, but as far as Sam was concerned, she was no match for Zora. Her natural looks might not be as dramatic as Shelly's, but, for Sam, Zora's looks, as well as her independent, feisty character, proved to be eminently more attractive.

They sat down at the table, and Sam reluctantly let Zora's hand go. He stifled a chuckle when he heard her small sigh of relief.

"Rachel," said Shelly, now addressing Zora, "you've got to watch out for your fiancé. He's an incorrigible flirt!"

Zora smiled at Sam and replied, "Oh, he's that and *so* much more."

Shelly laughed. "Well, you have a very healthy attitude about it, Rachel, after all, men will be men. My Milton loves to flirt also, but as he always tells me, in the end, he's going home with me."

Sam cleared his throat. This was not the direction he wanted the conversation to turn. "What smells so divine?" he asked.

"James, you are in for a treat. Tonight the chef has pepper shrimp soup, and curried lobster. Your taste buds, Mr. Brown, will be in ecstasy."

Shelly Wong didn't exaggerate about the quality of the food. In spite of the circumstances, Sam could not remember a time when he'd enjoyed a meal more. During dinner they kept the conversation light with Shelly regaling them with stories about the island, and its colorful people. Zora was quiet at the start of the meal, but by the time dessert came, she was talking with Sam and Shelly as if they were all old friends.

Sam decided during dessert that it was time to make his move. "I ran into Milton on the island a few days ago," he said casually.

"Milton, here?" Shelly stopped eating for a moment. "Surely you must be mistaken. He's still in the States. I just talked to him yesterday."

"You called him?" Sam cursed himself silently, the question was a little too sharp to be casual.

Shelly replied without too much apparent concern. "No, he called me. He travels constantly for his work, so its easier for him to get in touch with me. He's supposed to call me tomorrow sometime.

No, you couldn't have seen Milton. He's not on the island."

"Perhaps I was mistaken," said Sam.

"I'm sure you were, *dear.*" Zora smiled at him and touched his face lightly with her fingertips, in what was obviously an attempt at flirting. She didn't know how close she came to getting another kiss right there in the crowded restaurant.

"You're always mistaking people, James," Zora continued. "Just the other day you swore you saw Bob Marley in the supermarket—"

Sam smiled back at her. He appreciated her attempt at cleaning up what was obviously a mistake. When he told Shelly about seeing Milton, Sam had seen a look in her eyes of distrust. He'd moved too soon.

"Some people see Elvis in the supermarket, my James sees Bob Marley," said Zora.

"How exactly did you meet Milton, James?" asked Shelly, turning her full attention to Sam.

"Oh, we met through work," replied Sam. "We're in the same line of business."

"Ah, you must be in computers," said Shelly. "Do you know a lot about Milton's company?"

Sam cleared his throat. He had swallowed the creme too quickly. "Milton's company?"

"North Star," said Shelly, smiling. "If you know anything about Milton, you know that he's very proud of his company. He built it from scratch, you know. But that's my Milton, he has fire in the belly, eh? Rachel, do you know Milton?"

"No," Zora shook her head. "I don't know the man at all."

"Perhaps we can all get together at some point,"

said Shelly. "I've never been to America, although I'm anxious to see where Milton lives when he's there. But we're planning for me to go to New York at some point later this year. That's where Milton wants us to get married, in New York."

"You must get lonely with Milton away so much in the States," Sam commented, neutrally.

Shelly's eyes grew wistful. "Yes, indeed. I get lonely and I get jealous too, although Milton assures me that there's nothing for me to worry about. After all, all he does is work, eat, and sleep. But a man as good looking as Milton, I'm sure that there are lots of ladies who would want to spend time with him."

Sam looked over at Zora for her reaction. Her expression remained inscrutable, but Sam could see that she was clasping her hands tightly in her lap. He'd warned her that this would be difficult for her. He wished again that she wasn't so obstinate.

"Does Milton stay here when he comes to Jamaica?" asked Zora.

"Sometimes," replied Shelly. "But he goes all over the island, usually staying at friend's house or with his aunt. She doesn't like me, you know. Milton's aunt has no use for me."

"I'm sure you're mistaken," said Sam. "Who wouldn't like you?"

"My sentiments exactly!" Shelly said, with a light laugh. "I intend to win her over at some point, but right now I don't have the strength. I just stay out of her way. When Milton visits with her, I usually don't go along."

"Do you and Milton do a lot of traveling around the island?" Zora asked.

"Truthfully," said Shelly, "Milton doesn't like to take me traveling with him. He says that I'm too distracting."

"You must trust him a great deal," said Zora, quietly.

"Well, yes, I do. I'm sure there are many who would say I'm foolish to let my man roam all over without me being near, but when I love, I love big, and big love doesn't have room for jealousy."

The rest of the time, thankfully, passed quickly.

Justin Trahan sat in his apartment and opened his second beer for the evening. He was not a drinker by nature, but every once in a while he indulged. Tonight he was indulging. If the information he'd received was correct—and he had no reason to doubt that every word Frank DaSilva told him earlier tonight was gospel truth, as his grandmother used to say—then Sam and Milton's girlfriend had just thrown themselves into a very dangerous situation. Those were Frank's exact words, and Justin knew that he was not prone to exaggeration.

He'd first met Frank when he was in art school. At the time he was a successful art dealer who, despite his cloak of respectable citizen, was known to hang out with a decidedly rough crowd. Frank had his pulse on the art world. He knew who was selling, what was hot, and he had an unerring knack of determining who was up-and-coming and who would be history in the near future. There were rumors that some of the artwork that Frank had received was stolen, but he'd always been able to provide credentials for everything he sold. Although Justin attributed the gossip about Frank to jealousy, he suspected that there had to be some truth to the rumors. He valued Frank's friendship. In the competitive world of art dealers, he and Justin had managed to keep their friendship intact.

As soon as Justin learned that the Black Madonna was stolen, Frank was the first person he'd turned to and he promised that he'd do whatever he could to find out who was behind the theft. They both agreed that while the trail started at Milton Alexander, it didn't end there. There was someone else behind this, and there was someone—undoubtedly someone very wealthy—who wanted the painting. There had been many who'd wanted the Black Madonna. He'd heard this story often enough from his grandmother. Justin had been fascinated with the painting, but he was also interested in the legend of the diamonds. No one had ever discovered their whereabouts, but Justin suspected that whoever had murdered the artist, had taken the diamonds. Justin's thoughts turned back to Frank's warning.

"Tell your brother to be careful. He doesn't know who he's messing with."

Frank had left a message earlier on Justin's answering machine that he had information about the Black Madonna, and the person or persons who were negotiating with Milton to buy the painting. *"These folks are serious. Your brother just may have gotten himself into a dangerous situation. The word is that*

*the folks who want the painting are not above inflicting
bodily harm to get what they want. Call me, Justin."*

Justin had been trying to do that since he first
received the message, but he hadn't been able to
reach Frank. He'd called his mother to see if she
knew where Sam was staying, but she had no information. It was too late to call Sam's secretary, but
Justin would call her the first thing tomorrow morning to find out Sam's itinerary. He'd tried to call
Sam's cell phone, but he couldn't get through to
him. He kept getting a recorded message that the
cell phone customer was out of range. Justin had
no idea where his brother was, but he hoped that
his secretary would have his itinerary.

He hadn't told his mother about Frank's message, but she'd been suspicious. The relationship
between Justin and his brother had never been a
good one. As they'd grown older, their relationship had deteriorated to the point where they tol-
erated each other simply because they shared the
same blood. Justin tried to think back to a time
when they were close, but that was a long time ago.
He had to admit that the times they got along were
few and far between.

Sam was everything Justin hated about being a
Trahan. He was rigid. He thought his way was the
only way. Sam had tried to make him toe the
Trahan line—go to the best school, then go out to
make more money. As far as Justin was concerned,
the Trahans had more than enough money already. School had bored him. Making money
bored him even more. The only thing that he was
passionate about was art. Many of his art teachers
had encouraged him, but he hadn't sold many of

his paintings. He discovered that he was better at selling other people's art than his own, and he'd opened his art gallery. Sam had disapproved, of course, but Justin had stuck with it. Although Justin wasn't the success that his brother Sam was, he had enough money to do the things he wanted to do— travel to faraway places and buy artwork—both frivolous things as far as Sam was concerned.

"When are you going to grow up?" Sam would ask him this question several times. *"When are you going to get serious with your life?"*

The questions had stung, in large part because he'd thought these things himself. Selling art was not a passion. Painting was his passion, like his ancestor before him; except, his ancestor had been a success in his chosen profession. Sometimes, usually late at night when sleep eluded him, he would wonder what his life would have been like if he had kept on painting. One thing was certain, he wouldn't have been able to subsidize the lifestyle he now enjoyed. His grandmother, before she died, had tried to encourage him to start painting again, but he didn't have her strength, her resolute refusal to listen to the word "no." Sam was more like his grandmother than anyone else in the family. Like his grandmother, Sam was the rock on which the family leaned.

Justin had grown up resenting this inescapable fact. From the time he was born, he was compared to Sam; Sam was was the perfect one and Justin was far from perfect. Now Justin was in the position to help Sam. Whatever danger Sam was facing, Justin knew that it was serious. Frank might be a little dramatic but he told the truth. While Sam and Justin had never been close, they were still brothers, or, as his grandmother would say, they were blood. Blood did not turn its back on blood, and no matter what Justin felt about his brother, he wouldn't allow harm to come to him. He supposed that it was the Trahan way. His family always closed ranks when there was trouble—and Justin had a strong feeling that trouble was heading his brother's way.

9

Zora walked back to the hotel room in silence. Sam Trahan made a half-hearted attempt at conversation, but she was not in the mood to talk. They were no closer to finding Milton than they were when she boarded the airplane at JFK airport, back in New York. She hadn't expected that Milton would be easy to find, after all Sam Trahan had been looking for him for the past two months. However, she had expected that they would have discovered more information about Milton's whereabouts. Instead, they'd spent the evening with a perfectly lovely, not to mention beautiful, woman, who had the distinction of being the love of her ex-fiancé's life. While this experience was interesting, and ultimately disheartening, they had no new information about the art thief who had not only betrayed her, but had placed her in the position of becoming intimately acquainted with a jail cell.

"So what are we going to do now?" asked Zora, as they reached the hotel room door. They'd said good-bye to Shelly Wong in the dining room, parting with a promise to see her the next day.

"I don't know about you," said Sam, opening the door, and walking through it directly to the waiting bed. "But I plan on getting some sleep. We'll decide what to do in the morning."

"I'm not sleeping in the chair again," said Zora, closing the door behind her. She was bone tired. She needed to sleep, and she needed to sleep in a bed. He would just have to do the right thing, grab a blanket and sleep in the chair or on the floor.

"I certainly hope not," said Sam, as he started taking off his shirt. "It looked pretty uncomfortable."

"What're you doing?" asked Zora, alarmed at Sam's apparent intent to strip in front of her.

"I'm taking off my shirt," was his reply. "Do you mind?"

"Well, actually I do mind," said Zora, averting her eyes from a taut brown chest. "Is it absolutely necessary to strip naked in front of me?"

He had the nerve to laugh, "I'll only strip if you want me to, Zora."

"I certainly don't want you doing that!"

"Well, it's hot as hades in this room, so I'm taking everything off except for my underwear. If that offends you, I suggest you close your eyes."

Arrogant. Insufferable. Purposefully infuriating. All of those words sprang to her head, and it took more self-control than she would have previously thought she possessed to refrain from telling him exactly what she thought of him.

"I think you should sleep on the floor," said Zora, not giving up.

"Not in my lifetime," said Sam. "Or yours."

"If you were a gentleman you wouldn't sleep in the bed while I sleep on the floor."

"The way I see it," said Sam, who was now in a pair of sky blue boxers, "is that we both can share this bed. It's a big bed, Zora. I think we both can be very comfortable in it."

"I told you before," said Zora, "I won't sleep in the same bed with you."

"That's your prerogative," said Sam, as he turned off the lamp light beside the bed, throwing the room into immediate darkness.

"I don't mind saying that you are the rudest, most ill-mannered man that I have ever met," said Zora, giving in to her anger as she threw a blanket and a pillow on the floor. A soft snore was his only response.

Zora lay on the floor wondering how she was going to get out of this predicament. It was a long time before sleep finally claimed her.

Sometime later, she felt strong arms lift her up and place her in a soft, comfortable bed. Although she wasn't fully awake, she thought that she should at least register her protest. Instead, she settled, as if she'd been there many times before, into Sam's arms and drifted back into a deep sleep.

She felt right in his arms. She felt as if she belonged. Damn it, thought Sam as he tightened his arms around the sleeping Zora, she fit him perfectly. He'd never thought that anything like this would happen to him, these feelings that he couldn't explain, other than he was under some sort of tropical spell. He didn't want to let go of her. He wanted to take care of her. He wanted to wipe the sadness from her eyes. He wanted to watch a slow, lazy smile curve her lips. He wanted to dance with her to a long, impossibly corny love song.

She was lying with her back to him. His chin was resting on top of her head. She'd changed into a long nightgown. Something soft and made out of cotton. Practical. He expected nothing less from Zora Redwood; but notwithstanding the cotton nightgown, he felt as much passion and heat for her as if she were wearing one of those flimsy negligees that women wore when they had seduction in mind.

He wanted her. He supposed that he had known this from the time he first encountered her on that Brooklyn street. He wanted to wake up and see those brown eyes every morning. He wanted to grow old listening to that singsong accent that was a cross between Britain and the West Indies. He wanted to laugh with her, argue with her, kiss her, wrap his arms around her as if he were gift paper and she was a delectable present.

The realization that he was falling in love with Zora Redwood hit Sam hard. He needed to process this information, as he did with everything in his life. This wasn't love at first sight, but it came close. After two days he was falling in love. His grandmother was getting her wish. Stop, Sam said to himself, shaking his head. He needed to analyze his feelings for her. He needed to determine if this was some passing thing, or if this was something with the feel of permanence about it.

She stirred in her sleep and turned towards him. Sam felt whatever little self-control he had left drain swiftly away. He lowered his lips and started exploring her eyelids, then the tip of her nose, her earlobes, her stubborn chin. By the time he reached her lips, he felt her responding to his kiss. There was no tenderness to this kiss, only a deep sense of urgency. Her arms drew him closer, and she parted her lips wider so that he could explore more fully. His fingers reached for the buttons in front of the cotton nightdress, and her fingers pulled his head closer to hers. Her nightdress fell down her shoulders, and he moved his head downwards to a point just below her collarbone. He wanted to slow down, to savor the moment, but his urgency propelled him forward. He wanted more.

Common sense reared its ugly head. Sam pulled away before things went further. He wasn't sure he was ready for this. Hell, he wasn't sure that Zora was ready for it either. He only knew that once they made love things would never be the same. He knew, just as he knew that night followed day, that he would not let her go. Zora Redwood would not be a passing fling.

"We shouldn't do this," Zora whispered, even as she pulled him toward her.

"You're right," said Sam, right before he slammed his lips on hers, "we shouldn't do this."

The sound of four gunshots split the night air. Sam had heard that sound before and he knew its source. The shots sounded as if they were just below their window. He pulled away from Zora quickly.

"Don't get up," he said as he ran to the hotel window. Shelly Wong was lying on the ground by the pool. Her prostrate body was illuminated by the nightlight. She wasn't moving.

"Shelly's been shot," he called out to Zora. "Call emergency!"

Somehow he got his pants on, while running to the front door. He was barefoot, but there was no time to look for shoes. He tried not to think the worst, but from the view from his second floor window, Shelly was seriously hurt if not . . . he couldn't think about that possibility.

"Whatever you do," Sam said, "don't leave this room—and don't open this door for anyone else but me."

He didn't wait for her response.

A small crowd had gathered by the time Sam reached the back area of the hotel where Shelly lay on the ground by the pool. He made his way quickly through the crowd and knelt beside her. An older gentleman dressed in pajamas was holding her hands. Judging from the medical nature of the questions he was asking Shelly, Sam assumed that he was a doctor. Shelly was having a great deal of difficulty answering his questions.

Thank God she was alive, thought Sam. He could see her blood staining the ground on which she lay, and a feeling of anger flashed through him. What kind of person could do this? His thoughts went swiftly to Milton, but while Sam was certain that Milton was capable of stealing, he didn't believe that he could murder someone, especially someone he was supposedly in love with. Still, he was no authority on the man. If anyone had told him that Milton would steal the Black Madonna he would have laughed outright.

"James Brown," said Shelly, her gaze resting on his face, "you're a dear to come rushing to my rescue."

Her voice was weak, but her attempt at flirtation heartened Sam. She still had the fire in her he'd seen when he first met her. She was a fighter, this Shelly Wong. All thoughts of the Black Madonna evaporated. His only thoughts were of making sure that Shelly was going to be all right.

"Don't try to move," said the doctor, "the ambulance is on its way." He turned and said to Sam, "Who are you? Are you a friend of Shelly's?"

"He's a friend," said Shelly, her voice still weak, but to Sam's ears, surprisingly strong after everything she'd been through. "A new friend."

"Ah," said the doctor, once again turning his attention to Shelly. "Our Miss Shelly is a very lucky woman: from what I can tell, the bullet is lodged in her shoulder. Quite painful, I'm sure, but not life threatening. Thankfully, whoever did this was apparently not a good shot."

"Thank goodness!"

Sam turned around and found Zora standing over him, her attention focused on Shelly. She knelt beside him, holding Shelly's hand.

Sam didn't say any words to Zora, but he hoped that the look of anger in his eyes let her know that he was displeased. Very displeased. He had specifically told her to stay in the room. There might have been some connection between the shootings and

Milton's schemes, and if that was the case, then Zora might also be in danger.

"I'd ask you how you're feeling," Zora said to Shelly, "but I know that's a stupid question."

"For the record," said Shelly, with another grimace, "I feel like hell, but Doc here says I'll live, and quite frankly, I trust his opinion."

The sound of the siren told them that the ambulance was finally arriving. In a few moments two men in white coats ran towards them. They were carrying a stretcher.

Sam took this opportunity to speak to Zora. His heart twisted at the sight of her worried face. Where there had been passion earlier on, there was now only concern for her safety. He couldn't let anything happen to her. When he'd brought her into this mess, he never thought that he was putting her in danger. Now he knew that from here on, he'd have to find Milton without her help. He was putting her on an airplane to New York. Even though he couldn't be certain that Milton was involved in what had happened to Shelly, he wasn't about to gamble with Zora's life.

"I thought I told you to stay in the room," he said, turning to her. His voice was gentle, but it carried a clear note of disapproval.

"You did," replied Zora, as if stating a simple and entirely reasonable fact.

"Zora," Sam whispered, "I don't know what this is all about, but it might have something to do with Milton, and if it does, you could get hurt."

"So could you," said Zora.

"I can take care of myself," said Sam quickly,

"and don't you dare tell me that you can handle this. Look at what's happened to Shelly."

Zora raised a stubborn chin. "Don't you worry about me, and yes, I can take care of myself."

For a brief moment, Sam didn't know whether to scold her or to kiss her. He decided that neither course of action was appropriate. "We'll talk about this later."

She smiled at him, and his heart twisted again.

The ambulance attendants lifted Shelly in the stretcher, and the doctor stood up.

"Wait!" Shelly's voice was surprisingly strong. "I want Zora to come with me."

Sam didn't know if he was more surprised that Shelly knew Zora's real name, or that Shelly wanted Zora to accompany her to the hospital.

"We don't allow family or friends in the ambulance," said one of the attendants. "They can follow."

"I'm not going without her," said Shelly, her voice more firm than it ought to be, considering her present circumstances. "Zora comes with me!"

"Let her come," said the doctor. "I'll be there also."

Zora stood up and walked to the ambulance behind the attendants and the doctor. Sam followed her. He held her hand and she didn't pull it away.

"We're going to the hospital in St. Ann's Bay," the doctor said to Sam. "Anyone around here can tell you how to get there."

"Thanks," said Sam.

"Don't thank me," said the doctor, "anyone can see that Shelly wants you two to be around. Shelly's very dear to a lot of folks, including myself. I've been coming to her hotel for years."

Sam watched as the small group got in the ambulance.

"I'll meet you at the hospital," Sam called out to Zora. She turned around and smiled again directly at him. She should have stayed in the hotel room, away from danger—but he knew, just as he'd known from the first time he'd met her, that Zora Redwood was not a woman that anyone, even him, could push around.

10

The rain had continued falling for the past four hours and Milton's initial mild concern had now blossomed into full-blown alarm. He had tried unsucessfully to fall asleep, but the symphony of thunder and torrential rain had kept him awake. The wind slashed the raindrops against his window sounding as if someone were beating a drum. The lights in his house flickered on and off periodically, signaling the electricity blackout that was certain to come.

He had to get away. If Felice had found him, then the others were undoubtedly not far behind. Knowing Felice as he did, it wouldn't surprise him if she had joined forces with them. Milton cursed himself again for not hauling tail and running after the phone call from her. In light of the weather, his decision to wait a few hours while he determined his next move wasn't a wise one.

He hadn't wanted to make a move without a

clear plan. The folks who were after him were dangerous, and he needed to keep his wits about him. Besides, he had reasoned, it would be a few days before Felice made her way to the house. It was remote, and difficult to find even if you were from the island. Milton knew that Felice was shrewd and he had a sense that she would be arriving with other unexpected guests in the very near future.

He'd decided that his best plan was to go back to Runaway Bay the next day and lay low at Shelly's apartment. Shelly would protect him while he figured out his next move. The rain made the dirt roads that would take him back to the main highway, about thirty miles from his house, impossible to negotiate. This area was also known for its mud slides, and Milton wasn't going to take a chance getting his car stuck, literally in the middle of nowhere. He had no other choice but to sit and wait, but the more he sat the more frightened he became, knowing that they were closing in on him. Still, the thought that they couldn't reach him because of the same conditions that were keeping him trapped in this house, gave him some consolation.

Milton picked up a bottle of Red Stripe beer and brought it to his lips. He was glad that his hands no longer were shaking. He was regaining control. Things had gone awry. That's life, he thought, and there was absolutely nothing that he could do about it. He'd contacted the people who wanted the portrait and told them that he was raising the sale price. They hadn't been happy. A deal is a deal, they'd informed him. Some deals are meant to be broken, he had replied. Do you understand the predicament you've put us in, they'd told him. Not my problem, said Milton. *Your problems are just beginning.* That was what they'd said. Instead of agreeing to pay the extra money, they had broken off negotiations. These folk were not going to give up. They'd spent too much time and too much money already. Last week they had wired one million to an account in the Cayman Islands. They were to wire the remaining amount after they got the portrait.

Four million meant a lot to them, and Milton understood by their refusal to negotiate, that he had just given them four million reasons to kill him. It was time to go. The situation was now out of his control. He needed to think about his next move. He knew that they still wanted the Black Madonna. He also knew that they would use any force necessary to get what they wanted from him. Like Sam Trahan they were determined to get the Black Madonna, although Milton was certain that Sam Trahan would never do anything illegal. He was too much of a straight arrow for that. Sam was a man who lived by the rules, even as he made those rules work for him.

Milton thought about Sam Trahan, the man who had given him a chance by hiring him into his company. He knew that he should feel some guilt about Sam but Milton couldn't work up any feeling except disgust. Sam and his kind ruled the world, by virtue of their large bank accounts, and their ability to push others around. Although Sam had the reputation of being a fair man, Milton resented Trahan's power over him. Sam would always be in the "haves" group, while Milton was firmly aligned with the "have nots," until he'd seen a way to make quick money, almost too easy money. Now, as Milton sat in his home listening to the sound of the wind and the rain, he wondered just how easy it was to get this money. "*Nothing comes easy.*" The words of his aunt came back to him as clearly as if she had just spoken them. He supposed that in this, as in most things, she was right, and the thought gave him no consolation.

A vision of Zora's face flashed in his mind. Where had that come from, he wondered. He'd tried hard to put her out of his mind during these past few months. When it came to his heart, however, that was another matter. He wondered how Zora was dealing with the knowledge that he had deceived her. By now she must know about everything, including how he had used her to help his scheme. He knew that she would be hurt and he was sorry about that. There was no better person in the world than Zora. She was beautiful, loyal, compassionate, smart, all the things he wanted in a woman. He'd loved her from her sixteenth birthday, although she'd never understood his attraction to her. Zora underestimated her appeal, but to Milton, she was perfect. He was the imperfect one. The one who couldn't be faithful. It had nothing to do with his love for her, but in his heart, he knew that his aunt was right, Zora deserved better. She deserved a man who would live up to her trust. He pushed all thoughts of her out of his mind as he placed the beer bottle on the table. He had more pressing things to think about, specifically how he was going to get out of this situation alive.

* * *

The ambulance carrying Shelly careened down a darkened, country road to the nearest hospital, which was located in St. Ann's Bay, the capital of the parish of St. Ann. During the ambulance ride, Zora wondered on more than one occasion whether the ride was ultimately more dangerous to Shelly's health than the bullet. Although they needed to get to the hospital in a hurry, Zora wondered whether this rate of teeth-chattering speed was necessary, given that Shelly was not in any immediate danger.

"These ambulance drivers are tryin' to kill me," said Shelly, echoing Zora's thoughts.

"Well," Zora conceded with a faint smile, "the fact that they haven't killed all of us is close to a miracle."

Shelly laughed at Zora's statement, then quickly grimaced in pain.

"I'm sorry," said Zora. "Hopefully, we'll get to the hospital soon."

There was an awkward silence between the two women, as both the doctor and the medic fussed over Shelly. Zora sat silently in the background feeling both conspicuous and out of place.

"Shelly, what happened?" asked the doctor. "Do you know who did this to you?"

"The security guard—only I'd never seen him before. Every night I take a walk out back by the pool—it's safe—or so I thought—I noticed him, but not until it was too late—I realized that it wasn't George."

The doctor shook his head and muttered something about the world going straight to hell. Then, he checked Shelly's vital signs. Apparently satisfied with what he discovered, he sat back down. The medic followed his lead and sat next to the doctor. Both men started talking in low voices.

Shelly turned her face so that she was staring directly at Zora.

"Come close," she said, her voice low and urgent.

Zora walked over to where Shelly lay on a small, white cot. She sat on the floor of the vehicle, next to Shelly.

Keeping her voice low, Shelly said, "I think that Milton is mixed up in this."

Zora did not reply, but she was certain that Shelly was right. She couldn't figure out how Milton entered into the equation, but as certain as she was that the ambulance driver was reckless, she was just as certain that the shooting had something to do with Milton.

"What did Milton do?" asked Shelly, her voice breaking through Zora's thoughts.

Zora hesitated. She did not believe in adding to anyone's pain. She certainly didn't want Shelly to have to face the inevitable truth that she'd had to face two months ago—that Milton had betrayed them both, and not only was he unfaithful, he was a thief as well. It wasn't pretty, and it was the last thing Shelly needed to know in the condition she was in.

"I'm a big girl, Zora," said Shelly. "I can take it."

"How do you know who I am?" asked Zora, finally asking the question she'd wanted to ask as soon as Shelly had first used her real name.

"As soon as I saw you, I knew that you were his Zora. I've seen your picture. Milton said that you were a cousin, but I knew different."

"I didn't know about you," said Zora. "Not until recently. I didn't know."

Shelly grimaced again. "I know that. Tell me what Milton did."

"He stole a valuable painting," said Zora. "A painting of an African woman—have you seen it?"

Shelly shook her head.

"Does this picture belong to you?"

"No," replied Zora. "It belongs to Sam Trahan the person you know as James. I'm helping him find the painting."

"A thief," Shelly spoke slowly, as if trying to fully comprehend her own words. "Who would believe that Milton is a thief?"

Once again, Zora kept her opinions to herself.

She was quiet for a moment, then Shelly continued. "I knew that you were the woman that crowded Milton's heart so that there was no room for me."

Zora started to protest. She couldn't let Shelly think that Milton had any great love for her. It wasn't true; if anything, the opposite would be more accurate. Milton must have hated her to use and discard her the way he did.

As if reading her thoughts, Shelly said, "He loves you, Zora, as much as a man like Milton can love anyone. I knew about you, but I continued to hold on to him. I suppose you think I'm weak."

Zora shook her head. "I'm in no position to call anyone weak."

"Thank you for that," Shelly whispered. "Thank you for trying not to make me feel any worse than I already feel. And thank you for not leaving me."

"Don't thank me, Shelly."

"Zora, you must listen to me, eh? In my pocketbook is the key to my apartment. I live on the second floor of the Crystal Lake Apartments. Apartment 2A; it's on Busa Road. You must go there. You and Sam. You have to find Milton—I believe he's in trouble. Milton gave me a suitcase to keep for him the last time he was in Jamaica. The suitcase is in my closet. Maybe there is something there that can help us."

Shelly paused for a moment before she began speaking again.

"There've been people looking for him, and I know they don't mean him any good."

"Shelly, we're looking for Milton also."

"I don't know where he is," said Shelly. "But I know that he's in trouble. And I know that whoever shot me probably knows about you too. They may come after you, Zora. That is why you must move quickly. In the suitcase you might find information that will help you find Milton. You've got to do it, Zora. I'm of no use to Milton like this."

"I don't want to leave you alone at the hospital."

"My family will help me. I'll be well protected in the hospital. Just do what you can to find my Milton."

Shelly closed her eyes and seemed to fall into sleep.

St. Ann's Bay Hospital was located in the heart of St. Ann's Bay. The four-story building, with its gray stone exterior reminded Sam of an old prison. All the hospital needed were bars on the windows to make the picture complete. The inside of the building was somewhat more cheerful, with its blue walls and vivid paintings. There were nurses, and other medical officials rushing around. The whole scene seemed chaotic to Sam. He sat with Zora in a small waiting room, which was filled with other worried people.

He held her hand in his, and thanked God once again that while Shelly's wounds were serious, they weren't life threatening. Zora had insisted on remaining until she could speak with the doctor once more about Shelly's condition. Sam's thoughts returned to what had occurred between them earlier that evening. Neither of them had spoken about it, but something indefinable had changed between them and he was certain that she was feeling this also.

"Shelly says that we might be in danger as well," said Zora.

Sam laughed, "We *might* be in danger? May I suggest to you, Zora, that we are knee-deep in danger, judging from recent activity."

"This isn't funny," said Zora. She sat, holding on to Shelly's purse tightly.

"Do I look like I'm laughing to you?" asked Sam. "I'm serious. In fact, I'm dead serious, pardon the expression."

"Once we talk with Shelly's doctor, we need to get back to Shelly's apartment to look in Milton's suitcase."

Sam agreed with her, but he didn't want Zora mixed up in this anymore. He was going to put her on an airplane heading straight for New York, and hopefully, out of harm's way. She'd gotten him this far; he'd have to go the rest of the way on his own.

He could take care of himself, but he couldn't guarantee her safety. What had happened to Shelly could just as easily have happened to Zora. There was no way around it, he was sending her home.

The door to the waiting room opened and a doctor who, with his youthful appearance, looked as if he had just graduated from high school, called out, "Is James Brown here?"

There was a murmur in the waiting room as heads turned to see if the famous singer really was in a waiting room in St. Ann's Hospital. Sam had forgotten that he'd given them the name James Brown when he came to the hospital. Zora kicked Sam in his leg, prompting a response.

"Right here," Sam called out.

The doctor walked over to where Sam and Zora were sitting.

"I'm Dr. Kendricks," he said. "Ms. Wong's doctor. She's regained consciousness, and quite amazingly, she's doing fairly well, even with everything she's gone through. We've removed the bullets from her shoulder."

"Can we see her?" asked Zora.

"I'd rather you didn't," replied Dr. Kendricks. "Ms. Wong has to rest now. The best thing for you two to do now is go home and get some rest."

They thanked the doctor and watched as he quickly left the waiting room. As soon as the doctor left the room, two women walked over to Sam and Zora.

"Mr. Brown," said the first one, a short, round woman with thick glasses and short curly hair. "We're huge fans of yours!"

"Yes, indeed," replied the second woman, also short and round, but without thick glasses. "We have all your albums!"

"You look so different from your album covers!"

"Look," said Sam, "I'm not really James Brown."

The first woman giggled, "Oh, you don't have to pretend, Mr. Brown. We know the truth!"

"Ladies, I'm really not James Brown. He's about forty years older than me."

"Sure you aren't, Mr. Brown," said the second woman with a wink.

"Could you give us your autograph?" asked the first woman.

"Is that all you want from me?" asked Sam wearily.

One of the women giggled and said, "We're a little too old to be groupies, Mr. Brown."

The other woman held out a pen and some paper. "We'd be honored Mr. Brown, if you'd give us your autograph." After telling him that their names were Tina and Belle, respectively, Sam wrote *All the best, James Brown!* on the piece of paper.

As Tina and Belle thanked Sam for his graciousness, the door to the waiting room opened again and a medium built man in blue jeans and a navy jacket called out, "Are the people from Runaway Bay here? The ones that came with the lady that was shot?"

Sam stepped away from the two ladies and asked, "Who wants to know?"

"Inspector St. John, Runaway Bay Police Department."

"Here we are. We're the ones that witnessed the shooting," replied Sam,

Sam was aware that once again all pairs of eyes in the waiting room were fixed in his direction.

"Would you come this way, sir?" asked Inspector St. John.

Zora stood up. "I was with him also."

The policeman stopped and looked at Zora. Then, as recognition swept over him, he crossed the room quickly and stood directly in front of her.

"Zora Redwood, after all these years, you've finally come home," he said, with a huge grin on his face. "Don't you recognize me, Zora?"

Sam watched with disbelief as Zora threw her arms around the man with a shout. He felt a sudden surge of anger at seeing her in another man's arms. Jealousy. Another unfamiliar emotion. He didn't like it.

"Alistair, you are truly a sight for sore eyes!" said Zora.

"I didn't know that you knew Shelly Wong," the policeman replied. "I didn't even know you were on the island. What's going on?"

Zora shook her head. "I don't know where to begin."

Sam watched as tears started to roll down Zora's cheeks. He wanted to put his arms around her. Once again, he felt responsible for dragging her into this mess. In the short time he'd known her, he knew without a doubt that she had nothing to do with Milton's actions. He'd watched her as she cradled Shelly, without hesitation and with the same amount of care that one would handle a newborn, even though Shelly was one of Milton's other women. He'd also seen her as she fought with the doctors to stay with Shelly, only giving in when she was convinced that her presence would do Shelly's condition more harm than good. Zora Redwood was unlike any other woman, any other person he'd met, and he felt his admiration for her growing.

"Zora, are you all right?" Sam kept his tone neutral. He knew that showing any pity on his part was the last thing Zora needed.

She nodded her head, wiping her eyes. "I'm fine. Just nerves, that's all it is."

The policeman spoke up. "Zora, who is this? Don't tell me you got married and didn't give me no invitation for the wedding?"

Zora moved quickly to rid the policeman of this apparently foolish notion—too quickly, Sam thought.

"No, no, no. I'm not married. This is Sam Trahan . . . we're here on the island trying to find Milton. Sam Trahan, I would like you to meet an old childhood friend, Alistair St. John. Alistair lived next door to us when I was a teenager."

At the mention of Milton's name, Inspector St. John frowned. "You still messin' with that man?"

"It's a long story," said Zora quietly. "I hope that Shelly's really going to be all right."

"She'll be fine as soon as she does what you should do," replied Alistair. "Get rid of Milton."

Sam cleared his throat, "Inspector, you wanted to talk with us?"

"Ah, yes," said the inspector, "let's go to another room. I need some information from both of you."

Zora followed the policeman out of the room. As Sam walked behind them, an old woman, who sat on a chair in the corner with as much dignity as if she were sitting on a golden throne, shook her cane at him ominously.

"Me know James Brown," she said. "Me have all him records. Me seen he perform. You ain' no James Brown!"

Sam couldn't have put it better himself if he'd tried.

11

The security guard took the money from Terrence Phillips hands. He was nervous. He hadn't completed the job and he could tell from the man's eyes that he was displeased. The quicker he got away from him the better he would feel. As it was, his heart was hammering in his chest, his mouth was dry with fear. There was a coldness to this man that he had never encountered. He'd known all sorts of people, some of them, including himself, could be characterized as very bad, but he had never come across someone like the man who was standing before him. He looked as if he had seen the devil and was unafraid. This was not a man to take lightly. This was also not a man to cause any kind of displeasure.

"You didn't finish the job according to plan," said the man. His voice was barely above a whisper.

"No," admitted the security guard. "But the girlfriend is in the hospital. I know where she is, and I can finish the job there for you."

"I paid you to kill both of them," said Terrence, "I don't want any loose ends."

"I'll finish the job," said the security guard, earnestly. He did not like the way this man was looking at him, like a hunter zeroing on its prey.

"What about the other girlfriend?" asked the man. "What happened with her? She was right there—both of them under the same roof—an unexpected opportunity which you did not take advantage of."

The security guard cleared his throat nervously. "There were complications . . ."

"What sort of complications?"

"A man. There was a man who was with her—"

Terrence raised his hands. "No excuses. Take the money and go."

"What about finishing the job?" asked the security guard, a feeling of relief starting to wash over him.

"I'll take care of it," said the man, brusquely.

The security guard took the money and turned around to leave. He couldn't believe his luck. He'd thought that the man would have refused to pay him, or even worse. Instead, he was walking out of here a much richer man than he was when he entered. A smile crept to his lips. He had many plans for this money.

A shot in the middle of his back brought a quick and unexpected end to those plans.

*   *   *

Inspector Alistair St. John shook his head as he listened to Zora's story. Although he had no doubt that she'd left out some relevant information, like the hurt she felt about Milton's actions, he listened to her relay almost in clinical fashion that her fiancé had not only stolen from the man who was hovering protectively by her side, but Milton may very well have placed Shelly Wong's life in danger. There was no telling who Milton had made angry this time. The list was long. It seemed to Inspector St. John that Milton may have gone too far this time. Milton had crossed the wrong folk. Whoever shot Shelly was not playing. They meant business, and if Zora was right and there was some connection between what happened to Shelly and Milton's wrongdoing, then Zora might also be in harm's way.

He told her as much.

"I'll be fine," Zora responded quickly.

"I wouldn't be so sure."

Inspector St. John turned to Sam, who had spoken those words quietly. At least he had the good sense to be concerned for Zora's safety, even if she wasn't. Alistair wondered exactly what was the nature of their relationship. The Inspector had not missed the protective way Sam hovered around Zora. She deserved a man who would protect her. He hoped that at last Zora had given her heart to someone who deserved it. He'd hoped, at one time, to be the one for Zora, but she had never looked in his direction for anything other than friendship.

"Zora." The Inspector chose his words carefully. He didn't want to frighten her, but he was concerned. "There's a strong possibility that Milton is mixed up with what just happened to Shelly."

"Milton is many things, but he's not capable of shooting anyone," Zora replied.

"How can you be sure about that?" asked Sam. He stood in the corner of the small room, with his fists jammed in his pockets. His lips formed a thin line of disapproval.

The Inspector was a simple man. He was a man who tried to take pleasure in whatever circumstances he found himself in. He didn't wish for a bigger house. He didn't wish for more money. He didn't wish for a younger, thinner, prettier wife. He liked his full-figured, sweet wife. He liked his life just as it was—the life of a country policeman. But even a simple man like him could see and understand passion. It was obvious to him that the two people exchanging glares were passionate for each other, and if they hadn't already discovered that fact, the Inspector was certain that they soon would find out what he already knew.

"Milton may be capable of infidelity," said Zora, raising her chin, "and he may be capable of theft, but that doesn't mean he's a murderer."

Inspector St. John stepped in quickly to avoid an escalation of the conversation between Zora and Sam Trahan. "Even if Milton is not directly involved in this, I wouldn't discount that he's mixed up in this somehow. Perhaps he's made some other people angry."

"That could be true," Zora conceded.

"Just be careful, Zora," said Alistair. "We could've lost Shelly, and we don't want to lose you."

"I'll take care of Zora," said Sam in a voice that, though quiet, brooked no disagreement.

Inspector St. John struggled to suppress a smile of triumph. He was right all along. The man was sweet on Zora, and even though Zora was staring back at Sam Trahan as if she could happily throttle him, the Inspector was certain that Zora was sweet on him too. The Inspector didn't know Sam, but in the short time since he met him, he could tell that Sam Trahan was a vast improvement over Milton Alexander.

"I'd appreciate that," replied Alistair. "Zora is very dear to many people, including me."

"For Heaven's sake!" exclaimed Zora, placing one slender, brown hand on her waist. "You two he-men are acting as if I'm invisible! I can take care of myself, thank you very much."

"Well," said Inspector St. John, clearing his throat. "The point is that everybody has to be careful. I'll see what I can do from my end to help you find Milton. In the meantime, is there someplace that you two can be reached?"

"I would tell you to contact me on my cell phone, but it doesn't seem to work here," said Sam.

"It's going to be difficult to reach us," agreed Zora, "we're going to be on the move—but if you need to catch us, you can leave a message with Pastor Bee—you remember him, Alistair?"

"How could I forget?" the Inspector replied with a laugh. "His sermons were legendary. I remember one that went on for a good four hours."

"He doesn't know that I'm on the island—yet," said Zora. "But I'll contact him before the day is through. Anything you find out, make sure you tell him, Alistair. He can be trusted."

"I remember that you were the apple of his eye,"

he said. "Both him and Miss Essie used to fight over you. Have you seen Miss Essie?"

Zora's voice was tight, her reply terse. "Yes."

He decided to let that one go, although he suspected that somehow Milton had poisoned the relationship between Miss Essie and Zora. That man Milton, the Inspector thought, his lips turning down in disgust, was born to give trouble.

"I know where to reach you, Alistair," said Zora. "If I need you, I'll get in touch with the police station."

"Just be careful."

Zora smiled at him, and even though he was past grown, as his mother used to say, he felt like the same fourteen-year-old boy who'd pledged his undying affection to her, then he remembered his wife who was waiting for him at home. As beautiful as Zora was, neither she or anyone else could tempt him to break up his happy home.

Take care of her," the Inspector said, turning to Sam Trahan.

He watched as Sam put his arm around Zora's shoulder.

"Don't worry," replied Sam, his voice mirroring his grim expression. "I will."

12

"So what do we do now?" asked Sam.

They stood outside the front entrance of the hospital. In the distance, the sky was beginning to lighten to a shade of gray, the promise of dawn. The air had a stillness to it, and Sam realized that for the first time since coming to the island, there was no breeze in the air. The hospital stood on a narrow street filled with pastel-colored houses. From this vantage point, Sam could look down on the sleepy capital of the Parish of St. Ann, St. Ann's Bay. Below him, he could see the lights of those folks who were already awake at this ungodly hour—four fifteen in the morning. His body ached, and he longed for a bed. He didn't need much sleep, but a couple hours worth would do his body good.

"We go to Shelly's house and find out what's in Milton's suitcase," replied Zora, as she walked over to Miss Essie's red sports car, which Sam had parked down the street from the hospital.

"How about we get some sleep first," said Sam, as he followed behind her, "and then, we find out what's in the suitcase."

Zora stopped walking and turned around.

"I thought you wanted to find Milton," she said, her voice sharp.

"I do," replied Sam, "but I need to sleep, Zora. If you recall, I didn't get much sleep before this ordeal began."

At the mention of what had occurred between them the night before, Zora turned around and walked quickly to the car. He'd offended her, and that was not his intention. He was teasing her, attempting to bring levity to an otherwise serious situation.

By the time Sam reached the car, Zora was already sitting in the driver's seat, her face as impassive as an Ebo statue.

Sam got in the passenger side of the car and slammed the door shut.

"I think we need to talk about what happened back at the hotel room," he said.

"Please," said Zora, "there's nothing to talk about."

Sam lifted his hand and placed it under her chin. Using the slightest pressure, he turned her face towards him. He wanted to kiss her, to lose himself in her, just as he'd almost lost himself in her last night.

Instead, he said, "I think it's obvious that there is something going on between us."

Zora shook her head, "there's nothing going on between us. What happened in the hotel room shouldn't have happened. I apologize."

Sam counted to ten slowly, then counted again. He was going to explode. "You *apologize?*"

"Yes," she said, bravely, as if she were facing a firing squad. "It was all my fault. I threw myself at you. The fact that I was half asleep is no excuse."

Now he did explode.

"Half asleep?!" he roared.

"Yes," she said, staring him straight in the eyes, although he did note with some satisfaction, that her voice shook ever so slightly.

He removed his hand from her chin and stared stonily ahead. What kind of game was she playing? She didn't throw herself at him. It was he who had initiated things, and if anyone should apologize, he should be the one. And what was that nonsense about being half asleep? By the time he finished kissing her she was fully awake, and what's more, she enjoyed herself, just as much as he did.

"Sam—" Zora said tentatively. He felt her hand on his shoulder, but he remained focused on the street in front of him.

"I'm sorry," her voice sounded small. "I didn't mean to hurt your feelings."

"Do me a favor," said Sam, "don't apologize."

"But—"

"Zora, are you going to drive me to Shelly's apartment, or do I have to drive myself?"

"I thought you wanted to go back to the hotel to sleep," said Zora.

"I'm not sleepy anymore," Sam replied.

He heard the sound of the ignition almost immediately.

*   *   *

She was falling in love with him. Zora gripped the steering wheel and stared at the road in front of her as she carefully maneuvered Miss Essie's car on the wet surface. It had started to rain soon after they left St. Ann's Bay. At first the rain had come down in light, intermittent showers. Now, it was raining in earnest. The windshield wipers were working overtime, but still the rain slashed the windshield, obscuring her vision. The driving rain, however, was the least of her problems. The more pressing issue was her growing attraction to an unsuitable man, in an unsuitable place, and at an unsuitable time. How could she be in love with someone in such a short period of time? Things like this didn't happen to sensible, practical Zora.

She'd suspected that this was happening back in the hospital, when, in the midst of all the chaos, she'd wanted nothing other than to be with him and to draw from his strength. Her feelings, however, were confirmed as she sat in the car with him in front of the hospital, and thought about the feel of his hands on her face, the sound of his voice, his nearness, the way he'd looked at her with hooded, dark eyes. She wanted to be with him, in a way she had never experienced with Milton. True, her feelings for Milton had died long ago, but at one time she had cared deeply for him. Now, she realized that whatever she'd felt for Milton was not love.

How she had fallen in love with this brash, arrogant, stubborn man was a mystery to her, but was nonetheless, an inescapable fact. Out of the frying pan and deep into the fire. After giving her heart to a thief, she'd now given her heart to a blackmailer. A blackmailer, whose dark eyes made her think daring, inappropriate thoughts. A blackmailer whose kisses left her breathless and wanting more. A blackmailer whose wry smile and dark eyes made something deep inside her stomach flutter. She was in love with him.

The only silver lining in this unhappy situation was that he would never know. She'd never let him know that yet another unsuitable man had entered her heart. She wouldn't give him the chance to laugh at her, or worse, pity her. He'd never know what she felt for him. It would be a closely guarded secret, something that only she would have access to. There would be no confidences with friends. No chance for someone to tell her just how wrong he was for her. She already knew that and believed he was a ruthless man who'd stop at nothing to get exactly what he wanted. He wanted the Black Madonna and she was the one who was going to get it for him. She was simply a means to an end. She had no doubt that he enjoyed her company, but once he'd gotten what he wanted from her, then he would dispose of her, just like Milton had.

She'd done the only thing she could to save her pride. She'd hidden her feelings from him. It was easier to make him think that last night had meant nothing to her. She'd known that the apology would infuriate him and she was sorry. She'd only wanted to do something so outrageous that he'd turn those dark eyes from her permanently. Any sign of gentleness on his part, and they'd both be in trouble. She'd proven last night that she didn't have the strength or the inclination to resist him. Her only hope was to turn his attention elsewhere. She was betting that an angry Sam Trahan was bet-

ter than an amorous Sam Trahan. She could deal
with his anger. How was she going to deal with this
newfound knowledge that she was falling for him?

Terrence Phillips handed Felice the money in a
brown briefcase. As if reading her thoughts, he
said, "Go ahead and count it. I'm a man of my
word, unlike your boyfriend."

Felice hoped that the smile on her face hid her
nervousness. She didn't like being so transparent,
especially to someone as dangerous as the man
who was standing in front of her. Instinctively she
knew that to count the money in his presence would
be an insult. Felice was smart enough to know that
this was not someone with whose bad side she wanted
to be acquainted. Besides, there was enough time to
count the money. Before the final transaction, she
would make sure that every penny was accounted
for.

"That's not necessary," replied Felice, trying to
avoid his pale eyes. His irises were the color of pale
silver. They gave him the look of not being of this
world, as if he were some unpleasant, alien visitor.
She'd never seen eyes that color, and she decided,
as she stood in his hotel room, that after their transaction was complete, that she would make it her
business not to look into those pale eyes again.

"Very well, then," he said, "it's time to find Milton
Alexander."

"Yes," said Felice, "it's time."

* * *

The living room in Shelly Wong's apartment was a celebration of all things pink—bright pink curtains fluttering in the breeze from an open window, pale pink carpet, chairs and sofa in various shades of pink, pink pastel watercolors on the wall, pink teddy bears on the sofa, and lamps with pink shades. Hanging on the wall over the decorative fireplace, which Zora noted seemed odd in a tropical island, was a portrait, encased in a pink frame of Shelley and Milton. The artist had gotten a very good likeness of the pair. From the portrait, Milton's mocking eyes stared back at Zora, while Shelly, who was painted in profile, stared up at Milton's face.

So this was Milton's love nest, thought Zora as she sat down on what really was a comfortable sofa, despite its silly pink color. She thought she'd feel something, perhaps a sense of loss, even anger. Instead, she felt tired. She wanted to close her eyes and sink into oblivion, if only for a few moments. She looked over at Sam, standing in the corner of the room across from her. He looked as tired as she felt, yet she knew that if it were necessary, Sam could walk ten miles and then climb a mountain to get whatever it is he was seeking.

Sam cleared his throat. "I've been thinking . . ."

Zora knew that conversations which began with the words *I've been thinking* usually didn't end well.

Sam continued, "I've been thinking that you should go back to New York. Things are getting dangerous. I can handle matters from here."

These were words that yesterday Zora would have loved to hear. But that was yesterday. She couldn't explain it, but things had changed. She wanted to find Milton, and she wanted to find the painting he stole. All her life, she'd allowed people to walk over her, including Milton. She wanted to confront him. She wanted to find out why he'd treated her as shabbily as he did. She wanted to tell him what a terrible thing he had done, and how it had made her feel. She also wanted to be a part of finding the Black Madonna. It was time to stop going through life as a bystander. She was ready to participate.

"I'm not going anywhere," Zora replied, "until we find Milton."

She watched as Sam raked his hand through his short black curls in a clear indication of his exasperation.

"For God's sake, Zora! I'm trying to protect you!"

"I can protect myself, thank you for your concern."

Sam sighed. "It's late. Maybe tomorrow I'll be able to talk some sense into you."

Zora stared directly into Sam's eyes. "I wouldn't count on that."

"Why don't you get some sleep," he said, his eyes not leaving her face. "We'll deal with finding Milton later. You look exhausted."

These were the first kind words he had spoken to her since they left the hospital in St. Ann's Bay.

"I am exhausted," replied Zora, glad to change the subject, "but I don't know if I'll fall asleep. It's been a heck of a night."

"That's about right," Sam replied as he walked over and sat down on one of Shelly's pink chairs.

Zora thought about Milton's suitcase and for a brief moment considered looking for it right away, but she abandoned the idea, as exhaustion started to descend on her. There would be time enough to deal with the suitcase.

"You need to get some sleep also," she said, looking at the dark circles under his eyes.

Sam got up, walked over to where Zora sat and sat down next to her. "There's room enough on this couch for both of us," he said.

Her eyes flew to his in alarm, thoughts of last night flashed through her head.

"Don't worry," he said, his lips curved in an amused smile, "I won't ravish you again. You're safe with me."

"I don't think it's a good idea," said Zora, warily.

Sam lay down on the couch. "I'm going to sleep on the couch. You can stay here. You can go to the bedroom. You can sleep on the floor. Sweet dreams, Miss Redwood."

The thought of sleeping in Shelly's bed had less appeal to Zora than the thought of sleeping on the floor. She lay down next to Sam, with her back to his chest. She'd thought that his arms would encircle her, as they had done last night. But he remained quiet, and soon thereafter, his steady breathing let her know that he had fallen asleep. Despite her earlier protestations, she fell asleep.

The sound of rain hitting the windows awakened Zora from a deep sleep. She could smell the aroma of food being cooked. She sat up and looked around at her surroundings. Her eyes focused on the various pieces of pink furniture, and the picture of Milton with the beautiful Shelly. For a moment she was disoriented. The apartment with its overwhelmingly pink décor struck a jarring note. What on earth was she doing here? Then, memory came flooding back. She lay back down and stared at the ceiling fan spinning slowly overhead.

From the direction of the kitchen, she could smell eggs cooking, and ham, and other aromas that made her mouth water. Someone, and she assumed it was Sam, was an accomplished cook, judging from the smells caressing her senses. He was certainly a man who was full of surprises. She would have guessed that the busy tycoon that he was, he had no knowledge of what the inside of a kitchen looked like, let alone what to do when he got there.

"I thought you'd never wake up."

The sound of Sam's voice startled her. She turned to find him standing by the open door which led to Shelly's kitchen. In his hands was a tray with food, juice, and a cup of something that smelled like strong coffee.

"God bless Shelly," Sam said with a grin. "I love a woman with a well stocked kitchen."

He was dressed in the jeans he had on the night before, and nothing else. His body, like everything else about him, was obviously a product of discipline. No doubt, several hours in the gym, complete with the obligatory personal trainer. Stop staring, she told herself, but her eyes seemed to have a will of their own, and they were riveted to a chiseled brown chest. She remembered running her fingers down his chest and the blood rushed to her face.

He gave her a slow smile as if he could read her mind.

Zora refused to return his smile. She cleared her throat, and asked, "How long have I been asleep?"

He glanced down at the watch on his arm, and said, "I don't know exactly when you fell asleep, but I'd say it probably wasn't long after I did. So, my guess would be you've been asleep for about four hours."

He sat down entirely too close to her. Zora had to resist the urge to move as far away from him as she could, but any sign of weakness would show him just how much he had gotten to her, and that was the last thing she wanted him to know. He undoubtedly questioned her choice of men after what he found out about Milton. The Lord only knew what he'd think if he knew that she had fallen for him, yet another unsuitable man. He'd probably laugh at her, and raise one mocking black eyebrow. No doubt his overinflated ego would be pleased that yet another woman had fallen prey to his charms. As far as she was concerned, but Sam Trahan need never know that she'd fallen in love with him.

"We need to call the hospital to see how Shelly's doing," said Zora, forcing herself to keep her voice calm, even as her heart raced at the nearness of him.

"Resting comfortably," Sam replied as he picked up a piece of bacon from the plate on his lap and munched away. "I called this morning. Her doctor tells me that she is one lucky woman. If the bullet had been two inches lower it could have done some serious damage."

"Thank God for that," said Zora.

Sam finished his bacon and looked at her. "You're a remarkable woman, Zora. Frustrating. Infuriating. Intriguing. And remarkable."

Zora's eyes narrowed. She was used to the stubborn Sam Trahan. She was used to the angry Sam Trahan. She knew about the passionate Sam Trahan. But the Sam Trahan who flattered her, threw her decidedly off guard. What was he up to?

"I hardly think the word 'remarkable' describes me," replied Zora.

Sam placed the tray with a plate filled with scrambled eggs, bacon, and toast slathered with jelly, and a glass of orange juice, on her lap.

"Eat up," he said. "By the way, your false modesty is definitely not becoming."

"It's not false modesty," said Zora, digging into some of the best scrambled eggs she had ever tasted. "What's so remarkable about me?"

Sam shook his head slowly. "Someone really did a number on you, Zora Redwood."

He was watching intently as she ate, and she felt a wave of self-consciousness come over her.

"Let's change the subject," she said, in between bites. "These eggs are really wonderful."

Sam continued speaking as if he hadn't heard her. "Do you know why you're remarkable, Zora?"

"No," she said, moving on to the toast. "But I suppose you're going to tell me."

"I find you remarkable. You're in a terrible situation, and yet you have time to care about someone else who is in trouble. Most of the women I've known would be far too concerned about landing in prison to be concerned about a woman with whom their boyfriend had an affair. I find that remarkable."

Zora remained silent for a moment. She wasn't sure what to say in response to Sam's words. She forced herself to think about food and not about Sam Trahan.

"There's nothing remarkable about caring about people," said Zora. "You ought to try it sometime."

Instead of being insulted, he let out a low chuckle. "Good old Zora, always ready to put me in my place."

Good old Zora. That phrase went a long way, Zora was sure, in explaining Milton's inability to be faithful to her. She didn't compare to the exciting Shelly, or the sensuous, conniving Felice. Good old Zora. Coming from Sam, the man who was making her heart race, those words smarted.

She finished the toast. "Let's find the suitcase. The sooner this ordeal is over for me, the better."

"The weather's pretty bad outside," said Sam. "I was over at the hotel this morning, and the receptionist said that they're expecting a pretty bad storm. They've already had power outages on the island. We may be detained here for awhile."

"I don't want to stay here any longer than I have to," said Zora. Milton and Shelly's pink love nest made her uncomfortable. It stood as a mocking symbol of what she hadn't been able to have—and would probably never have. She didn't fool herself about the kiss she shared with Sam back at the hotel. She knew that the night's passion with Sam was transient, undoubtedly fueled by the desperate circumstances they found themselves in. In the harsh light of day, Zora was certain that her favorite tycoon would say a polite thank-you to the nursery school teacher and promptly forget about her once he'd gotten what he wanted.

"I can understand that," said Sam. "Frankly, all this pink is giving me a headache. Why don't you finish your juice, and then we'll go find Milton's suitcase."

She drained her orange juice. It was freshly squeezed. She was impressed. Sam had more talents than she had given him credit for.

"I brought our things back from the hotel," said Sam. "Do you want to change?"

Zora shook her head. "Let's find out what's in the suitcase first, hopefully it will lead us directly to Milton, and the Black Madonna."

"Zora, we talked about that last night. I thought that after a good night's sleep, you'd have a clearer perspective about all this. I called the airlines this morning and I've made arrangements for you to get on the evening flight to New York."

"You made arrangements without checking with me?"

"Zora, be reasonable. This is getting dangerous."

"You're not running away, Sam, why should I."

"Because this is something that concerns me. Milton stole from me."

"And Milton stole from me, also," Zora replied. "And what he stole from me is just as valuable as your painting. He stole my good name. If we don't find him we'll have a tougher job finding the Black Madonna and I'll have a tougher time clearing my name. I don't want to be known as a thief."

"You're not a thief," Sam said, "for heaven's sake, he duped you."

"Then I'll be known as a stupid thief," said Zora. "Which doesn't make things any better, by the way."

"No one need know about your involvement in Milton's schemes . . ."

"How long do you think it'll be before Felice tells the police about my part in all of this. She told you about it. Why wouldn't she tell the police?"

Sam was quiet as he digested this undeniable point.

Then, he said, "I'll protect you."

"Don't take this the wrong way, Sam, but my days of relying on men to protect me are over."

"Zora . . ."

She stood up. "I'm going after Milton with you or without you."

Sam shook his head, "You're being unreasonable, foolhardy, reckless and you might want to throw in stubborn."

He took a step forward, so that there was no distance between them. He put a hand under her chin and lifted her head, moving his face so that their faces were mere inches apart from one another. She thought he was going to kiss her. Her heart sank when she realized that she wanted nothing more than for him to kiss her.

He moved his mouth close to hers, then he said slowly and deliberately, " Do you know, Zora, how much I want to make love to you right this very second?"

Zora's eyes narrowed. He was using the undeniable attraction they felt for each other to get his way.

"Are you in the habit of forcing yourself on women?" she asked.

She saw his dark eyes harden. She'd gone too far, but she was powerless to stop.

"There would be no force involved and you and I both know that," he said quietly.

"It's true that we are attracted to each other," admitted Zora, "but that doesn't give you the right to treat me as if I were some of the people you pay to order around. From this point on, you won't take what I haven't freely given."

"What are you saying?"

"I'm saying," said Zora, "that you will not kiss me or do anything else with me unless I give you express permission."

He threw his head back and laughed. This was not the reaction Zora was hoping for. He stood in the middle of Shelly's living room and laughed until tears rolled down his face.

Zora stared at him as if he had lost his natural mind. She saw nothing remotely humorous about her declaration.

Sam wiped his eyes once his laughter stopped.

"My dear Zora," he said, "you have my word that there'll be no more stolen kisses or anything else, unless you ask—no, beg me. If you want my kisses, Zora, you're going to have to beg me."

Zora's spine stiffened. He had taken nerve and arrogance to another dimension.

"That day," said Zora, "will never come."

"As I told you before," said Sam, with a broad, arrogant smile, "never is a very long time."

*   *   *

The suitcase wasn't difficult to find. Located in the back of Shelly's bedroom closet, it was obvious to Sam that no one had made any great effort to conceal its existence. It was old, and brown, and was covered with faded stickers of various places where it had accompanied its owner: Geneva, Montreal, Niagara Falls, Panama City, Rio. The owner of this suitcase was apparently well traveled.

Sam lifted it out of the closet. Despite its appearance, it was surprisingly light. He carried it to Shelly's bed, where he lay it down carefully. This could be the first break they'd had since landing on the island. Across the bedroom, which, like the rest of the apartment, was done in various shades of pink, Zora watched him quietly. She was annoyed with him, and that was just fine with Sam. He hadn't meant to tell her that he wanted her to beg for his kisses, but the stubborn set of her chin, and her ridiculous declaration that he should ask her permission before he tasted those lips again warranted an equally ridiculous statement. No matter what she said, they both knew that the passion, the feeling that was between them, was something that could not, would not, be denied.

"Open the suitcase, Sam," she said. She sounded annoyed.

Sam obeyed her order immediately. He wanted to find out what was in the suitcase as much as she did. The suitcase was filled with mens clothing. Sam dug through the clothing quickly until his hands reached a thin manilla envelope. Success. Zora was beside him then.

"Sam, for goodness sake, open it," said Zora, and although Sam took issue with the dictatorial tone of her voice and her words, he opened the envelope quickly. At some point in the near future, he was going to have to teach the little nursery school teacher who was the boss in this relationship. Even if she couldn't acknowledge what was going on between them, Sam was certain that she would come to understand that she belonged right there by his side, just as he belonged by her side. They had things that had to be taken care of first, Milton and the retrieval of the Black Madonna, but Sam was certain that Miss Redwood would come to see that they fit together. It was inevitable.

But, thought Sam, first things first. He opened the envelope in one swift movement and stared at its contents. A real estate brochure; a business card for Calvin Michel, real estate agent; and a set of keys. Sam recognized Milton's writing. He handed the brochure to Zora.

"We need to call this Calvin," said Sam.

"Let me do this," said Zora. "If you go asking too many questions, he might be suspicious. He also might not help us."

"So what do you suggest?" asked Sam.

Zora didn't reply. Instead she walked over to the end table next to Shelly's bed and dialed the number on the card. Then, as Sam watched with growing admiration, and amusement, Zora's proper Jamaican accent lapsed into the singsong dialect of someone who clearly was not a nursery school teacher.

"'Elo!" said Zora into the phone, "Ah need to talk to Mister Michel . . . Who me? Mi name Dolly . . . Dolly Parker . . . I help him take care of the house.

No, I'm the new house cleaner. He fired the other
one. She steal his stuff too much! Is why you ask so
much questions?! Jus' get mi de man—is an emergency! Hurry, do!"

A few moments passed, which to Sam seemed
near an eternity, and Zora began talking again. "Oh,
Mister Michel . . . thank de Lord in His heaven is
you . . . who me? Mi name is Dolly . . . but that not
important! Ah have a real emergency, man . . . well,
to be frank, and . . ."

Here, Zora paused dramatically before she began
speaking again. "Ah mus' be frank, Milton Alexander
is in a whole lot of trouble! . . . If you mus' know,
Ah'm his maid, an' a few other things, but that ain't
important. What is important is that he needs me
to clean his house . . . de one you sold him—yes,
that's right—Ah have de key but Ah don't have de
address—what's the problem? The problem is—
an' please, Mister Michel—dis mustn't go nooooo
further—Milton's been there with a lady friend—
an' the evidence of this is all over de place—but,
Milton is bringing his fiancée to de place—yes, the
one in America, de school teacher, Mm-hm. You
see de problem. I don't want no troubles there—if
Ah don't clean that house today, *today*—not only
will I be out of a good paying job, an' you know
how difficult it is sometimes to get a good payin'
job—but Milton will be out of a wife—if you un-
derstan'—de chickens will come home to roost!"

There were more moments of silence, while
Sam held his breath and prayed that Calvin Michel
bought Zora's act.

Then, Zora began speaking again. "I agree . . .

yes, yes, we wouldn't want no trouble—yes. All right. O.K. O.K. Thank you, de Lord will bless you an' . . . what's dat? Ah'll be sure to tell him that you helped . . . Yes, thanks again."

Zora hung up the phone with a look of triumph in her eyes.

"He's near Highgate," said Zora.

"Highgate?" replied Sam, who had never heard of the place.

"Yes, Highgate," replied Zora. "Give me ten minutes to shower and get ready. We're going to find Milton."

She stood with the phone in her hand, her dark eyes shining, her lips parted and curved in a smile. To his eyes, she was beautiful. To his eyes, there was no other woman who could compare. He wanted to kiss her again, but then he remembered his own words—that she would have to beg him for his kisses.

Perhaps he'd spoken too hastily.

13

Celia Trahan stared into her brother Justin's eyes when she asked the question. Although he was not much older than she was, Justin treated her as if she were his child, and not his sister. He usually told her the truth, but the few times he'd been less than honest always occurred when he wanted to spare her from being upset.

"Is Sam in any danger?"

Justin stood up, and walked around his desk to where his sister sat on one of the pillows thrown on the floor of his office. He'd never bothered getting much furniture for his office. Instead, he'd spent his money on art. His office was dominated by paintings and sculptures by several up-and-coming artists, and a few established ones which hung on stark, white walls. Competing with the secondhand desk, chair, and multi-colored pillows he'd found at a thrift store in the East Village were the various art pieces that he'd invested in and the

various framed sketches done by his own hand.
Only Celia knew that he was the artist who'd
sketched these pieces.

There was no harmony to the sketches. Their
style was eclectic. A mixture of post-modernist and
traditional—from sketches of nudes, to abstract
shapes done in no particular style, to sketches of
barren landscapes. Some of his customers had offered to buy the sketches, but they were personal
and Justin felt protective of them. He was not
ready to part with them. The only person he'd
given any of his work to was Celia. She'd fallen in
love with a sketch of his grandmother in profile.
He'd managed to capture the strength and the
pride in the old woman, God rest her soul. Celia
had asked for it. He'd given her the sketch without hesitation, as he would now give her the truth
to her question.

"Yes," replied Justin. "Sam's in danger."

He knew his sister better than to expect her to
dissolve in either tears or hysterics. In times of cri-
sis, she was cool, levelheaded, and direct.

"What can I do?" Celia asked.

"I don't know what either of us can do," said
Justin. "We don't know where Sam is or how to
contact him. I can't get through to him on his cell
phone . . . I'm guessing that even if we could find
him, Sam is so damned bullheaded I doubt that
he'd listen to us."

Celia took a deep breath, then she said, "Tell
me what you know."

It wasn't much, but it was enough to alarm
Justin, and enough for him to summon his sister to
his office. "My friend Frank DaSilva called me. He

told me that the folks that are after the Black Madonna are not the sort you want to tangle with."

Frank had contacted him this afternoon, and the news he had wasn't good. His sources, whom he refused to disclose, had informed him that the folks who were now after the Black Madonna were ruthless—and deadly. The last two dealers who had sold to the buyers had ended up dead. They'd been asking different dealers about the Black Madonna, until the portrait was stolen. The last dealer whom they inquired about the Black Madonna was murdered. Milton was over his head with these folks, and Sam was now in the direct line of danger.

Justin gave Celia the short version. "The folks who are after the Black Madonna are not averse to getting physical if that will get them what they want."

Celia raised an eyebrow, and in that moment she gave a perfect, unconscious imitation of Sam. "Getting physical?"

"Yes," replied Justin. "They're the prime suspects in the murder of at least two art dealers."

Celia sucked in her breath, and then blew it out slowly. "Who are these people?"

"No one knows for certain. They do their business through intermediaries, who disappear after the transaction is completed."

"Aren't they checked out before the transaction?"

Justin gave a dry laugh. "They deal in cold, hard cash. There are a lot of dealers who'll take the money—and not ask any questions."

"We've got to find Sam," said Celia. "We've got to warn him."

"Yeah, we do."

Suddenly, a memory that was long repressed, surfaced. When Justin was in grade school, he got his lunch money taken every day for a week. He'd been silent about it, but somehow his brother found out. The next week, instead of having his lunch money taken, the bully started giving Justin his lunch money. Justin had refused to take it, but the terror in the bully's eyes when Justin refused his money had caused him to relent. On the third day of getting the lunch money from his former tormentor, Justin learned what was going on. Sam had threatened to beat the boy within an inch of his life if he didn't leave his younger brother alone. Neither Sam, nor Justin had ever discussed the incident, and they kept fighting with each other. But the message was clear; no matter what was going on between himself and his brother, Sam was not going to let an outsider hurt anyone in his family. The message wasn't lost on Justin then, nor was it lost on him now. He was going to Jamaica to find him, and warn him.

"I've tried to reach him on his cell phone, but my calls aren't going through," said Justin, "and I called his secretary. He didn't give her an itinerary and he hasn't checked in since he left for Jamaica. I'm flying down there this evening."

"I'm going with you," said Celia.

Justin was about to tell her that things might be dangerous and he wasn't about to bring his sister into a dangerous situation, but he knew better. He'd have an easier task holding back a hurricane, than keeping Celia away from someone she loved who was in trouble.

"All right," said Justin. "Go home and pack. We leave for Jamaica this evening."

Sam Trahan sat behind the steering wheel of Miss Essie's sports car and put the key in the ignition, but he made no attempt to move the car from where it was parked in the lot behind Shelly's apartment building. He was stalling. A new technique for him. He'd spent his life dealing with his problems head on, and he had done quite well as a result. But now, every time he started saying what he wanted to say, the words got stuck somewhere in the middle of his throat. He knew what he wanted to tell Zora, but he wasn't sure how she was going to deal with his words, and he wondered if those words would be the last he spoke to her.

He was granting her a reprieve. He hadn't slept much in Shelly's pink palace. Instead, he'd lain awake staring at the sleeping Zora, resisting the urge to pull her into his arms. He remembered all too well what had happened the last time he'd done that. He wanted to be clear about his decisions, and it was a difficult thing to do with Zora around.

"What are you waiting for?" asked Zora. "The weather's bad, and its only going to get worse. Mudslides do not make for good, or safe, journeys."

The rain was heavier now. The weather announcer on radio station RJR, Jamaica's national radio station, had cheerfully announced rain for most of the island, becoming increasingly heavier and accompanied by high winds. "It's not a hurricane," said the announcer, "but it'll sure feel like one."

Sam took a deep breath. Now was as good a time as any to tell Zora what he needed to tell her.

"Zora, I'm taking you back to the airport. It's the right thing to do."

He watched as her eyes widened in surprise. She didn't look pleased about the news. Far from it.

"We've talked about this already," said Zora. "I'm not going back to New York . . . not until I find Milton."

"I'm sorry, Zora but I'm taking you back to the airport. This is getting too dangerous for you. If anything happened to you I wouldn't forgive myself. I can handle finding Milton by myself."

Her tone was measured. "What about your threats to throw me in jail if I didn't help you?"

Sam took a deep breath. "I needed your help, and I thought that telling you that would be the most expedient way to get your help."

She might as well know the truth, thought Sam. Even if she never wanted to lay eyes on him again, he wanted her to know that he would never have put her in jail. From the beginning he knew that she was a pawn in Milton's game, just as he'd been.

"Expedient?" Her voice, though calm, lowered an octave. "So now I'm *expedient?*"

He was walking into dangerous territory now, and he knew it. He hadn't the slightest idea how to extricate himself from this mess without her thinking even worse of him, but he was willing to give it a try.

"I didn't say that you're expedient," Sam tried to explain, "I said that the situation was expedient—look, you've gotten me this far, and I'm grateful. I'm certain that I'm going to find Milton. You're free to go."

"Free to go?" Now her voice rose an octave.

Her eyes were blazing, and she seemed to be having difficulty breathing. His nursery school teacher was passionate outside of the bedroom also.

Sam tried a new tactic and appealed to her reasonable side. "Zora, I really don't understand why you're acting this way—I'd think that you'd be happy to get away from me, and from this whole situation."

"In other words," said Zora, "my services are no longer required."

"Well, I wouldn't put it that way," said Sam. He felt foolish. He wasn't used to explaining his actions to anyone, and he was certain that he didn't like it. In his world, people explained themselves to him, not the other way around.

"Which way would you put it, Sam?"

Damn it all, she was being unreasonable! He had just handed her a way out of this mess, and instead of leaping at the chance—with the appropriate amount of gratitude, no less—she was glaring at him as if he had just insulted her.

"Zora," he said, forcing his voice to remain calm, after all, she had been through a lot, perhaps the last few days had taken their toll on her. "You sound as if you're disappointed that I'm no longer blackmailing you."

Her voice was tight and her response was clipped. "I just don't like being used."

He was completely exasperated. Any patience that he was holding on to completely evaporated. He was sitting in the middle of a rainstorm trying to keep her safe and she had the audacity to be angry about it.

"I'm not using you," said Sam. "You're free to return to your life."

A thick wall of silence greeted Sam's words. Zora stared in front of her at the windshield with a fixed and determined glare.

"I had no idea that I'd be putting you in danger," said Sam. "If I'd known, I would never have gotten you to come to Jamaica with me. You mean too much to me, Zora. I can't stand by and watch you get hurt."

He'd said too much. Sam had spent his life carefully crafting his words, but he had just spilled out his heart like a hopeless schoolboy. She was turning his life upside down. He hadn't meant to tell her how he felt about her. Not yet, after everything she'd been through. He knew she'd have a hard time trusting and believing him.

Sending her back to New York was the best thing for her, and if she couldn't see it now, she'd see it later—and even if she never agreed with him, he knew that what he was doing was right and, for now, that was all that mattered.

"Don't pretend you care about what happens to me," said Zora. He'd expected her to greet his declaration with something other than the glowering anger she was now directing his way. "You've decided that I'm in the way, and so now it's time for me to go."

"I do care, Zora. More than you know."

She laughed at that. "You don't care about me, Sam Trahan. I'm a convenient means to an end, and now I'm not so convenient—it's time for me to go!"

The whole thing was ridiculous. He was not going to argue with her on this. His mind was made up, and by God, they both had to live with it.

"I'm taking you to the airport," he said, his voice low and controlled, but his black eyes mirrored his anger, frustration, and his confusion. If he lived to be a hundred and one, he would never understand women, and he certainly would never understand Zora Redwood, even though at this particular moment he wanted her more than he'd ever wanted any woman.

She turned and glared back at him. "Suit yourself. I won't get on the plane."

"What?!" his voice roared and competed with a crack of lightning in the distance.

"I said," she replied, staring back at his eyes, "I won't get on the plane. You got me mixed up in this mess, and I'm not going to walk away until it's finished."

"You spent the past few weeks happily ensconced in New York. You weren't worried about finding Milton then."

"First," she said through clenched teeth, "I wasn't happy. Second, and more important, I hadn't been implicated in Milton's actions until you came along. That changed things. I need to find Milton, maybe for different reasons than you do, but believe me, it's just as important. I'm not going anywhere."

No one had ever stood up to him in that manner. Even his grandmother knew when to back down—knew when too far was too far. Instead,

Zora had proceeded with abandon into a territory where most people tread very carefully, if at all. He fought the grudging admiration for her spirit that was mixed up in his anger. It was no use fighting the attraction he felt for her. If he could have made passionate love to her right there in the parking lot he would've done so. Instead, he baited her.

"Are you sure that the real reason you want to find Milton is not to ask him to take you back?"

In one swift motion, she pulled his head to hers, and placed her lips on his.

"Kiss me, Sam," she said.

He fought with his self-control. He wanted to do more than just kiss those full lips.

Sam kept his lips on hers, but refused to obey her order. He said, "That sounds like an order, Zora. No one orders me around."

"Like hell," was the immediate response, although she didn't move her lips from his. "You've been ordering me around from the moment you met me."

He was losing all control, if ever he'd had it with Zora.

"Well, then," said Sam. "Ask me. Nicely."

She pulled away from him and said softly, "Sam, would you kiss me?"

He dragged her to his side and lowered his lips on their intended target. The world spun around him, and he felt the pull of gravity slip away. He was falling into a dark abyss in which he had no control, and he didn't care. He fell deeper and he was taking her with him. She matched his response. He could feel her hands, at first tentative, but now sure and steady, on his chest, his face, his back— her fingers splayed open. He put his hands on the sides of her face, and drew her into him. She groaned, and that undid all self-control.

"Sam," she moaned his name, and he knew then that he could not let her go. He would never let Zora go.

She pulled away from him, her breath coming in fast, hard gasps. Then, she said, "Do you still think that I want to beg Milton to take me back?"

He shook his head. "I think you've effectively dispelled that notion."

He watched as her lips curved into a smile. By God, he wanted to kiss her again.

"I'm glad that's settled," she replied. "Are you still going to send me away?"

"No," said Sam, "God help me, I'm not sending you away. We started this journey together, and we're going to finish it."

He couldn't let her go. His good sense had flown out of his head with one kiss. Lord, help me, he thought as he looked at the woman he'd fallen in love with.

Zora smiled at him and any hope he had of sticking to his guns and sending her home was lost.

"Well," said Zora, "what are we waiting for? Let's go catch ourselves an art thief."

14

The rain pelted the windows in Milton's house. The lights in the small bedroom flickered off and on intermittently and Milton knew that it was only a matter of time before he lost all electricity. He was familiar with these types of rainstorms. He remembered many nights where he and his aunt had nothing but candles and kerosene lamps to provide light. As soon as it began raining, he'd searched the pantry and found candles and a box of damp matches which miraculously still worked.

The feeling of isolation was starting to get to him. It didn't escape his wry sense of humor, or what little of it was left, that he'd chosen this place because of its isolation. Now the thought that for miles there was not another soul around unnerved him. It was late afternoon, and the rain had been coming down steadily since last night. He knew that the roads down to Highgate, the closest town to the house, would be dangerous. Miles and miles of dirt road, which would soon become an impassable sea of mud; his only consolation was that if it was difficult for him to get away, it was equally difficult for folks to get to him.

It had taken months of planning, and Felice had provided invaluable assistance. Milton had access to Sam's office. Sam ran things loosely. He prided himself on his accessibility to his employees. It was ultimately his downfall. It hadn't been difficult for Felice to find the combination to disarm the alarm system. Three nights with the head of corporate security had been enough for him to let his guard down. The rest was easy. Felice had gotten the key to the safe which held the combination numbers for the alarm, and Milton had done the rest.

Now the Black Madonna was in a safe place, and buyers who found him, also through Felice, had promised to make him a very wealthy man. He'd known from the beginning that he would not share the money from the sale of the painting with her. She was just a means to a very lucrative end. He'd also known that if he didn't get away from Felice, she would be dangerous. She'd bring attention to herself, and ultimately Sam Trahan would find them. He couldn't afford that. There was a ruthlessness in Sam Trahan that Milton recognized and admired. He did not, however, want to be on the receiving end of this ruthlessness. So he'd lay low, even as the buyers expressed annoyance and anger increased. They'd threatened him, but he had something that they wanted and he'd hold the painting hostage until he was good and ready.

Milton would be the first to admit that greed had gotten to him. The original sum of money, though great, wasn't enough. The buyers had been angry, but they wanted the portrait and they agreed, reluctantly, to his price. But as Felice had warned him, these folks were not used to being double-crossed and he was going to have to live the rest of his life looking out for them, as well as looking out for Sam Trahan. It was worth it. Financial independence had been something he'd dreamed of since childhood, and it had never before been within his reach. He understood that with this newfound financial independence he was going to have to leave some people behind, even if these were people he cared for. He did not use the word love. He didn't believe in that emotion.

Milton was clear-eyed in his approach to relationships. He cared for Shelly, but he didn't love her. She was beautiful, a wonderful ornament on his arm. He craved the look of envy he got from other men when they saw him with her. As for Zora, things got a little more complicated. He'd often thought that if he were capable of loving someone, it would be Zora. There were other women more beautiful, more compliant, more everything than Zora, but it was Zora who came closest to capturing his heart. He would never understand it, and it would be one of his life's regrets that he'd betrayed her trust. She loved deeply, and she trusted deeply, and Milton knew that because of his actions, that part of her nature would change. She was an unavoidable casualty of war—he believed the correct term was collateral damage.

Perhaps one day, years from now, they would meet again. It was a fantasy of his. He would see her in some faraway place by chance and he would be able to explain that, like the scorpion who tricked the frog into trusting him, he couldn't change who he was. It was in his nature to be deceitful; it was something he knew he would regret but the truth was he was quite comfortable with himself.

On impulse, he picked up the telephone and dialed a number. He wanted to hear another voice, the voice of someone who was always kind to him, even when she was dissapointed in him, as she often was.

She picked up on the first ring, as if she were expecting his call.

"Hello, Milton."

"Aunt Essie, how did you know it was me?"

Her voice sounded tired, and Milton became ashamed, as he knew that he was the cause for the fatigue in her voice.

"I was hoping it was you," she said. She got to the point. "There's folks looking for you, Milton."

His response was automatic. "Don't believe what you hear. Its all lies."

"There were two people who had the ring of truth—Sam Trahan, and Zora. Sweet, sweet, Zora—Milton, how you treat de chile like dat?"

Whenever Aunt Essie lapsed from the Queen's English to patois, it was a clear sign that she was agitated.

"Aunt Essie, some things you don't understand, so its best to keep quiet on them."

Miss Essie's voice rose. "Don't sass me, boy! Is I raise you, an' I ain't too old to tell you that right is right, and wrong is wrong, and what you did is plain wrong. I didn't raise you to carry on like this, I tell you!"

What did he expect? That after she found out the truth, she'd welcome him with open arms? Even Aunt Essie had her limits. He decided it was best not to fight this battle. He would not win.

"Who else was there looking for me?"

"A man with funny eyes," said Miss Essie, "kind of pale-silver eyes. He came right after Zora and her man left."

Zora's man? Aunt Essie was turning foolish in her old age. Sam Trahan, with his millions, could have any woman he wanted. What on earth would he be doing with a nursery school teacher, even if she was pretty, and had a mouth that invited kisses? Sam dated models, actresses, women whose faces graced the covers of magazines. Nursery school teachers who volunteered at homeless shelters and would rather curl up with a good book than a good man were definitely not his style.

Miss Essie's voice interrupted his thoughts.

"The man that follow Zora . . . the one with the evil eyes . . . he carry the mark of death," said Miss Essie. "Plain as day, Milton. He carry the mark of death."

The phone line went dead, and spared Milton from having to respond to that superstitious nonsense. Superstition or not, however, his blood ran cold at the thought of Miss Essie's words. Turning his attention away from Zora, he wondered—who was this man with the silver eyes?

Things had changed between them. Zora looked over at the man to whom she'd given her heart, who was now concentrating on the road which was slick with rain. The narrow coastal road had several areas where the sea was less than a few feet away. They were about thirty miles away from Magotty, and the rain was now coming down harder. At times, the car seemed to skim over water. Zora held her breath while Sam, who she'd discovered was an excellent driver, kept them from skidding off the road. She wasn't surprised that Sam approached the treacherous drive without fear or hesitation. She'd wager her last dollar that this was the way in which he faced all opponents.

In a perfect world, he would be the kind of partner she wanted to spend her life with. A man who did not let hard circumstances deter him from his goal. Milton was often flustered by what Zora considered to be minor setbacks, but she had not yet seen Sam flustered. She'd seen him angry, frustrated, bewildered, but he had always managed to keep his emotions under control. She shook her head as if to rid herself of foolish thoughts. Any thought of her building a future with Sam Trahan was foolish. Instead, she forced herself to focus on finding Milton. She could not fool herself that Sam Trahan could build a relationship with her.

Sam looked at her and smiled.

"Stop worrying," he said.

She couldn't help but return his smile.

"I'm not worrying," she lied.

"Then stop doing whatever it is to cause that pretty mouth of yours to turn into a frown."

He was impossible—beautiful, exciting, passionate, and impossible.

Sam turned his attention back to the road. "What in the world?" he murmured, his eyes narrowing in concern.

Zora followed his gaze and saw that there appeared to be a roadblock with soldiers in the middle of the road.

Sam slowed the car to a halt and waited for the soldier who was walking quickly toward the car. He wore a green rain slicker, which Zora guessed was probably standard army issue.

Sam rolled down the window.

"What's going on?" asked Sam. His tone didn't imply even the hint of annoyance.

"The road's washed away a few miles down, you'll have to go back to Pembrook, and take a detour through Orange Hill. Do you know how to get to Pembrook?"

Zora spoke up. "I do, I'll get us back there. I'm familiar with the area."

"Where are you headed?" asked the soldier.

"To Magotty," she replied, without hesitation.

"If I were you, I'd tarry awhile in Pembrook, or in Orange Hill for the night. Things are pretty bad in Magotty—a lot of flooding and there's been a few mudslides."

Zora thanked the soldier quickly, and directed Sam back to Pembrook. She was grateful for all the drives she took with her family as a child. She knew almost every part of the island, and even though it had been several years since she'd last driven these roads, she was still comfortable with navigating the sometimes confusing roadways.

By the time they reached Pembrook, the rains were accompanied by high winds, which shook Miss Essie's sports car without mercy.

"I think we need to tarry awhile," said Zora, echoing the soldier's words.

"My feelings exactly," said Sam. "I don't suppose you know anyplace we can stay?"

Zora shook her head. "I've never stayed here, although I've driven through Pembrook many times."

Sam eased the car into a gas station, and a Rastafarian attendant holding a red, black, and green umbrella appeared almost instantly at the driver's side of the car. Sam rolled down the window and said, "We don't need any gas, but we do need some information."

"I'll see what I can do for you, mon."

"Any place to spend the night around here?"

"Well, we don't have much in the way of hotels here, you know, but there's a guest house just down the road or so."

Zora had grown up in Jamaica and she knew that "just down the road or so" could mean around the corner—or several miles away.

"Where exactly can we find this guest house?"

"Just go down the road right here and when you get to King Street, there'll be a yellow church on the corner, you hang left and it'll be the third house on the right. There's a big mango tree in the yard."

They thanked him for his directions, which were remarkably clear. In less than ten minutes, they were pulling into the yard of a white, two-story house where there was a mango tree laden with yellow and orange mangos. There was a sign in front of the house which read *Refuge Guest House,* which Zora hoped was an accurate description of the place.

They were welcomed with true Jamaican hospitality, despite their bedraggled appearance and their lack of a reservation.

"Of course we have room," said the proprietress, a friendly, plump woman with graying hair and a pleasant disposition. "It's not fancy, but it's clean and, what's more, it'll provide you both with a warm, dry place to lay your head until this storm ends."

Her name was Carolyn, but she informed them as she walked with them to their room, everyone called her Caro; it was her dead husband's nickname for her, God rest his soul. She thought that Zora and Sam were married, and neither person corrected her assumption.

The room she provided them took Zora's breath away. It was simple and it was exquisite. There was a king size brass bed in the middle of the room, with an ornate white and gold bedspread. Beside the bed stood two antique brass lamps which were lit. The lamps blanketed the room in a warm, golden light. In the far corner was a dark wood dresser. On the other side of the room were two chairs made out of the same dark wood as the dresser with white and gold cushions. In the windows, pale gold, sheer curtains completed the picture of elegance.

"I hope you like the room," said Caro. "It's got a private veranda which looks out on the patio in the back. It's got a great view of the hills also, but right now all you folks will see is rain if you venture to the windows."

"It's beautiful," said Zora. Sam remained silent.

"I'll leave you two love birds alone," said Caro. "There isn't a phone in the room, but I suppose it doesn't matter—the phone lines have been down for a few hours now."

She left them with a promise of a good, hot meal in the evening. "I'm making some curry shrimp and some rice and peas. If you'd care to join me for dinner, I eat promptly at seven. If you have other plans, don't worry. I won't be offended."

Zora stood staring at Sam. She'd thought that being alone with him in this beautiful room would arouse the passion between them, but instead she felt an unfamiliar shyness creep over her. This was the kind of room she would have envisioned spending her wedding night in, and the thought that she would in all likelihood never have a wedding night with Sam Trahan or anyone else brought an almost unbearable sense of sadness and regret.

"Are you afraid of me, Zora?" he asked, looking at her warily.

"No," she said, honestly. "I'm not afraid of you." Inside, she added, *I'm afraid of what I feel for you.*

"Good," he said, "because I don't want you to

fear me. That would displease me, greatly. Come here, Zora."

She obeyed him and walked in front of him. He put his arms around her and drew her close to him.

He whispered in her ear, "I won't hurt you, Zora."

Milton had said those words also, and he'd betrayed her. She now knew that no matter what it was she felt for Milton, it wasn't love, and while his betrayal hurt, she realized that what hurt the most was her pride. With Sam, any hurt would be real, and undeniably painful.

"Come to bed with me, Zora," he said. "We won't do anything that you don't want us to do. You know how I feel about you, but you have to know that I won't come to you until you're completely ready. Last night was great, spectacular even, but I don't think that either of us were ready for what happened. The next time, and there will be a next time, Zora, I want us both to be ready."

In spite of her better judgment, she followed him to bed and lay down next to him. He kept his word. He held her, and from time to time she felt his kisses on her hair, but he seemed to know that she wasn't ready for anything else.

Zora fell asleep to the sound of rain.

Sam watched Zora as she slept. In sleep, with her features relaxed, she looked like a little girl to him. He wondered what Zora must have been like as a child. He suspected that she was probably the same as he'd found her to be on a Brooklyn street—smart, sassy and incapable of being brow-beaten. There was also something else about her, a sadness hidden somewhere deep within those dark eyes of hers. He wondered if that sadness had been there when Zora was a child.

As if she knew he had been looking at her, Zora opened her eyes and stared at him. Her lips curved into a small smile.

"Spying on me when I'm at my most vulnerable?" she asked, still smiling.

Sam decided right there and then that he would never tire of hearing that West Indian lilt.

"You might say that," answered Sam. "Actually, I was enjoying the peace and quiet, if you want to know the truth."

She laughed then, and said, "Are you trying to tell me that I talk too much?"

"No," said Sam, "but when you're awake, you're usually fighting me—so if it takes having you fall asleep to have a little peace, then I suppose I'll take it any way I can get it."

Her expression turned serious. "I'm not fighting you now, Sam."

He wasn't sure if he was reading the signals right. It had been a long time since he'd been in a relationship, and although it was far too early to characterize what they had as a relationship, he knew that was what he wanted with Zora. He would settle for no less.

"What are you saying, Zora?" His voice was hoarse, as he struggled with the almost irresistible urge to drag her into his arms.

Zora sat up and placed her lips on his. She

gave him a light kiss, with an implicit promise of more.

"Is that plain enough for you?" she asked.

He pulled her towards him, with an urgency which surprised them both. His hands roved freely, as did hers—touching faces, necks, arms, stomachs, hands upon hands, flesh upon lips, legs entwined. Her fingers unbuttoned his shirt and as the garment fell away, she leaned forward and placed light kisses on his chest. It was his undoing.

"Zora," he murmured, struggling to speak coherently, "are you sure? Are you completely certain that you want this?"

Zora nodded her head. "Yes, I'm certain."

Outside, he could hear the raindrops pelting the window with a fierceness that matched his feelings for this woman.

He felt like an awkward schoolboy. He felt as if this were the first time.

"I have protection," he said. "I bought some when I stopped off at the store this morning."

Instead of the outrage he'd expected, he got a soft giggle from Zora.

"Leave it to you to always be prepared, Sam," said Zora.

He wrapped his arms around her. "I used to be a Boy Scout," he said.

Zora whispered in his ear, "Lucky me."

When evening finally came, after the rain had stopped falling, and after they had eaten a feast of Jamaican food courtesy of their gracious—and, judging from the two roses that accompanied their meal, romantic-minded—hostess, Zora lay in bed listening to the sounds of a night in the Caribbean. These sounds of crickets intermingled with occasional calls of a nocturnal bird were familiar to her. She had grown up listening to the noises of the night. She remembered many times being frightened by the darkness and the sounds that came from outside her bedroom window; her mother would lay in bed with her until she fell asleep.

"What are you thinking about?" Sam's voice interrupted Zora's thoughts.

"Yesterday," replied Zora.

They were lying next to each other, and Zora was surprised at how comfortable she felt in this position. It was as if they were well acquainted with each other in a way that would only occur through a shared history. The last time she'd felt this safe, this cherished, had been as a young child in the arms of her parents. She reached out and touched his smooth, brown face, tracing her hands lightly down the length of his nose and over his lips. How had it escaped her how beautiful this smooth, brown, arrogant face was? He wasn't handsome in the conventional cookie-cutter, movie-star glamour look that one saw in magazines and in the movies. His face, with its prominent nose, full lips, strong chin, and piercing dark eyes was much more interesting, much more compelling than that. Zora knew that there were many women who would find Sam Trahan attractive simply because of the aura of power and money which surrounded him. His wealth as well as his business acumen were well known. But Zora knew that if Sam Trahan had been a fisherman on a boat in the middle of the sea without a penny to his name, she would still find the face of the man lying beside her beautiful and, more than that, she knew that what she felt for this man—and she knew it was love—would not change even if tomorrow brought a change in his fortunes. Her heart belonged to him.

"Does yesterday bring you sadness?" he asked.

She nodded her head.

He wrapped his arms around her and she moved closer to him. She lay her head against his chest and she could hear the strong, steady sound of his heartbeat.

"Tomorrow will be better," he said, his voice carried a confidence that Zora wished she shared. "Tomorrow after tomorrow after tomorrow after tomorrow . . ."

Zora could not look to tomorrow. Tomorrow would bring Milton, and the Lord only knew what else. Still, she would cherish this night, as long as her memory held her.

They were coming. This was the end. Milton felt the taste of fear in his mouth and something else. Regret. He sat in his bedroom as he heard the footsteps come closer. For a fleeting moment, he thought that perhaps he should try to run for it, but in his heart he knew that it was too late. He'd played a game and he'd lost. He'd lost the woman he now realized that he loved. Had losing Zora been worth the price of the Black Madonna? He now knew that it wasn't.

He'd known that if they found him, they would

kill him—and they'd found him. The time for bargaining was over. He'd betrayed them just as he'd betrayed Zora. Now he was going to pay the ultimate price. He was going to pay with his life. The footsteps were coming closer now. There was no place to run. *I'm sorry,* he whispered to Zora. *I'm sorry.* He realized now what she meant to him, and that he'd put her directly in the line of danger. Think, think, he told himself as his heart hammered in his chest. His hand reached for a piece of paper on the nightstand beside his bed and wrote down the words he knew that would ultimately protect her and possibly get her out of the mess he'd created.

As the door to his bedroom burst open, he prayed that his aunt was right when she told him that God still listened to the prayers of sinners.

Justin Trahan fastened his seat belt and watched as a pretty young stewardess cautioned the passengers on the Air Jamaica flight about emergency exits, and water landings, and other information which did not interest him. Beside him, his sister sat reading a medical journal as if it were a paperback novel. She was riveted. He knew that Celia was trying to shift her attention away from her concern for Sam.

"Don't worry, Doc," Justin said, using his nickname for Celia. "Sam is too hardheaded, and too arrogant to let anything happen to him."

Celia closed the medical book and looked at Justin. Her eyes, which were so much like her grandmother Ma Louise that it was difficult even now for Justin to look into them, were worried.

"It's his arrogance that worries me," replied Celia. "It could make him too confident in a situation where he should be careful."

Justin secretly agreed with his sister's assessment of their brother, but he didn't want to say anything to increase the worry that crowded her eyes.

"Well, the cavalry is on the way to save him," said Justin, as the roar of the jet engines increased. They were ready for takeoff.

15

The Tuesday morning sun that greeted Sam when he awoke was in direct contrast to the previous day's rainstorm. Sam and Zora had left Carolyn's guest house after breakfast promising to return. As they drove along roads that were strewn with debris from falling trees, and roads that were still in some places covered with water, Sam could see that Mother Nature had unleashed her fury yesterday. Today, however, the sun was shining and, although it was just past ten in the morning, the temperature was somewhere between hot and steaming.

Miss Essie's sports car was far from comfortable and the air-conditioning was nonexistent; still, they were making good time. They were five miles out of Highgate. Once there, they would have to find Milton's house, but Zora had an address, and she was nothing if not resourceful. Sam knew that in a matter of hours he would be standing face to face with Milton Alexander.

Beside him, Zora sat staring out of the window. Her face was pensive. She had awakened this morning silent and withdrawn. Her knew the reason for her mood. Milton. He wondered if she still had feelings for him. Last night, he'd been convinced that Milton was not only out of her heart, but out of her head. Today, however, her eyes were clouded with what he could only guess were memories. They'd called the St. Ann's Bay hospital from a pay phone this morning to see how Shelly was doing. The nurse with whom they'd spoken had assured them that Shelly was doing "as well as could be expected," which was good news. Still, Zora was apprehensive. He'd wanted to hold her and tell her that everything would be all right, but as he sat in this cramped red sports car, he wondered what would happen after this whole mess was sorted out.

The countryside around him was spectacular. He wished, not for the first time, that he were in a position where he could enjoy the sight of the vivid green hills that surrounded the road, or the sight of the palm trees and wide-winged birds with their bright colors. He wanted to see this place through Zora's eyes, eyes which hopefully one day would not look at the world through a lens of betrayal and distrust.

"Sam, slow down here," said Zora, "you're going to have to make a turn just past the pink house over there. I think that should be King Street."

Her voice sounded cool and businesslike. Sam's thoughts flashed to a recent time when she was neither. When they woke up, she'd seemed shy, but a quick kiss had melted the ice. He knew that they were getting closer to Milton and he was certain that this contributed to Zora's mood.

Forcing his thoughts back to the present and to more immediate matters, he asked, "What's on King Street?"

"Not what," she replied. "Who. There's a shop called Charlie's that my parents used to go to. It's where everyone in Highgate at one time passes through. That's the quickest way to find out where Milton's house is. The realtor says its outside of Highgate, up in the hills. I need to figure out how to get there. These country roads can be tricky."

"We don't have much to go on."

"We have enough to find Milton," Zora replied.

He had to trust that Zora knew what she was doing. He had no choice. Still, as difficult as it was for him—a person who had ultimate control over every aspect of his life and his business—to give up control to a woman whom admittedly he cared for, he now had to rely on her to help him get the Black Madonna back to his family.

He followed her directions and a few minutes later he was double-parked on a busy main street, watching her disappear into the doors of a large store. He watched as people swarmed around the street, vendors hauling their wares in large straw baskets; market women balancing baskets of fruit on their heads; Rastafarians, with their long dreadlocks, walking regally down the street. In the distance, he could hear the sounds of reggae music coming from someone's radio. He was a world away from the streets of New York and, despite the circumstances, or perhaps because of them, he had a feeling of well-being, a feeling that no matter what, everything was going to be all right. He thought about finding a telephone to call his secretary. He hadn't checked in with her in days. This was the first time he could remember that his work hadn't taken first priority in his thoughts. Sam decided that he would call his secretary later that day.

Twenty minutes later, Sam watched Zora walking quickly towards the car. In her hand was a piece of paper which she held in front of her as if it were some sort of trophy. She opened the car door, and slid into the seat beside him.

"He's not too far away from here," she said, "and I've got the directions."

He shouldn't have doubted her. In the past few days he'd known her, she'd proven not only to be completely irresistible to him but also to be resourceful. To say that the delectable Miss Zora Redwood had many talents would only be underestimating her.

Following Zora's directions, they drove through a street that cut through the middle of the small town. After leaving Magotty, they took a road which veered right and started their ascent into the hills. The driving became much more difficult then, as the winding dirt road was in many places turned to mud from the rains the day before. The houses that clung to the sides of the hill varied from shacks with tin roofs that seemed so frail that Sam wondered how they managed to remain upright, to more spectacular villas that somehow managed not to look out of place. Soon, they left the houses behind, as the road became steeper and narrower. There was nothing out here but an occasional herd of wild goats. The countryside was beautiful, but remote.

In the distance, they could see a white house on the crest of the hill. Unlike the villas that they had passed on the road, with their cool, inviting pastel colors, this house looked as if it belonged to another time, and another place. This was a home which belonged in Europe, or somewhere with colder climates, a house which looked as if it had come, via a time capsule, directly from the eighteenth century.

"That's the house," said Zora, her voice tight.

This seemed as good a time as any to say what he should have said to Zora this morning. He pulled the car over to the side of the road, and shut the engine off.

Turning to Zora, whose face remained in profile as she stared at the house, Sam said, "No matter what happens here Zora, I want you know how much I appreciate your help. I want you to know that."

She turned and looked at him. "I did what I had to do."

The words slapped him just as surely as if she'd taken her hand and slapped his face. The coldness in her voice surprised him. She seemed angry with him, and he couldn't understand it. Last night they'd been as close as two people could be, and today she was acting as if he were an enemy.

"You did what you had to do?" he repeated her words slowly. He wanted to give her a chance to take them back. Immediately.

She didn't seize the opportunity. "Yes, I did what I had to do."

The words left his lips before he had a chance to censure them. "Did that include last night, Zora? Were you doing what you had to do last night?"

She turned and looked at him then. She opened her mouth as if to respond, but nothing came out.

"Answer me, Zora!" Sam was insistent.

"Wow," said Zora. "Last night was real."

Sam wanted to hold her tight. He wanted to protect her from whatever was waiting for them in Milton's house. But he had to concentrate on the business at hand. Once that was taken care of, he would pursue Zora Redwood with a singleminded focus. Even if she continued running from him, he was going to show her that they belonged together. He had never failed in any task he set out to do, and he wasn't about to start now. He turned on the engine and moved the car forward. He had unfinished business to attend to, and once that was accomplished he was determined to convince Zora that he belonged in her life, and she belonged in his.

The house stood in front of them, an imposing white mansion. It looked as if it belonged on a wide, sweeping plantation. Zora felt her heart pound in her chest, whether from fear or anticipation, she wasn't sure. There was an air of neglect that clung to the house, from the unkempt grounds and overgrown bushes in the front to the grass which looked as if it had not been cut in months. The house was in need of paint and the front wooden steps on which they were standing were cracked and broken in many places.

There was no sign of life coming from within the house. The windows in the front of the two-story house were all closed, and it appeared to be in complete darkness. Were they too late? Zora wondered. Had Milton left already? She pushed that possibility out of her mind quickly. The thought that they had traveled this far, and had gotten to this place, only to end up where they began, with no Milton, was unfathomable to her.

Sam turned to her. From the hard, serious look on his face, Zora could tell that his mind was on finding Milton. All thoughts of yesterday's diversions were far away.

"I want you to stay outside here while I go inside first," he said. "We don't know what or who's inside. Let me handle things from here."

She bristled at the he-man act. He wouldn't have gotten to this point without her help. She didn't take kindly to being told to step aside, as if she would be in the way.

"I'm going inside with you," she said.

His voice became ice. "This isn't negotiable, Zora. I want you to stay here until I call you."

"I don't take orders," she retorted, keeping her voice even, although she wanted nothing more than to yell at him at the top of her lungs.

"I don't have time for this," said Sam. "Quite frankly, neither do you. Milton is a dangerous man and there's no telling what he'll do when I confront him. If there's one thing I know about Milton it's that he's going to go for my weak spot. You're my weak spot, Zora. Do you understand? I can't let anything happen to you. Milton is smart. He'll see that and he'll try to use that to his advantage. I won't let that happen."

It was the closest thing to a declaration of love. She wasn't sure if she was hearing the words correctly, but Sam Trahan had just told her he cared about her, or so she thought. Being compared to a weak spot wasn't the most romantic thing she'd ever heard and maybe he wasn't in love with her, as she was in love with him, but he cared for her. In the midst of the most unlikely of circumstances, Zora felt her heart soar.

"Do you understand me, Zora?" Sam asked, his voice less harsh now, but still determined.

She nodded her head. "I'll stay here for awhile, but if you don't come out I'm coming in there for you."

Zora watched Sam wage an internal war. She knew he didn't want her to go into the house under any circumstances, but if the circumstances called for it, she would be in there with Sam. No matter what he thought, or no matter what common sense called for.

He leaned over and kissed her lightly. "Are you supposed to be my very own personal bodyguard?"

"Something like that," Zora replied.

Sam sighed. "What am I going to do with you?" he asked as he exited the car.

Zora watched as Sam walked quickly up the front pathway and up the wooden stairs towards the imposing white doors. He grasped the large brass knocker which protruded from a brass lion's head. He knocked on the door loud enough to rouse the dead or summon the inhabitants of the house. There was no response.

Sam turned the brass doorknob and the front door opened easily. He hesitated for a moment then he walked inside and closed the door behind him.

Zora felt her heart start to hammer in her chest and her mouth go dry with fear. What if Milton tried something crazy? What if he tried to hurt Sam? Milton would have to be desperate. Desperate to keep Sam's property, and desperate to keep himself out of prison.

Zora whispered a quick prayer, and hoped fervently that Sam would forgive her for not keeping her word to stay put. Besides, she reasoned to herself as she raced up the stairs before her common sense caught up with her, what kind of person would she be if she allowed Sam to face what was certainly a dangerous situation, alone?

Zora opened the door and found herself facing a darkened room. She could hear footsteps on the second floor, and Sam's voice calling out for Milton. Her eyes quickly grew accustomed to the darkness and she saw that she was standing in a living room, only this room looked as if it was the scene of a recent riot. Furniture was pushed in haphazard patterns, some overturned, and the ones that were upright were strewn around the room in a way that indicated chaos. She turned and looked for a light switch on the wall. Finding none, she picked up a lamp from the debris on the ground and pulled on its switch.

As the light from the lamp spilled into the room she heard Sam's footsteps overhead come to a sudden halt. Without hesitation, she ran towards the wooden stairs that led to the second floor and took the stairs two and three at a time. Her only thoughts were a silent and single-minded prayer to let Sam be all right. At the landing of the second floor she turned in the direction where she had just heard his footsteps, now silent.

"Sam!" she called out, but her words were greeted by complete silence. The light in the narrow hallway of the second floor was turned on and Zora walked quickly down the hallway to an open door located almost at the end. Through the open door, she could see Sam kneeling down—at the same moment, the sense of dread with which she had awakened this morning rose within her and she felt her breath come in ragged gasps. Where was Milton?

She had expected to see his face, arrogant and contemptuous, staring at her. He would be surprised to find her in his element; perhaps he would even create a scene. She was prepared for this. What she wasn't prepared for was the sight of Sam kneeling over the prostrate body of a person she knew was Milton.

"Don't come in, Zora!" Sam turned and looked at her, the blood drained from his face, his mouth a thin, grim line. "For God's sake, don't come in!"

She stood rooted in the doorway. From where she stood, she could see Milton clearly now. He was lying on his side, as if he had just fallen in that position and had chosen to remain there. He was wearing blue jeans, and a white oxford shirt. His feet were bare.

"Zora, please!" Sam's voice was pleading. "Don't come in."

Zora wanted to turn and run, but she couldn't. Instead, she took a deep breath, and walked into the room and knelt beside Sam. Her eyes then rested on Milton's face. His lifeless eyes which stared into her own answered her unasked question. She averted her gaze from his face and saw that the front of his white shirt was stained with blood, which had now turned a deep rust color. There was a small hole in his shirt.

"He's been shot," Sam said simply.

Zora felt the room suddenly grow hot and the floor seemed unsteady. She couldn't breathe. She had never fainted before, but the ringing in her ears and the way the room swayed before her heralded that she was very close to passing out. Oblivion was welcome now. She welcomed the darkness which was surely near. But a part of her, the stubborn part that she supposed was due to her heritage, and to the way she was raised, fought the easy way out.

Sam put his arms around her and pulled her to him. "I'm sorry," he said.

Zora reached out to hold Milton's hand. Had he suffered? she wondered. No matter how he'd hurt her, he didn't deserve this end to his story. She'd hoped that the courts would have sorted things out. This was no justice. Not for Milton. Not for Sam. Not for anyone involved. Her heart ached as she thought of Miss Essie. She knew that although Miss Essie had her differences with her nephew, she loved him dearly.

"Oh, Milton—" she whispered.

This was someone she'd loved once, someone she had planned to spend her life with. She felt the bitterness she'd held towards him, from the moment she'd found out about his betrayal, drain away and leave in its place a sense of loss of what could have been—not for them, for she knew as certainly as she was sitting in this neat and dreadful room, that they had not not been meant for each other.

Zora looked at Sam and said, "I need to say good-bye."

He pulled her tightly towards him as if he didn't want to let her go, then as suddenly as he embraced her, he released her. He left the room.

She wanted to say something, perhaps offer a prayer for Milton. But, nothing coherent came to mind; instead, she took his hand in hers. She felt a piece of paper and she pulled her hand away in surprise. The paper fell on the floor beside him. In his neat handwriting, she saw the words: *three palms*.

Zora began crying then, tears mixed with cries. Milton had come through in his last moments. He had redeemed himself. He had led her to the Black Madonna. She was certain of it.

She didn't know how long she sat there crying, and holding his cold hand. "Good-bye," she cried, "good-bye."

She didn't know when Sam entered the room, but she became aware of his presence behind her. Solid, waiting, comforting. Sam Trahan. She stood and walked towards where he waited in the same doorway she had stood earlier.

"I've found it," she said. "I've found the Black Madonna."

"Don't worry about the Black Madonna," he said, "are you all right?"

She shook her head and said, "No, I'm not all right—but I will be."

He pulled her into his arms again. "Zora, we'll find the Black Madonna; right now I just want to make sure you're going to be O.K."

She looked up into his face and said, "I'm going to be just fine but Milton has just given us the answer we've been looking for. He's led us to the Black Madonna."

"Zora, let me handle this . . ."

"No." Zora's voice was firm. "You made a promise to your grandmother to get back what belongs to your family, and I'm going to help you keep that promise."

16

"How far is Rose Hall?"

The question startled Felice. Terrence Phillips had been silent since they'd left Milton's house. At the thought of Milton, and what had happened to him, Felice felt her chest tighten with a strange pain. Terrence had taken a gun, squeezed its trigger, and ended Milton's life. In retrospect, Felice should not have been surprised by this ending. She had heard that he was brutal, and that the people he worked for were equally brutal and unforgiving. Milton had double-crossed them, and in so doing, he had paid with his life. She'd thought that they would have taken the information from Milton by force. She'd been angry at Milton, and the thought that he would be roughed up had not overly concerned her. But Milton's violent death had shocked her. Still, Milton was gone and she wasn't going to waste any time worrying about him; what

did concern her was the thought that she'd meet
the same violent end.

She had to get away. The money no longer interested her. What good was the money if she
wouldn't be around to spend it? She had underestimated these people, but now she saw them—and
the situation she was in—very clearly. She knew
that the only reason she was still alive was because
she was still useful to them. Unlike Milton, however, Felice was determined to get out of this situation very much alive.

"How far is Rose Hall?" Terrence asked the question again, this time his voice rose slightly.

"Not far." Felice tried to stop her hands from shaking. "From what I can tell on this map, it's about
seventy miles away."

"The roads aren't in good condition after the
rains," said Terrence. "It'll take us some time to
get there."

Felice made no comment, instead she concentrated on finding a way to get far, far away from
this madman. Despite his outwardly calm appearance, she'd seen firsthand the violence he was capable of. At first Milton had refused to tell them
where the Black Madonna was hidden despite her
entreaties, and Terrence's threats. Then, Terrence
had opened a briefcase filled with more cash than
Felice had ever seen. *If you give me the information,*
he'd said, *I'll not only let you live, you'll walk away a
very rich man.*

The sight of the money had foolishly loosened
Milton's tongue. It was a trick, and Felice had seen
through it, but in his desperation Milton had foolishly opened his mouth and given away the infor-

mation that ultimately led to his downfall. Milton had grasped the briefcase in his hand, and told them that the portrait was in a back room in the Rose Hall mansion, a former plantation that was now used as a musuem. "That's the safest place for the portrait to be," Milton had declared. "Most people on the island believe that the house is haunted, and apart from a few brave tourists who come to the museum to see the sights, no one is going to go wandering around that place. Even the people that work there—certain rooms are just off limits. It's in a closet in the basement."

Those were the last words spoken by Milton. Terrence had the shot Milton once in the chest. He had fallen to the ground, his surprise at being double-crossed shadowing his eyes. When they left he was still alive, but Felice knew that the end for Milton was very near.

"Under other circumstances," Terrence had informed her, as he took her by the arm and led her out of Milton's white house, "I would've made sure that he was dead before I left him, but I want him to think about his actions and how they led to this end, before he dies."

Felice had asked him then, "Are you going to kill me too?"

He had answered without hesitation, "I haven't decided. I need you to help me find the painting—I was rash shooting Milton when I did. I should've waited to determine whether or not he was telling the truth—but, to be frank, I lost control. Something that rarely happens. So, for now we're stuck with each other. For better, or for worse."

For better, or for worse. At one time, she'd thought she'd hear those words in a wedding ceremony with Milton. She'd cared for him, although she couldn't say that she loved him. They were good together. He'd excited her in ways that other men had failed to do. She'd been intrigued by him. Like her, he had a vision that life owed him much more than he'd been given, and he was ruthless enough, conniving enough, to do everything in his power to get whatever it was he felt that he deserved. Now, he lay dead, she was certain of this, in the bedroom of a house far in the hills.

The car suddenly slowed down, and Felice saw two policemen in the middle of the road, in front of them, waving at them to stop.

Freedom! Felice's hopes soared. *Freedom!*

Just as suddenly she felt something cold and hard by her side and looked down to see the gun Terrence had used to shoot Milton.

"Don't be foolish," he said calmly, his eyes steady on the road in front of him.

He placed the gun on the seat beside him and rested one hand over it.

"Hullo!" the policeman called out to them, as they came to a stop in the road. One of the policemen walked over to them, and leaned in the window. The other stood in the road looking out for approaching cars.

"What can I do for you, Officer?" Terrence asked, with a wide smile.

"Jus' want to warn you to take it real easy on the road—two miles down, the road wash away a little bit—got a lotta mud over there. You can make it, but you must drive real slow. Already there is a whole lot of car accidents! Folks driving like they plain old crazy or confused!"

"Thank you for the warning, Officer," said Terrence, as the policeman stepped aside and waved them through. "And may I commend you on a fine job that you're doing. It's officers like you that give the Jamaican police the deservedly fine reputation they have!"

Felice felt her heart sink into the base of her stomach, as she watched the officer's face beam in response to the false compliment.

"The decision to remain silent was a wise move on your part," said Terrence as they drove away.

Felice wasn't so sure.

As if to underscore his words, he continued, "Had you chosen to get dramatic, there would have been two dead policemen, and that would have been most unfortunate."

17

"How can you be sure that the painting is in Rose Hall?" Sam asked as they drove down the dirt road, away from Milton's house. The sight of Milton's body lying on the bedroom floor flashed in Sam's mind as he concentrated on manuevering Miss Essie's car on the dirt road, on their way back to Highgate and then to Rose Hall.

He looked over at Zora, her face reflecting the grief he knew that she was feeling.

"When we were children," replied Zora, "we used to hear stories about the White Witch of Rose Hall—Annie Palmer. She lived at the plantation in the nineteenth century. According to the legend, she killed her husbands and her lovers. There's a story that her husbands are buried under three palm trees just down the hill from the house. The house is a big tourist attraction now, but when we were growing up, folks tended to stay away from the house—because it is haunted, or so everyone believed. Milton was fascinated by Rose Hall and the stories that surrounded the place. I'm convinced that was what the note about three palms was about—it was Milton's way of trying to lead us back to the Black Madonna."

The whole thing seemed far-fetched to Sam. Witches. Haunted houses. Palm trees. Still, Zora was absolutely convinced that the portrait was in Rose Hall. In the short time he'd come both to know Zora and to fall in love with her, he'd also learned to trust her. If she believed that Milton had left her a message from the grave, then Sam accepted that this was, in fact, true.

He glanced at her again. He'd had a difficult time convincing her to leave Milton at the house. She'd wanted to call the authorities and wait for their arrival, but the telephone service had been interrupted by the storm. In the end they decided to go back to Highgate and then contact the police. An anonymous call would be best, Sam stated, as the last thing they needed was to be tangled up in Milton's mess. There would be questions, and perhaps, suspicion—two things they didn't need.

"How are we going to find the portrait? It could be anywhere in the house or on the property," said Sam.

"We'll figure it out once we get there," said Zora. "Right now we need to get to Highgate to let the police know what's happened to Milton."

Night fell before Felice and Terrence reached Rose Hall Plantation. Situated on a hill, the mansion, with its stark, white, Georgian architecture and its several dark windows, looked forbidding to Felice. She felt a sharp chill race up her spine at the sight of the Rose Hall mansion. Was this the place where she was going to die?

They drove to the gate at the foot of the hill, where a night watchman shined his flashlight into the car.

"We're close, mon!" he said, annoyed that anyone should be bothering him at this late hour. "Come back tomorrow!"

Terrence rolled down the window and called out, "Is it too late for a house tour, my good man?"

The watchman laughed. "Tour over from four o'clock, and only someone really mad will want to take a tour at this time. You don't know that this house haunted?"

"I don't believe in ghosts," Terrence stated.

"Is that right?" asked the watchman. He seemed unimpressed by this statement.

"I don't suppose you could give me a private tour?" asked Terrence. "I'd make it worth your while."

The watchman shook his head vigorously. "No amount of money could make me go in there at night. Even the folk that work in the house get out by nightfall. Come back, tomorrow. We open at ten."

Terrence thanked the watchman and drove away.

Felice had expected that her companion would have tried to kill him, but she'd been surprised that he'd simply driven away.

"He's a lucky man," Terrence commented, as if

he were responding to the question. "Under any other circumstances, he'd be dead—but I want to take the portrait with as little commotion as possible. A dead night watchman, would certainly cause a commotion."

Felice remained silent, as she'd done for much of the journey.

Terrence continued his one-sided conversation. "We'll just have to take the tour tomorrow morning—breaking in houses is not my particular specialty. Tomorrow we'll have to wander through the house until we find what I've come to this island for."

Felice exhaled a long breath. She'd live to see the next day.

Zora stood in the shower and let the warm water wash over her body. Sam had driven to the hotel. They had decided that Rose Hall would be closed by the time they got there; they would go to Rose Hall the following day. She closed her eyes and let the water wash away the feelings of sadness, disbelief, fear, and anger, but nothing helped. The warm water didn't offer any relief. Even now, she couldn't believe that Milton was dead. Although she'd seen him with her own eyes, there was still a part of her that expected that any minute he would come to her and tell her that it was all a big mistake—that he didn't betray her, that he didn't steal from Sam, that the body she saw lying on the bedroom floor was not him.

Sam had made the decision to spend the night

in a hotel near Highgate. There's nothing we can do tonight about getting the Black Madonna back, he had reasoned. Besides, the long drive from Highgate to Rose Hall on darkened roads made unsafe by the recent flooding wasn't wise.

Zora had wanted to keep going. There was something in her that urged her to push on, to find the portrait that had cost Milton his life, and which had perhaps put her life, and Sam's as well, in danger. There was another part of her that wanted to turn and run—to play it safe. But she suspected that until this whole ordeal was resolved, neither she nor Sam would know peace or safety.

She thought about Sam, and felt a rush of gratitude. Before, she'd resented his attitude, the way he forced his will on her, either through blackmail, or more recently, through charm. But now, she was grateful. He'd realized that what she needed to do was to stop running, even though her mind screamed at her to do otherwise. He'd also realized that she couldn't handle talking to a strange policeman about Milton's murder. Sam had made the necessary telephone calls once they checked into the hotel. She'd heard part of the conversation.

He had notified the police without identifying himself. Although Zora understood the reason Sam was being so secretive—he could not risk any connection to Milton's murder, particularly when he was so close to finding the Black Madonna—it had struck her as cold. It hadn't seemed right, but if there was one thing she'd learned since first encountering Sam Trahan on a Brooklyn street it was that sometimes it was better to be flexible than to be right.

She didn't know how long she stood there with the water rushing over her. She could have been standing there for a few hours or a few minutes. She let her mind go blank as she forced images of Milton out of her head. There was a decisive knock on the door and then she heard Sam's voice call out.

"Zora, are you all right?"

"Don't worry about me!" she yelled back over the sound of the water.

"You've been in there a while Zora."

"Yes," she agreed, turning off the water. Suddenly, she felt a heavy fatigue wash over her body. She wanted nothing more than to crawl into the king-size bed that was in the next room, and pull the covers over her.

Stepping out of the shower stall, Zora walked quickly over the cold tile and wrapped herself in a thick, white towel. She hurriedly dried herself, and slipped into a pink terry cloth robe which was mono-grammed with the name of the hotel.

Looking at herself in the mirror, she thought that the pink robe looked ridiculous, but she didn't care. The urge to keep running, which had started after they'd found Milton, had now left her. All she wanted to do was go to sleep and wait for oblivion to overtake her.

Zora walked over to the bathroom door and opened it. Sam was sitting on the bed, looking at the bathroom door as if he'd been waiting for her to emerge. His eyes looked tired, but his concern for her was clear.

"Do you want to be alone?" he asked. "I could take a walk, or I could get another room. I thought that maybe you'd want my company, but maybe it would be better if I just left you alone."

She loved him. Once again the realization hit her. Hard. In the midst of what would have to qualify as the worst day of her life, her feelings for him had not diminished.

"I don't want to be alone, Sam."

He walked over to her. For a moment he stood silently in front of her. She thought, or perhaps it was just hope, that she saw in his eyes a reciprocation of what he must surely see in her eyes. Then, he bent over and lifted her up, as gently as a parent lifts a sleeping child. He carried her to the bed and laid her down on it. Then he lay next to her. He made no move to touch her, he simply was there, providing silent comfort, until she fell into a much needed, dreamless sleep.

Sam awoke early the next morning. As a child his grandmother had taught him that "nothing comes to sleepers, but a dream." She had also taught him that while it was important to dream, he had to be awake to put those dreams into reality. As a result, he had always been an early riser. For Sam, getting up at six in the morning was sleeping in. No matter what situation he found himself in, his eyes always opened promptly at five, just like his grandmother. He thought about her now, as he lay awake next to the sleeping Zora, and he felt the grief that overwhelmed him when she died, wash slowly over him.

"I need you here with me, Gram," he whispered. "I need your counsel."

His grandmother had always been there for him. She was the first person to whom he'd turn for advice, and even though some of her advice was difficult to take, she'd always been right, and she wasn't too afraid, or too bashful, to point out that particular truth to anyone who would listen. He'd let her down when the painting was stolen. She never saw it that way, of course. She attributed the theft of the painting to Milton's wicked ways. Still, Sam knew how deeply his grandmother felt about the painting.

"It's part of our family's history," she would say. *"It's part of our birthright. Our people have had much taken away from us, but we've always held on to each other. We've always held on to our birthright. What the Black Madonna went through—slavery, as many of our ancestors did, cannot be forgotten— must not be forgotten. We cannot forget our birthright—it's our pride, our assurance that we are survivors. In the midst of everything that has happened to us, we have survived. That is what the Black Madonna is, our past, our present, and God willing, our future."*

Sam still didn't understand her words, but he recognized the ring of truth in them. In his heart, he felt that he was close to finding the Black Madonna, but at what price? He looked over at Zora and felt his chest tighten with fear. If anything happened to her, he could not live with himself but, like his grandmother, she was not a woman who could be made to do something she didn't want to do. Zora had made it clear that they were in this together. She was not going to leave his side.

Nothing comes to sleepers, but a dream.

Sam pulled the covers back, and got out of the bed. The hotel suite had a small living room area off to the side of the bathroom. Careful not to awaken Zora, Sam walked quietly over the immaculately polished wooden floor into the living room.

It was small, with just enough room for a love seat and a television. He walked over to the television and switched it on then he sat down to see what was going on with the rest of the world, or at least, with the rest of Jamaica.

He sat for some time staring at the screen, watching images on the television while his mind was occupied with figuring out how to get into the mansion at Rose Hall, and how to find the Black Madonna. As far as Sam could best determine, looking for the Black Madonna in an old, haunted mansion was just as easy as finding the proverbial needle in a haystack.

He began drifting back to sleep when a familiar voice made his closed eyes fly open.

"They killed him, my Milton. Sam Trahan and Zora Redwood killed him. When they left me, they had vengeance in their eyes, and I know in my heart that they were the ones that did it!" A weeping Shelly Wong, who managed to look gorgeous dressed in a cream hospital gown, was sitting in a hospital bed, propped up by pillows.

The reporter, turning to the camera, spoke in hushed tones. "Milton Alexander was found dead yesterday in a location just outside Magotty. Informed sources say that Mr. Alexander was shot once through the heart, but again, that has not been confirmed. These sources also indicate that an anonymous call tipped the authorities to this heinous murder. This is the first murder in the Highgate area in over five years . . ."

The reporter then turned and said to Shelly, "What makes you so sure that Mr. Trahan and Ms. Redwood are involved in this crime?"

Shelly's tears ceased, as she looked into the camera. Her voice trembled and there were several times that it seemed Miss Wong would once again dissolve into tears but she managed to keep her tears away while she spoke. "I'm certain they're involved. Mr. Trahan had convinced himself that Milton stole his property—but I know Milton, he just wasn't capable of theft! There was no finer man than my Milton! And, as for that—that Zora Redwood . . . well, Milton had recently left her for me, and well, you know what they say . . . hell has no fury like a woman scorned! And believe me, he had scorned Zora Redwood!"

"I'm going to wring her neck!"

Sam turned to see Zora standing in the doorway, her eyes blazing.

The reporter continued, "Both Ms. Redwood and Mr. Trahan are wanted for questioning in regards to the murder, however, at this point, authorities state that neither are suspects."

"A fine time for a disclaimer!" said Zora as she sat down next to Sam on the love seat.

Sam picked up the remote on the small table next to the love seat and turned off the television. Turning to Zora, he shook his head in amazement. He had always prided himself on being a good judge of character, but twice he had been taken by surprise by people he'd underestimated. First, with Milton; and now, with Shelly Wong.

He turned his attention to Zora. "I know that this is a stupid question, in light of everything you've been through, but are you all right?"

Zora's voice was firm, "I'm not happy, but I'm all right."

Sam knew that this was the best he could hope for under the circumstances. A sudden thought flashed through his mind. "We've got to get out of here, I checked in with my credit card, under my real name . . ."

Zora finished the sentence, "So it's only a matter of time before someone on the staff puts two and two together and we end up in the police station, while whoever killed Milton is free to get the Black Madonna, and possibly to kill again."

Sam stood up, propelled by another thought, equally sudden, and more disturbing than the first. "If the police can get to us, then so can Milton's killer. I don't know why Milton was killed, but I do know that it had something to do with the Black Madonna. This wasn't some random violent act— Shelly led us to Milton. I don't know if she's involved in his murder, but she's mixed up in all of this."

Zora looked at Sam, "It doesn't make sense. Someone shot Shelly—maybe whoever shot Shelly, also shot Milton."

Sam's internal alarm bells were ringing. He was certain that Shelly had set them up, whether it was to take the fall for Milton's murder, or to be mur-

der victims themselves. Either way, Sam was not
staying around the hotel long enough to figure it
out.

"How soon can you be ready to leave?" asked
Sam.

Zora stood up. "Give me ten minutes."

18

"She's lying."

There were few things in life that Justin Trahan was certain of, but he was certain that Shelly Wong was a liar.

"Of course she's lying," his sister Celia agreed, her voice remaining calm. "But she's putting on a very good act. We're looking at an Academy Award performance here."

The small guest house in Montego Bay, which had been given a ringing endorsement by the customs agent in the airport, had one black-and-white television with two working stations. Justin didn't watch much television, but last night he'd had difficulty sleeping and he'd watched a spirited soccer match between Jamaica and Guyana. When he'd finally fallen asleep, the match had been dead even, and he'd awakened this morning curious about the outcome.

He'd turned the television on hoping to catch

234 Janette McCarthy Louard

the eight o'clock morning news. Celia, who had been sleeping in one of the two twin beds in the small room, was already awake, her face in a medical journal. The current story about the murder of Milton had caught their immediate attention.

"We've got to find Sam," said Celia, "before he runs into whoever killed Milton. My guess is that this is the person that took the Black Madonna—or at least is somehow involved in the whole mess."

Justin hoped that Sam hadn't already encountered the person who had killed Milton. It had been days since anyone had heard from Sam and Justin's alarms were sounding. *What should we do?* his mind raced over the names of the few contacts in the art world that Frank had told him were on the island and could be helpful.

Celia narrowed her eyes in thought, a sure sign to those who knew and loved her that she was methodically working on solving a difficult problem. She was silent for awhile, and Justin thought that Celia had finally met a problem she couldn't fix.

Then a determined smile curved her lips and, for a fleeting moment, she looked exactly like her departed grandmother as triumph lit her light brown eyes.

"What is it?" asked Justin.

"We'll find Shelly Wong. I know that she has to be involved in this; there's no other reason why she'd make up those lies about Sam."

"How are we going to find her, Celia? We have no idea who she is, or where she is."

Celia remained undaunted by Justin's words. "She was interviewed in a hospital. There can't be that many hospitals on the island. We'll just call around until we find the one where Ms. Wong is located."

The tour guide at Rose Hall Great House was thrilled. At last, she'd found someone who shared her passion about Rose Hall and its history. Most people who took the tour were visitors to the island that came off tourist buses eager to gawk at a little bit of history and hear scary stories. This man asked pertinent, searching questions, and more importantly, gave the tour guide a chance to show off all she knew on this subject.

She was fascinated by the story of the White Witch of Rose Hall, the late Annie Palmer.

She had told the story numerous times, how Annie came from Haiti and married a wealthy English planter, John Palmer, and buried him, as well as two other husbands. Yes, there were rumors that Annie had murdered her husbands, and countless slaves, but this had never been proven, and besides, she herself was twice-divorced and she could well understand a wife's homicidal urges.

"What is the significance of the three palm trees?" the man asked, and the tour guide's heart lifted with joy. In the five years she'd worked at this job, no one had ever asked her about the three palms. Only a true scholar on the subject of Rose Hall would know about the three palm trees.

The other folks on the tour all looked bored or tired. The tour guide had heard a few muttering about the tour taking too much time, but she wanted to prolong this experience.

"There is a legend," said the tour guide, pausing for dramatic effect, "that Annie Palmer buried her three husbands under three palm trees."

The man asked more questions as the tour progressed. He was fascinated by the architecture of the house, the history of the house, as well as the history of its inhabitants, and the guide willingly gave him the benefit of all her information.

"Is the house really haunted?" asked one of the other tourists in the small group.

The tour guide laughed at this. These people really were ridiculous to ask her about ghost stories when there was so much more to learn. She'd heard this question a thousand times, she was sure, and each time she would use a smile to cover up her disgust. She didn't know that on more than one occasion, an astute tourist would notice that her smile never reached her eyes.

"Do you believe in ghosts?" asked the tour guide.

There was nervous laughter in the group. The tour continued and then, all too soon, it was time to part.

"I very much enjoyed speaking with you," the man who shared the tour guide's interest in Rose Hall said to her.

"Believe me," she gushed, "it was an absolute joy to talk with you."

The tour guide noticed the woman who had never left the side of this wonderful man. She looked downright unhappy and, at times, nervous. The tour guide thought if she had a man as handsome and as obviously scholarly as this man was, she would have a happier look on her face. She noticed that the man never let go of the nervous woman's hand. What a lucky woman, thought the guide. For her, romance was a distant and vaguely unpleasant memory.

"I don't suppose you give private tours?" asked the man, lowering his voice as the tour group went their various ways.

"We usually arrange private tours on weekends," she said.

He looked crestfallen. "I'm leaving for the States tomorrow. I was wondering if later on today—I'd make it worth your while."

"What is it that you want to see?" the tour guide asked, now clearly intrigued.

"I'd love to explore the different rooms at my leisure—I noticed that there were some rooms that weren't shown on the tour."

"Yes," said the tour guide, "those rooms are off limits to the public, usually because they haven't been completely redone . . ."

"It would be exciting to see those rooms without the artificial enhancement of someone's vision of what the room should look like."

The tour guide's heart sang out again. There was someone else in the world that shared her vision and her absolute love for this mansion.

"The last tour ends at six. Meet me by the guard's booth at about nine tonight—by then, the cleaning people should be gone."

"The guard told me he wouldn't let me in last night," said the man.

"Don't worry about him. He'll let you in—he's in love with me, and he'll do what I say. Bring a twenty dollar bill, just in case."

The man beamed at her. "I'm truly grateful Mrs.—"

"It's Miss," the tour guide responded. "Miss Forsythe, but please call me Pearl."

It wasn't until they left that Pearl Forsythe realized that neither of the two people had given her their names.

Zora drove Miss Essie's red car as if the devil himself were following close behind. Down narrow dirt roads, that snaked around the mountains and then through an emerald green countryside where the foliage grew wild. She remembered taking drives through these remote parts of the island with her parents. These were places where tourists seldom ventured, but where the rugged beauty rivaled any of the perfect hotels with their manicured lawns and immaculately kept grounds. She had spent many happy hours on winding country roads listening to her father describe a childhood spent in a place where he knew the names of all the wildflowers that grew around him. She knew these roads intimately and she silently thanked her father for taking her along on those car rides. She knew where she was going and she knew that it would be impossible to get there using the main coastal highway. By now, the highway would be filled with police searching for them.

They'd left the hotel in a hurry, packing their suitcases, and then taking them down the back stairs. It had still been early and there were not too many people around to notice their abrupt departure. Zora had gotten in the driver's seat, and Sam had immediately argued that, after everything she'd just been through, he should be the one to drive to Rose Hall.

"I can get us where we need to go without running into the police. Can you do that?" she'd asked him. She'd been gratified to see that he had come to his senses quickly and didn't need any more convincing.

He got in the passenger seat, strapped himself in, and said, "Let's get to Rose Hall."

She hadn't replied to his directive, but she knew that he'd assumed that in fact she was driving to Rose Hall. Eventually, Zora thought, they'd get to Rose Hall, but there was someplace else she had to go first. She hadn't mentioned it to him because she didn't want an argument, but she knew that the argument was inevitable once he found out what her plans were. Taking a deep breath, she decided to get it over with.

"I'm going to talk to Miss Essie," she said.

"Zora, we need to get to Rose Hall right away!"

"We need to go to Miss Essie's house first," replied Zora. She'd expected him to be impatient and she was not overly concerned about it. "I need to talk with her to make sure that she knows that we had nothing to do with Milton's murder."

"Can't we do that later?" asked Sam. "After we get the Black Madonna, and after we clear our name with the police."

"I understand that it's important for you to get the Black Madonna back, but it's just as important to me to make sure that Miss Essie—a woman that has meant a lot to me, just as your grandmother meant to you—knows that we had nothing to do with Milton's murder. I'll be happy to drop you off at Rose Hall and you can do whatever it is you need to do to get the painting back."

Her suggestion to him that perhaps they should now part ways seemed to take the wind out of him. He stared open-mouthed at her for a moment, then he clamped his lips shut in a tight line.

"I don't want to prevent you from getting back what's yours, Sam. Please don't prevent me from doing what I need to do."

"I won't let you rush headlong into disaster," he said, in a voice that let her know that the matter was not open for discussion.

"I understand you need to go," said Zora, trying to reason with him. "You can go your way, and I'll go mine."

Sam's voice rose, "Milton is dead, and the police are looking for us. Whoever did this is more than likely looking for us. Do you think I'm going to let you out of my sight?"

Zora slammed her foot on the brakes, and they lurched forward. There was a herd of wild goats in the middle of the road.

"If you feel that way," said Zora, "then come with me to Miss Essie's house. This is something I need to do."

Why was it that whenever he was around this woman he lost control of his emotions? He never yelled at anyone—even when they deserved it, but here he was, yelling at her like a maniac, and, just as suddenly, another feeling, more urgent, came over him. His lips found hers as they sat in the car with wild goats passing all around them. He eased the gear into park with one hand, and with the other, he drew her closer to him.

"Zora," he whispered against her lips, "what am I going to do with you?"

She pulled back and stared into his eyes. She said, "You are going to kiss me, and then you are going to come with me to Miss Essie's house, and then we're going to find the Black Madonna."

Miss Essie didn't look surprised to see Zora and Sam standing at her front door.

"Come in," she said. Her face was drawn tight, and the circles under her eyes told Zora that Miss Essie had not been able to sleep last night.

A sharp wave of guilt swept over her. She remembered the last time she'd seen Miss Essie, and how curt she'd been to the old woman. Looking back, she saw that her reaction to Miss Essie had been unfair. Milton had been her nephew. How could she have expected Miss Essie to turn against him? Hadn't Miss Essie warned her that Milton wasn't right for her? The warning should have been enough, but it wasn't. She'd rushed headfirst to certain heartache, just as Milton had rushed to his own sad fate.

She put her arms around Miss Essie.

"I'm sorry," said Zora, hoping that Miss Essie would understand. She was sorry for her loss. She was sorry for Milton's wasted life. She was sorry that she'd never be able to make peace with Milton now that he was dead, and she was sorry for hurting Miss Essie the last time they met.

Miss Essie clung to Zora and, although her body shook, she did not cry. "We're all sorry. My Milton, if only he'd lived up to his promise. Life is full of 'if onlys,' eh?" Miss Essie pulled away from Zora without waiting for a response. "Mr. Trahan," she said in greeting.

Sam stepped forward and took Miss Essie's hand. "I'm sorry for your loss," he said.

"Thank you for that," said Miss Essie. Then she turned and walked back inside the house through the flower-filled living room to the back porch where they had had their last conversation together.

Zora followed Miss Essie to the porch, but Sam remained in the living room.

"I'm here if you need me," said Sam.

He couldn't know what those words meant to her. There had been no one that she could turn to when she'd needed reassurance. Her parents, as much as she loved them, had not provided the kind of comfort that Sam now offered.

She looked at him, his face now so familiar, from the stubborn chin to the kind eyes that now looked into hers. She was in no position to look toward the future with this man. There was too much yet to accomplish before that could happen, but her heart lifted in hope that maybe there was some small part of him that envisioned a place for her in his life.

"Thank you, Sam," she said, and then she went to the back porch to talk with Miss Essie.

Miss Essie sat in a wicker rocking chair, her eyes gazing at the hillside that sloped down into the green valley. It was a beautiful view, and one that

Zora was intimately familiar with, having spent countless hours in this back porch, either talking with Miss Essie, or courting with Milton.

"Sit down, child," said Miss Essie. "We need to talk."

Zora sat on a matching white wicker rocking chair across from her.

"Miss Essie," Zora knew she sounded awkward, but she wanted to get the words out as fast as she could. "I don't know if you saw the news with Shelly Wong—what she says is false, Miss Essie. Neither Sam nor I have anything to do with Milton's murder."

Miss Essie's eyes were sad, but Zora thought she saw a flicker of resignation in their depths, as if she was reconciled to the painful part of life.

"I know that, child," replied Miss Essie. "That Shelly Wong ain't nothing but a whole heap of trouble, and don't believe I didn't tell that to Milton— but God bless the dead, Milton ears was hard and so it goes . . ."

"I don't know why Shelly's saying these things," said Zora.

Miss Essie's voice rose in indignation. "She's lying on you to protect herself. Believe you me, that Shelly Wong is involved in what happened to Milton!"

"I know that Shelly Wong is a liar," said Zora, "but I can't believe that she is mixed up in Milton's murder. She loved him."

Miss Essie sucked her teeth in a clear expression of disgust.

"Love? What does Shelly know about love?" Miss Essie said. "She is mixed up with this as sure as night follow day! Take my words and mark them well, Zora—it may save you and your young man inside from troubles. Still, in the midst of all this trouble, I'm glad that you found your way to love, Zora."

"How did you know?"

"I knew before either of you did," said Miss Essie. "I saw the way he looked at you when you all were last here, and I saw the way you looked at him. It was only a matter of time before you all figured it out, and I for one am glad to see it. I fancy myself a good judge of character, and your Sam is worthy of you. Milton, God bless the dead, wasn't."

"I'm in love with Sam, Miss Essie."

"I know you are, child."

"But there's unfinished business to take care of before either of us can think about what a relationship would mean . . . we're from different worlds . . ."

Miss Essie's voice rose again. "Different worlds, eh? A whole lot of rubbish that is! Don't shut this man out of your life because others hurt you. Don't make that mistake, child."

Zora found that there were tears in her eyes. Wiping her eyes, she said, "I came here to comfort you, and here you end up comforting me."

"Darling Zora," said Miss Essie. "You have always been a comfort to me. From the time you were a little girl asking all those impossible questions about the world, you gave me comfort. I remember how you used to make up all those stories and you'd tell them to me, and I'd lose myself in your stories, Zora. For those moments, I'd forget about the world for just a little while. You were a comfort then, and believe me, child—you're a comfort now."

"Thank you, Miss Essie."

"Don't thank me, child—not yet. Like you say, you have unfinished business. You have to write the end of this story, Zora. You have to go and find that painting—the one Milton lost his life over. You have to do it for yourself."

Zora nodded her head. "I just wanted to make sure that you were all right. I wanted to make sure that you didn't believe those terrible things Shelly Wong said about me."

Miss Essie rose and walked over to where Zora sat. She placed her hands on the sides of Zora's face and said, "I've always had faith in you, Zora. It's time you start having faith in yourself. Go and finish the end of this story, Zora."

Zora felt that familiar fear in the pit of her stomach.

"What if I fail?" she whispered.

"Let me tell you something," said Miss Essie. "Everybody fails at something. You will, too—but you won't fail at this. I promise you."

There was a quick knock on the back door, and then Sam opened the door without waiting for a response.

"The police pulled up into the driveway," he said.

Miss Essie came to life.

"I'll let them in and while they comfort the grieving Auntie, Zora, you need to go on down the hill to Lena Phipp's house. You remember the house, eh? You stay there, and I'll send someone down with a car for you as soon as I get rid of the policemen. The key is in the pot out front in her yard—in the pot that carries the begonias. Don't worry, eh? Lena is in America visiting her son. Stay there until I send someone. Hurry now!"

Zora gave Miss Essie a quick kiss just as the front doorbell rang.

"Take care of my Zora," Miss Essie turned and said to Sam.

"Yes, ma'am," replied Sam.

Satisfied with his response, Miss Essie made her way back inside the house, on her way to meet the policemen. The doorbell rang again.

19

"Where the heck are the begonias?"

Zora stood in the front yard of Lena Phipp's powder blue house and looked at the flowerpots on the porch. There were at least ten flowerpots and Zora did not relish digging in the dirt to find the keys for the front door. Mindful of the police at Miss Essie's house as well as Lena's neighbors, the thought flashed through Zora's mind that perhaps it would be more expedient to break through a back window and climb in.

She watched as Sam walked up the wooden front stairs, its bright red color incongruous at best with the powder blue exterior, and headed across the porch to one of the clay flower-bearing pots. He leaned over, rolled up his sleeves, and put his hand in the dirt.

"Sam," said Zora, as she looked around her, and said a silent prayer that there were no nosy neighbors looking at them, "let's just go around the back. I'm sure we can find a way to get in the house without going on this wild key chase."

Sam stood up, flashing a triumphant smile on his face, and a set of copper-colored keys in his right hand.

"You need to have more faith in me, Zora," he said with a smile that made her heart do things that were inappropriate considering their present circumstances.

"How did you know which of those flowers were begonias?" asked Zora, wondering if there was anything that Sam Trahan could do that would surprise her. "Don't tell me that you're a closet horticulturist."

"As a matter of fact," drawled Sam, refusing to take the grin off his face, "my mother prided herself on raising well-rounded sons, so along with the usual baseball and football games came music lessons, art lessons, and horticulture."

Zora found herself grinning back at him. "So are you going to tell me that you also do ballet?"

"Now that," said Sam, as he turned and put the key in the lock in the front door, "is where she apparently drew the line."

He turned the knob once and the door swung open like a waiting friend.

"Are you coming?" Sam asked, with a quick grin. "Or do I have to send you an engraved invitation?"

Zora walked quickly across the yard, then up the stairs. Sam stood by the open door and looked at her. She could not decipher the look in his eyes, but she noted that he was no longer smiling. Once again, she felt the invisible hand pull her towards him, and she wondered what had happened to her free will. Whenever he was around, it seemed to evaporate, like rain falling on hot stones.

"Stop looking at me like that," said Sam.

They were close enough for her to reach out and touch him, and she could think of nothing else at that moment that she wanted to do but to once again lose herself in his touch.

"How am I looking at you?" asked Zora, growing bolder.

He grabbed her and pulled her inside Lena Phipp's house. Closing the door behind her, Zora found herself thrust into complete darkness, except for a thin shaft of light that came from one of the few windows that wasn't completely obscured by the closed curtains.

She felt his lips on hers and her remaining shred of resolve disappeared. This was madness. It had to be insanity, tropical fever, temporary delusion, something completely out of her control that made her act this way. She felt an urgency in his caresses. There was passion, but there was something else, a feeling that events were swirling around them, out of their control, that had pushed them together, but could also tear them apart.

Milton. The name seared itself in her mind, violently. Milton. Milton had been murdered and whoever had murdered him might be after them next. Zora pulled away from Sam.

"No," she said, shaking her head. "No, we can't do this. Not now. Not here."

She could hear as Sam's breath came in short, hard gasps.

"I'm sorry," he said, his voice hoarse. "I feel like I'm taking advantage of you. Believe me, this usually isn't how I operate."

She touched him then, moving her hand across his cheek.

"You didn't take advantage of me," she said quietly. "Everything that happened here, I wanted, and more—to tell the truth. But we need to get the Black Madonna and we need to find out what happened to Milton, before this can continue."

He pulled her to him, and held her.

"I can't lose you, Zora," he said simply. "I can't lose you."

Zora tilted her head to look at the man whom she knew she would love forever. She could make out his features in the darkness. Her fingers traced the frown on his lips.

"You're not going to lose me, Sam Trahan," said Zora. "Cross my heart, and hope to die."

She immediately regretted her choice of words.

"Let's hope that day doesn't come for a long, long time," Sam replied.

Justin Trahan was often amazed by other people's reaction to his sister. From his earliest memories folks went out of their way to be accommodating to her. She had been a beautiful child, with an even more beautiful spirit, and therefore, in Justin's eyes, it was not surprising that people would be drawn to her, but her beauty, even combined as it was with brains, compassion, and a healthy dose of common sense, did not account for the way most people ended up doing exactly what it was that Celia wanted them to do. Another person would have abused this gift, or at the very least, would have taken it for granted, but Celia did neither. She would react with gratitude, which Justin knew was sincere.

There weren't many hospitals on the island, and it hadn't been difficult for them to locate Shelly Wong. St. Ann's Bay was a few hours' drive, and after a taxi ride through some of the most lush, beautiful countryside Justin had ever seen, they found themselves standing in front of St. Ann's Bay Hospital. The taxi driver, who by this time was smitten with Celia, promised them that he would wait for their return. He had even suggested that perhaps the young lady was hungry and he could find something suitable for her to eat, completely ignoring Justin's stomach which was rumbling loud enough for the taxi driver to hear. Celia had declined the offer of food politely, and the sight of her open, easy smile had been enough to set the taxi driver blushing and stammering.

Justin had finally taken pity on the poor man and ushered Celia inside the hospital lobby where they encountered a taciturn, and apparently harassed, employee at the patient information desk. Justin had explained to the woman, who was apparently settling into an unpleasant middle age, judging from her sour expression, that they were looking for Shelly Wong.

"Are you family?" she had asked, looking directly into Justin's eyes, as if daring him to lie.

"No," replied Justin.

"Only family is allowed to see Miss Wong," said the nurse, her eyes narrowed as if she were annoyed that he was wasting her precious time.

Justin tried to explain that they had come all the way from America, and that they needed information from Miss Wong. The nurse replied that she didn't care if he had come from Jupiter by way of Mars, the doctors' orders were strict that only family was allowed to see Miss Wong.

He felt his temper rise, but just as he opened his mouth to tell the nurse exactly what he thought of her and her poor manners, Celia gently pushed him aside and stood smiling in front of the nurse.

"Please excuse my brother's tone," said Celia, keeping her voice soft and even. "We've just come to the island yesterday, and so far, the trip hasn't been an easy one."

The nurse looked at Celia warily, as if she couldn't quite figure her out. Justin had expected a smart comment to fly out of the nurse's mouth, as he had recently experienced; instead, the nurse gave a noncommittal grunt. From where Justin stood, that was progress.

Celia explained that she was a medical resident, and that she understood that the patient's progress was paramount. She also explained that under any other circumstances she would not disturb this inviolate rule that the patient's needs and the hospital's rules always come first, but as her brother and another innocent young lady's life might be in danger, it was vital that she speak with Miss Wong.

Justin held his breath as he waited for an explosion which did not come. Instead, the nurse told her what room Shelly was in.

"You should have tol' me is a matter of family business. Nothing more important than that. I have a brother too an' I would do anything for him. Shelly is in Room 408, but I must warn you, she is a difficult woman."

"Well," said Celia, "she's been through a lot."

The nurse sucked her teeth. "She ain' been through that much. She been talking to reporters all day."

"I thought you said only family could see her," said Justin, feeling his temper rise in spite of himself.

"Family, and those who know how to grease a lady's palms," she replied, without missing a beat. "The elevator is down at the end of this hallway, take it to the fourth floor."

Celia thanked the nurse, and pulled Justin away before he could make any further comments. They walked quickly down the hallway as if they were both afraid that the nurse would change her mind and stop them before they had a chance to find Shelly Wong.

It was a long shot that they would get anything from Shelly Wong, but Justin suspected that Shelly was the best way they had to finding and helping Sam. He thought about his grandmother and his lips curved in a rueful smile. All her life she'd tried to get him to stop fighting with his brother. Blood matters, she would say so many times that he'd lost count, but resentment, and some jealousy had stopped any closeness that had a chance of growing between Justin and Sam. Sam's stubborn insistence on telling everyone around him, including Justin, how to run their lives certainly did not help strengthen any familial bond. Still, no matter what the differences were between them, Justin knew that he would never stand by and let anything happen to his brother. Perhaps after all these years, his grandmother's words about the importance of family were finally ringing true.

The elevator door opened and Justin stepped aside to let his sister enter first. He hesitated for a moment before going inside. His internal alarm bells were ringing loudly. Justin always had a knack for sensing impending danger. His grandmother had had the same gift. It was probably the only thing they'd had in common. He stepped inside the elevator, shrugging off the disturbing thoughts. He had to focus on finding Sam, and standing around worrying was not his style. He wondered what kind of person this Shelly Wong was, and whether she would be able to help them locate Sam.

The directions to Shelly's room turned out not to be as direct as the nurse had originally indicated. After walking down a series of hallways, and making several wrong turns, Justin finally found himself standing in front of Room 408. He knocked on the door, and almost immediately he heard a husky voice call out, "Come in, what took you so long?"

He opened the door to the small hospital room and entered, with Celia following behind him. Sunlight streamed through an open window, and framed what had to be, in Justin's opinion, one of the most beautiful women he'd ever laid eyes on. The television had not done her justice. She was standing by the bed, dressed completely in white, with one hand on her hip, and the other in a sling. Her brown hair was pulled back from her face and large, dark eyes and a full mouth which was now set in a pout, jumped out at him.

"Who the hell are you?" asked this vision.

Celia spoke up, "Miss Wong, my name is Celia Trahan, and this is my brother Justin. We're here to ask you some questions about our brother, Sam. We know that this is a terrible time for you, but we're desperately worried about Sam, Miss Wong and well—we really don't have anywhere else to turn."

Justin had expected an explosion, a demand to get out of her room, hysterics, anything but the brilliant smile that curved Miss Wong's lips. She looked positively inviting.

"I should have seen the resemblance," said Shelly Wong, looking directly at Justin.

Justin knew that this was an act. He looked nothing like his brother, or the rest of his family. Miss Wong was up to no good, and Justin was convinced now more than ever, that the key to finding his brother lay right here with Shelly Wong. He decided to play along.

"Yeah, we've been told that we could pass for twins," said Justin.

"You certainly both have charm," replied Miss Wong, eyeing him like a bee closing in on an open jar of honey.

"Miss Wong," asked Celia, dragging her attention back to more immediate matters, "have you seen our brother?"

Shelly Wong sighed and sat down heavily on the bed. "Yes, I've seen him, and his girlfriend."

"His girlfriend," asked Celia. "Sam doesn't have a girlfriend."

"Oh yes, he does," replied Shelly, her dark eyes now glittering with what looked to Justin like spite, "that little woman that Milton threw away. Zora Redwood."

"Milton's girlfriend?" Now Justin spoke. "Sam's mixed up with Milton's girlfriend?"

Shelly's lips curved into a smile, which didn't quite reach her eyes. "It seems this Zora Redwood works fast. She charmed Milton, until he got wise and realized that she was only out to use him, and now apparently, she's moved on to your brother."

"When did you see them?" asked Celia.

"Yesterday, before they killed Milton."

"Miss Wong, I can't speak for Zora Redwood, but I know my brother. I know he's capable of many things, but I also know that he's not capable of murder."

"I know that he killed my Milton," said Shelly, her eyes filling up with tears.

Celia was unmoved. "What proof do you have that our brother killed Milton Alexander?"

Shelly Wong wiped her eyes with the back of a trembling hand. Taking a deep breath, she said, "I wasn't there, of course, but I know what I saw in Sam Trahan's eyes—I saw murder."

Justin stifled a quick retort, and instead asked, "Where did you see Sam?"

"At my hotel," said Shelly. "He was there with his little friend. He was there when I was shot."

"Are you saying that Sam had something to do with the person that shot you?" asked Celia, her rising voice clearly showing the anger that greeted Shelly Wong's words.

"Well," she purred, "I can't swear on it, but since meeting Sam Trahan, I've been shot at, and my fiancé has been murdered. There's a connection between all these events, and I won't rest until I make sure that your brother and his girlfriend are punished for what I know that he did."

"Let's get out of here," said Celia. "This whole thing is a ridiculous waste of time. Sam had nothing to do with anyone getting shot or killed."

"Where is Sam now?" Justin asked Shelly Wong. "Do you know where he is?"

"I have no idea, but believe me, if I knew where that murderer was, I would have informed the police by now!"

Justin's eyes rested on a closed suitcase by the foot of Shelly's bed.

"Are you going somewhere, Miss Wong?"

"As a matter of fact, I am," replied Miss Wong. "The doctors are against it, of course, but I'm leaving the hospital. I don't feel safe here—a friend is coming by to drive me somewhere where even your resourceful brother won't find me. I don't believe I'm safe here."

"Come on," said Justin to his sister, "let's go." It was clear that they weren't going to get any more information out of Shelly Wong. "Good-bye, Miss Wong," said Justin. "Good luck to you."

As they left the room, Shelly Wong called out to Justin, "Mr. Trahan, it's a pity we didn't meet under different circumstances."

Justin turned and looked at Shelly Wong before

walking out of the hospital door. He saw the perfectly made-up, perfectly shaped face of a hard woman. He wondered how he had found her beautiful just a few short moments ago.

"I wish I could say the same, Miss Wong."

He followed Celia out of the room, and closed the door behind him. Even the antiseptic hallway in which they stood seemed like a breath of fresh air compared to Shelly Wong's room. Justin sensed that he had just been in the presence of someone either truly evil or truly sick.

"Talk about your merry widow," said Celia, shaking her head. "Her dearly departed fiancé is hardly gone from the scene before she turned her bright lights on you."

"I'm still convinced that Shelly is mixed up with all of this, and we need her to find Sam."

"I don't know how we're going to do that," replied Celia.

"Well, we have no other choice," said Justin. "Sam needs our help, and unfortunately for him, and for us, Shelly Wong is the best shot we have at finding Sam before trouble does."

A knock on the front door awakened Zora from a sound sleep. She'd fallen asleep in the arms of Sam Trahan, as they both lay on Lena Phipp's narrow, and decidedly ancient, couch. Her body felt stiff, and she blinked her eyes in the unaccustomed darkness that covered the room. Sam switched on a lamp on an adjacent table, and Miss Phipp's questionable decorating tastes—which included a healthy dose of plastic lawn furniture, framed posters of Bob

Marley and Billy Dee Williams (before he permed his hair), and psychedelic-colored chairs that had been in style back in the sixties—came into view.

Sam looked down at Zora and put his index finger on his lip. "Shh," he murmured. "We don't know who this is."

There was another knock on the door, louder this time. Then a voice called out. "Miss Zora, is me, Ambrose Lethe! I work for Miss Essie! She sen' me with the car for you to take!"

Zora sat up.

"It's all right," she said, "I know him. He's worked for Miss Essie for years."

She walked over and opened the front door to find a smiling Ambrose on the porch. It had been years since she'd last seen him. An indefatigable ladies' man back when Zora was growing up, Zora'd heard that Ambrose's wife had finally gotten tired of his womanizing and had moved away to another part of the island where, apparently, she'd found true love. Ambrose, for his part, had turned his sights on the Church where he'd become born-again.

Zora gave him a quick kiss on his cheek. "Ambrose, its good to see you."

He was one of the few people who'd complimented her as she grew up. He'd always told her that she'd grow into a beauty, and although she never believed him—after all, Ambrose was an indefatigable flatterer—she was grateful then, as she was even now.

"Not as good as it is to see you, Miss Zora," replied Ambrose. "You're as beautiful as ever!"

Old habits, thought Zora with a smile, die hard.

"Come in," she said, stepping aside to allow him to enter.

Ambrose entered the room and Zora closed the door behind him. He stopped when he saw Sam.

"You must be Miss Zora's manfriend," he said, extending his hand.

"Yes," said Sam, without any hesitation, grasping Ambrose's hand and shaking it heartily.

"Well, it's good to meet you!" said Ambrose. Turning to Zora, he said, "Not to speak ill of the dead, this one is a definite improvement, Miss Zora. But don't tell Miss Essie I told you so."

Zora cleared her throat. She was embarrassed at what this must look like. Her fiancé was dead and here she was in someone else's house with a man who was not her fiancé, hiding from the law. Her only consolation was that her parents were far away from the island and they had no clue about the actions of their only child.

"Is the car parked outside?" asked Zora.

"It is," said Ambrose. "It's my car, not as fancy as Miss Essie's."

Zora protested, "We can't take your car, Ambrose!"

"Why not?" he said. "It might not be as spiffy as Miss Essie's, and it's old as—well, heck, but it rides like a dream!"

"That's not what I meant," said Zora, feeling embarassed. "I'm sure your car is perfect, but it isn't right to take your car. What will you use?"

"Why Miss Essie's red sports car, of course," replied Ambrose. "I can't wait to take it for a spin. Miss Essie feels that if you're driving her car you all might be—well, more conspicuous."

"She's got a point," said Sam. Turning to Ambrose, he said, "Thank you for your kindness, sir. We appreciate it."

Ambrose grinned. "It's nothing. I watched little Zora here grow up into a wonderful young woman and if there's anything I can do to help her, then I'll do it."

Zora gave Ambrose a quick hug. "Thank you."

He smiled at her and said, "You mustn't hold me too close, now—your manfriend will get a little jealous."

He handed her a set of keys and a blue lunch pail with the yellow, green, and black Jamaican flag painted on it. "From Miss Essie," said Ambrose.

After placing a kiss on Zora's cheek and a quick good-bye, Ambrose left.

Zora handed the keys to Sam, then she opened the pail. Inside were corned beef sandwiches made with still-warm, harddough bread, a childhood favorite of Zora's. Miss Essie had also packed some meat patties, also warm, some cocoa bread, some sweet pastry, and two bottles of fruit juice.

"God bless that woman," said Sam, eyeing the contents of the lunch pail. "I hadn't realized just how hungry I am."

In the midst of her own personal tragedy, Miss Essie had time to think about others. Zora's eyes welled up with tears.

She felt Sam's arms encircle her waist and his head rested on her hair. "Come on, princess," he said, "let's eat some of this good food."

Zora stared at Sam for a moment and found it difficult to imagine that a few short days ago, he was just a name and a picture on the society pages of the newspaper. Today, he was someone she couldn't imagine living without. She didn't know if her future included Sam Trahan, but she was glad that he was still in her present. He had a way of pulling her out of herself, of refusing to allow her to dwell too much in self-pity. He was, she thought as she pulled out a corned beef sandwich, just what the doctor ordered.

20

"You're a beautiful woman, Felice," said Terrence Phillips, "but a stupid one."

Felice turned to face him. They were sitting in a parked car, just down the road from the Rose Hall Great House.

"And stupid women," Terrence continued, "take foolish risks."

"What are you going to do with me?" asked Felice, all the while scanning her surroundings for the possibility of help. The country road on which they were parked was devoid of cars, or any passersby. They were, as Felice thought unhappily, in the middle of nowhere. Even if someone happened to come anywhere near the parked car, Felice knew that her companion would not hesitate to use the loaded gun that lay in his lap, both on the passerby and on herself.

"I don't know," said Terrence. "But I do know that if you do anything stupid, I will be forced to, well, hurt you. It's not something I particularly relish, Felice."

The look in his eyes told her otherwise. Felice knew with a certainty that made her heart race, that he would kill her if she did not get away from him.

"I won't do anything stupid," she replied, staring into his cold eyes.

"That's good, my dear," he said. "You'll live longer that way."

Ambrose's car had seen better days. An old, beat-up four-door Chevy Impala whose color was somewhere between black, gray and dark blue, Sam thanked the Almighty that although the engine sounded as if it would give up the ghost at any moment and the car would intermittently start shaking for no apparent reason that Sam could tell, it was still running. After driving the car for a nerve-wracking hour, Sam could only attribute Ambrose's declaration that it "ran like a dream" to a car owner's blind affection.

"I'm not sure that this car is going to make it," he said. "How much longer do we have until we get to Rose Hall?"

"We should be there soon," replied Zora. "Another hour or so."

The smell of the sea, which Sam had now become accustomed to, provided him with inexplicable comfort. In another life, thought Sam as the car began to shake again, he must have been a sailor. Through the open car windows he could hear the crickets start their loud melody and the wind felt good on his face. Soon the world around him would be covered with darkness. Night fell quickly, and without warning, on the island.

"It's not too late for you to back out of this," said Sam. "I can handle things on my own. It could get very dangerous."

"Still trying to get rid of me?" said Zora. Her voice betrayed nothing of the tension Sam knew that she had to be feeling.

"I'm not trying to get rid of you," replied Sam, "I'm trying to protect you."

"I can take care of myself," was the quick retort.

He glanced over at the stubborn profile that he had become familiar with. The set of the jaw, the clenched mouth, the downright arrogant tilt of the head that was Zora. He took a deep breath. He did not want to offend her; hell, he only wanted to take care of her. He wanted to make sure that she didn't risk that beautiful neck of hers. The Black Madonna was his responsibility. Still, he knew that the woman that he loved would not back down, and he reluctantly admitted to himself that this was part of her inestimable charm.

Sam chose to turn to another topic.

"Tell me about the legend of Annie Palmer and Rose Hall," he said. Zora had alluded to the island folklore that the Rose Hall mansion was haunted.

"Annie Palmer, the original mistress of Rose Hall came to Jamaica from Haiti back in the 1800s. She married a painter, John Palmer and, according to the legend, she killed him and two other husbands."

"Lovely," Sam commented.

"She was a cruel woman," Zora continued. "There

are numerous stories of tortured slaves and black magic. She was murdered by her slave lover. Annie has been haunting the place ever since and there are folks who claim that they see her riding horse-back at night. The mansion, and you'll see what I mean, is downright spooky. As a child, my heart used to pound with fear whenever we passed it—it's just off the highway, for all to see."

"Why on earth would Milton hide the Black Madonna there?" asked Sam, wondering what kind of sick mind would hide a valuable painting in an old haunted mansion. It was clear to him that Milton either was not thinking with all of his God-given faculties or he had a strange sense of humor.

"Milton loved the story of Annie Palmer," said Zora. "He was fascinated by it—looking back, I think her cruelty appealed to him."

Sam couldn't stop himself from asking the next question.

"What did you see in Milton? True, he was good-looking, but he was completely different from you. I can't see you having the least bit of interest in black magic or haunted mansions or murder."

Zora was quiet for a moment, then she said, "There was another side to Milton. A funny side. He had an absolutely wonderful sense of humor and, believe it or not, he was capable of great kind-ness. When we were young, other children used to tease me, and Milton was always there, my biggest defender. He looked at me and saw someone beau-tiful, even though most of the rest of the world dis-missed me."

"They were either blind or crazy," replied Sam. "Where were you when I was going through teenage angst?" asked Zora. "Anyway, I knew there were other sides to Milton—the selfish side and, if I were honest with myself back then, I knew that Milton could not be trusted. I'd seen him lie effortlessly to others—oh, always about little, inconsequential things, but I should have wondered about the ease with which he spun completely false tales to get him out of trouble. I should also have wondered about the way he treated people, as if they were disposable. I should have wondered about his long periods of absence—absences without explanation or warning. I should have wondered."

She was blaming herself for Milton's actions and Sam would not allow that. Milton had used her, just as he had used others, including Sam. Zora was not the cause for Milton's betrayals, nor could she have saved him from his own vices and demons.

"I thought that I could change him," said Zora, her voice filled with sadness. "I thought that I could make him be the wonderful person that I wanted him to be."

"You're not the first person to make that mistake," said Sam. "Milton was responsible for his actions. There was nothing you could have done either to stop him or save him. He was a man bound to self-destruct—I'm just grateful that he didn't take you with him."

"Sam," said Zora, her voice suddenly urgent, "tell me that you're a different man from Milton. Please tell me that, Sam."

Sam slowed the car down. Turning to look into Zora's eyes, he said, "I promise you Zora, I am not Milton. First, I would never throw away what Milton threw away. I would never walk away from you, Zora. I couldn't walk away from you if I tried. Second, I promise you Zora that I will always be faithful to you. There is no other woman for me, Zora. Third, I love you, Zora Redwood and I'm sorry to say that Milton in all likelihood didn't know the meaning of love. He didn't treat you the way that you deserved. I am not Milton, Zora. I promise you that."

She smiled then—a slow, steady smile that traveled from full lips all the way to her large, dark eyes, which sparkled at him. What was it about this woman? Certainly, he'd seen better-looking women—women versed in the art of seducing men—who had turned his head, but there was absolutely no other woman who had captured his heart the way Zora Redwood had apparently so effortlessly done.

"Do you love me, Sam?" Her words were spoken carefully, deliberately. "Are you sure, Sam?"

"I've never been more sure of anything in my entire life," said Sam.

She didn't say anything in reply to his declaration, but the tears in her eyes told Sam everything he needed to know.

21

Located just off the main north coast highway, even when seen from a distance, Rose Hall was an imposing structure. The white mansion on the hill brought back old childhood fears that Zora thought were long laid to rest. Every child on the island had grown up with the stories of the dreaded witch of Rose Hall, Annie Palmer. For Zora, the house was a tangible reminder of ghost stories and nightmares in the dark. She remembered returning home from Montego Bay with her parents late at night. At first sight of the white house, Zora would close her eyes and pretend to sleep. She never wanted her parents to know of her fear of Annie Palmer. It would only confirm their general opinion that she was weak. The only person she'd confided in had been Milton, who had laughed at her.

"Do you believe that ghosts can hurt you, Zora? Believe me, don't be afraid of the dead, it's the living that you should worry about."

His words came back to her just as plainly as if he'd spoken them. She remembered his fascination with Rose Hall and Annie Palmer. He'd visited the mansion many times and he'd bought several books on the subject. Zora had thought that this fascination with such a cruel character had bordered on the perverse. But Milton had had many strange ways and, for Zora, this was just one more thing about him that she didn't understand.

Zora watched as Sam turned the car north and began the ascent up the road which led to the home of Annie Palmer. The road was much narrower than the highway. It was wide enough for one car, but Zora knew that cars traveled on the road in both directions. Sam eased his foot slightly off the gas pedal and the car proceeded at a slower pace up the narrow dirt road.

Night had fallen and the dark road was illuminated only by the headlights of the car. The overwhelming darkness and the sudden curves made the drive up the hill a difficult one.

Sam turned and said, "I don't suppose that you'll let me do this alone?"

Zora shook her head. "No. We're in this together."

Sam sighed, "I thought that you might say that."

He drove around another sharp curve and began an even steeper climb until they reached the wrought iron gate entrance to the mansion. Zora had never been here, but there was a sudden feeling of familiarity, a sense that she had been here before, perhaps in her dreams. A small path led from the gate to the front steps of the mansion.

The path was illuminated with gas lanterns, which gave the house an eerie glow.

Sam parked the car in the clearing by the gate. "We're here. It's strange," Sam said, staring at the house. "I could have sworn I saw a light in the upstairs window, but now it's completely dark."

"I don't mind telling you that the hairs on the back of my neck are beginning to rise. This place gives new meaning to the word creepy," said Zora.

"It's not too late to back out now," said Sam.

"Not on your life," said Zora. "You can't get rid of me that easily. Besides, Annie Palmer has been dead for over two hundred years. There's nothing in that house that can hurt us now."

"Slow down!" said Celia. "She'll figure out that we're following her."

Justin was driving at speeds upwards of seventy miles per hour. The small rental car shook uncontrollably, and the engine was making noises that were not at all reassuring.

To make matters worse, they were driving on the wrong side of the road.

"If I drive any slower, I'll lose her," replied Justin. "She's driving like a bat out of hell!"

They'd been following Shelly Wong from the time she'd left the hospital. A black car with a very good looking man had picked Shelly up from the hospital. From there, they'd gone to the bank in St. Ann's Bay. After that, they went to an apartment building in Runaway Bay where, several hours later, Shelly had emerged alone. Getting into the same black car that had picked her up, Shelly began her race down the north coast highway. There was really no other word to describe Shelly's driving. It was amazing that this woman had been shot recently, thought Celia. She drove the car as if she were a race car driver on his final lap.

"Besides," said Justin, "in case you haven't noticed, all the cars around us, including Shelly's, are speeding."

He had a very good point, thought Celia. Still, she didn't want to take the chance of being discovered—Shelly was the best chance they had to find Sam.

"Well, just be careful," said Celia. "Try not to get us killed in the process."

"Little sister," said Justin, as the speedometer shot past eighty and the engine began screaming in earnest, "you worry too much!"

Sam opened the front door of Rose Hall Mansion easily. He'd expected that he'd have to do something dramatic like jimmy a window, enter through the cellar, or at least pick a lock, which he actually did quite well. Instead, the door opened as soon as he turned the doorknob. It was almost too easy.

"Here," said Zora, thrusting a small flashlight into his hand, "you'll need this to find the light switch."

Sam turned to look at her with open admiration. "Where on earth did you get this?"

"I bought this back at the store in Highgate," replied Zora. "I always come prepared."

Sam entered the foyer and turned on the flashlight. Quickly scanning the walls, he found what he was looking for and flipped on the light switch. Someone had gone to great pains to restore the mansion to its earlier glory. The mahogany floors gleamed as if they were just polished. A chandelier hung majestically from a wooden ceiling. The lights from the chandelier shot diamond patterns on the pale silk wallpaper. It was beautiful. For a moment, Sam felt as if he had stepped back in time. There were two antique mahogany chairs with floral patterned seats and a brass lamp with a lampshade made of the same pale silk as the wallpaper.

Sam stood transfixed until he heard Zora's words, "Let's go find our needle in the haystack."

"Where do we start?"

There were two closed wooden doors on either side of the foyer, and a curved staircase which led to the second story.

Zora turned to the door at her right and opened it. "Let's start here."

Zora stepped inside the room and immediately fell silent. She stood there as if rooted to the spot.

"What's the matter, Zora?" Sam asked, as he entered the room. "Have you seen a ghost?"

The voice that answered Sam's question was not Zora's voice, but it was a voice that was nonetheless very familiar to him.

"Not a ghost, Mr. Trahan. Unfortunately for both of you, we're all too real."

The man turned the light on and Sam found himself staring at Terrence Phillips, the private detective who had failed to find Milton. He looked different now—his head was shaved bald, and his eyes, which Sam remembered as being a non-descript brown, were a pale silver. He was dressed in black jeans, with a crisp, white cotton shirt. It's open collar gave Terrence the air of a casual vacationer, an appearance which was at odds with the gun that he held in his hand.

"What is this all about?" asked Sam, pulling Zora next to him. He surveyed the room and saw that there were three people sitting on a sofa in the corner of the room. Their hands were tied in front of them with some sort of rope. Their mouths were taped shut. He recognized Felice, but the other two people sitting next to her were strangers to him.

"You're a smart man, Sam. Surely you can figure this all out."

Sam shook his head. "I hired you to find the Black Madonna, and to find Milton. You accomplished neither, and now I see you here in Jamaica with a gun in your hand. Perhaps you should explain to me just what the hell is going on here."

"Why don't you and the lovely Miss Redwood have a seat."

Sam's grip on Zora's arm tightened. "No, thank you, Terrence—if you don't mind, we'll stay right where we are."

"Mr. Trahan, do I have to remind you that the one with the gun is the one who gives the orders. If I tell you to sit, then you'll do it, and quickly."

"No," said Sam, quietly. "I won't. If you're going to shoot me, go ahead and do it. I don't take orders from any man."

"Sam, please, for heaven's sake, if this lunatic says sit down, then that's what we need to do," said Zora.

Sam didn't respond but instead stared directly into Terrence Phillip's eyes. He thought he saw a glimmer of admiration there, but he was sure he had just imagined it.

"If you want to stand, suit yourself. But believe me, Sam, this whole process will go a lot smoother if you just do what I say."

"Sam, who is this man?" asked Zora. "How does he know me?"

"Why don't you tell her, Sam," said Terrence Phillips.

"I don't know who you are," said Sam. "It's apparent that the man I thought you were never existed."

Terrence Phillips laughed. "True enough, Sam Trahan. True enough. Miss Redwood, my name, at least for your purposes, is Terrence Phillips. It's not the name my mother gave me, but that secret has gone with her to her grave, I'm afraid. I run a well known, and equally well respected private investigation service. I am, also, Miss Redwood, and this is the part that you might find interesting, or at least relevant to your particular situation, an art historian and an art thief. A very successful art thief. I steal expensive paintings, and I sell them to people who don't care where the paintings came from, wealthy people, Miss Redwood."

"You stole the Black Madonna?" asked Sam, his voice quiet and deadly.

"Well, not exactly—I had some help," replied Terrence Phillips. "The charming Felice approached some friends of mine with a proposition which for me was irresistible—the Black Madonna. She said that she could get it for us. The Black Madonna

has always been, for me, something of an elusive
prize—it's well known that the Trahan family has
refused a fortune just to hold on to the painting,
and it's equally well known that the painting carries with it a certain cache. Do you know about the
legend of the Black Madonna, Miss Redwood?
Perhaps Sam neglected to tell you about the diamonds."

"What diamonds?" asked Zora.

"The ones that were stolen from my great-great-
grandfather before he was murdered?" asked Sam.
"What does that have to do with the painting?"

"The story is that the map to the diamonds, which
must be worth quite a fortune today, is hidden somewhere in the portrait."

"That's nonsense!" Sam's voice rose in anger.
"My family has had that painting for generations.
If there was a map to those diamonds, someone
would have found it by now."

"Perhaps," said Terrence, "but it is intriguing,
nonetheless. I've studied the work of your illustri-
ous ancestor. The stories about him are legendary.
He was as resourceful as he was talented. The key
to those diamonds lies in the painting of the Black
Madonna, and I aim to find out one way or another. At the very least, I will have a painting
that is worth a great deal of money. At best, I
will have a bag of diamonds that will enable me
to become the independently wealthy man I deserve to be."

Sam shook his head. The man was mad. He was
crazy. Diamonds? What diamonds? "The diamonds
have never been found. In all likelihood, the murderer took the diamonds."

"Enough talk, Sam Trahan. It's time to find the Black Madonna. It seems that even in death Milton double crossed me. The room where he indicated we would find the painting is empty."

"I'm not helping you, Terrence. If you want to find the damned painting, you can bloody well do it yourself," said Sam.

"Ah," said Terrence, "that's where you're wrong, Sam. You see, both you and Miss Redwood are going to help me. If you don't, I start shooting people."

"Go ahead and shoot me," said Sam. "You're going to do it anyway."

"Perhaps you're right about that," replied Terrence. "But right now, it won't be you that I'll shoot. I'll start with Felice over here—even though she's a large part of the reason why you're in this predicament, I'm sure you don't want her blood on your hands. Then, I'll continue with the museum guide, whose only crime was that she trusted the wrong people. You know a little bit about that, Sam. Next, I'll shoot the guard, who has already told me that he is responsible for six young mouths to feed, with another on the way. Isn't that right, Winston?"

The guard, whose mouth was covered with tape and whose eyes were wide with fear, nodded his head vigorously.

"Finally, I'll shoot Miss Redwood, who—judging from the way you are currently clinging to her arm—has become quite dear to you."

"Damn you, Terrence," Sam said quietly.

"True enough," he said. "Are you going to start listening to me, or do I have to start shooting?"

"What guarantees do we have that even when we help you, you won't kill us?" asked Zora.

"There are no guarantees here, Zora," replied Terrence. "The only guarantee that I can give you is if you don't do what I say, then the killing will begin. I've already killed someone that you used to be very close to, don't think that it will be that hard for me to kill again."

"What do you want us to do?" asked Zora.

"I want you to find the Black Madonna. You have two hours. By my watch it's 9:05 p.m. At 11:05, I start shooting—and Zora, I'll insist that both you and Sam watch. Do I make myself clear?"

"Two hours?!" Sam exclaimed. "How do you expect us to find the painting in just two hours?!"

"That, as they say, is your problem. I'll be watching you both," said Terrence. "And if anyone does anything foolish, I start shooting. No questions asked."

Zora had never been in a house with so many rooms. By her count, they'd already looked in seventeen rooms, including the cellar, and there was no sign of the Black Madonna. They looked in closets, behind tapestries, under beds, knocked on walls to see if any hollow spaces contained the portrait, but still they could not find it.

"We need more than two hours to find the painting," Zora said, turning to the pale-eyed man who followed their every move. Sam continued rolling aside a heavy Oriental rug, focused on the task at hand.

"My watch indicates that you have less than fifteen minutes to find the Black Madonna before bodies start hitting the floor. I wouldn't waste time trying to bargain for more time with me, I would be working harder to find the portrait."

"Help me with this rug, Zora," said Sam, stopping momentarily. "It's heavier than it looks."

Zora walked to where Sam stood and leaned over, placing her hands on the partially rolled carpet.

"Sam what do expect to find under the rug?" asked Zora. Her nerves were frayed, and the knowledge that there was a madman with a gun pointing in their direction did not help.

"Sometimes these old homes have floors that have hidden compartments. Usually, they contained jewels or other valuables. We've looked just about everywhere else—it's worth a shot."

Zora marveled at his composure, and his focus. He remained calm, unruffled and determined, while she quietly fell apart. She wasn't afraid for her own safety, although she knew that if she had any sense left at all, she should realize that this could be her very last night on this earth. Her fear was that she would never see this man again, a man who just a few short days ago was just a name and a face on the society pages, but who now meant more to her than any man before him. She was quite certain that even if a miracle happened and she survived this night, there would never be another man after him.

"Help me roll the carpet, Zora," Sam said softly. He was watching her intently now.

She saw the quiet strength in those eyes and, unless she imagined it, she saw mirrored the love she felt. Taking a deep breath she moved closer to Sam and began to roll the carpet.

"Ten minutes!" Terrence called out. "Ten minutes left!"

Sam moved his mouth close to her ear. Brushing a soft kiss on her forehead, he said, "Don't lose faith. We're going to get out of this alive. Just focus. Focus on finding the portrait."

But how can we do the impossible? she wanted to ask. *We need days, not minutes.*

She nodded her head, drawing strength from him. She would not give in to fear. She'd lived her whole life ruled by fear—fear of her parents' disapproval, fear that others would not like her, fear that she would fail in school, fear that her looks would never be as good as her mother's. What had fear done for her except allow her to live a life which gave her contentment but left her lonely? *Poor Zora*, Milton had said, *always on the outside looking in.*

"*Always on the outside, looking in.*" Zora repeated the words out loud. *Always on the outside, looking in.* Milton's words came back to her, along with the realization of where he'd hidden the Black Madonna. She turned to face Sam.

Keeping her voice low, Zora said, "I know where the Black Madonna is, or, at least I think I have a pretty good idea."

"Well," said Sam, "I hope you're right. We've got seven minutes before this maniac decides to make good on his threat."

"What are you two whispering about?" Terrence asked sharply.

Zora looked at Sam. Should she let Terrence Phillips know that she had finally realized where Milton had hidden the Black Madonna? Should she use this knowledge as a bargaining tool in exchange for their freedom? What about his threat to start shooting the three people downstairs?

"Tell him," Sam said quietly. "Tell him. We'll get through this, but we won't have a chance if we don't deliver the painting to him."

"I've got a good idea where the Black Madonna is," said Zora, turning to face her captor.

"If this is some sort of ploy to buy time . . ."

"It isn't," said Zora. "Which bedroom belonged to Annie Palmer?"

"How the hell should I know?" asked Terrence, now showing signs of strain.

"What difference does that make, Zora?" asked Sam.

"Milton told me that Annie Palmer used to watch her lovers in her bedroom without them knowing it. He said that she would spy on them from inside a wall in the bedroom. I thought that was just embellishment to an already over-the-top legend, but according to Milton, there had recently been a discovery of a wall that led to a hidden room. I need to find out which one of the bedrooms belonged to Annie Palmer."

"The museum guide should know," said Sam.

"I'm way ahead of you," replied Zora, as she hurried out of the room and ran down the stairs to the room where Felice and the museum guide and the guard were still sitting tied up. She quickly crossed the room and untied the kerchief which bound the woman's mouth.

"Which one is Annie Palmer's room?" asked Zora.

Pearl Forsythe remained silent. Her eyes defiant.

"Please," said Zora. "If you don't help me, he'll kill us all."

Pearl spoke bitterly. "He'll kill us anyway. I'm not helping him, or you, find this damned painting!"

Sam walked into the room and knelt beside the woman. "Ma'am, if you don't help us, your death, and everyone else's death, is a certainty. If you do help us, there may be hope, and hope, no matter how remote, is all we have going for us right now."

Pearl stared at him for a moment, then she replied, "It's at the top of the stairs, the second room to the right."

"Do you know anything about the secret chamber in Annie's bedroom?" asked Zora.

Pearl scoffed, "Of course I do! After all, I am a historian and my particular specialty is Rose Hall. There is a chamber located just behind the wall behind her dresser. Anyone who knows anything about the history of this place knows about that room!!!"

"Thank you," said Zora. "You may just have saved all our lives."

Pearl scoffed. "I wouldn't count on it. This is an evil man we're dealing with. We're not getting out of here alive!"

Zora ignored those words. Followed closely by Sam, she brushed by Terrence Phillips who stood surveying the scene with a grim smile playing about his lips. Bounding up the stairs and down the hallway, she ran through the open door into Annie Palmer's bedroom. The room had mahogany floors like the other rooms in the house, and it was dominated by a large four poster bed. The silk wallpaper was a pale shade of pink and the walls were covered with pictures of various tropical flowers. There was a wooden dresser in the corner, and a small writing table with an antique chair on the other side of the bed. Sheer white curtains danced in the breeze coming through an open window.

"O.K.," said Sam, "help me push the dresser aside."

Zora moved quickly. They had three minutes left until 11:05. She forced those thoughts out of her mind. She couldn't let herself be ruled by fear! They had come this far. Somehow, some way, they were going to get out of this alive. They pushed the dresser to one side to find a wall that looked like any other wall in the room.

Zora's heart sank. She'd thought the wall would open as if by magic, but it did not part like the Dead Sea. Then she remembered what Milton had told her: *Annie would knock on the wall, and then it would move.*

Zora pounded on the wall with her fists frantically and nothing happened. For a moment her mind seemed to reel with the possibility that she had been wrong and so had Milton and in less than three minutes she would be responsible for the deaths of three people.

Taking a deep breath, she tried again. Knocking on the wall in earnest, she yelled, "Open up! Open up!"

She knew that she sounded like a crazy woman but she was past the point of caring. This had to be where the portrait was located. It just had to be! Just as she was ready to admit defeat, the wall moved slowly to the side and she found herself facing a room no larger than a closet. Inside the dark room was the outline of what she knew in her heart was the Black Madonna.

"You did it," said Sam.

"Yes," Terrence Phillips said, behind her, "you did it. You're a remarkable woman, Zora Redwood."

Zora walked in the room and lifted up the portrait. It was covered with a large silk cloth.

She took the portrait out of the room and placed it on Annie Palmer's bed.

"Unwrap it," Terrence Phillips said, barely containing his anticipation.

Zora forced her hands to remain steady. She removed the cloth from the picture, and revealed the Black Madonna. Sam stood next to the bed looking down at the portrait. Terrence Phillips remained in the doorway.

"Give it to me," said Terrence. His voice sounded cold and deadly to Zora's ears.

Zora lifted the portrait carefully and carried it to Terrence Phillips. Glancing at Sam, she saw that his face remained impassive. She could not tell from his eyes what he was thinking.

Terrence grabbed the portrait from Zora's hands. For a moment he studied it carefully, as if determining if the portrait was real. Then, with a slow, smile, he pronounced, "Milton is to be commended. He took good care of the Black Madonna. It seems to be in perfect condition."

Sam spoke up. "What do you intend to do with my property?"

Terrence regarded him coolly. "I suppose that's a fair question," he said. "You do, after all, have a right to know. I intend to sell it for a great deal of money, but not before I've examined it to see if there really is a map which shows where the diamonds are."

"That story is old news," said Sam. "If there was a map hidden in the portrait, don't you think that my family would have found it by now?"

"Perhaps," said Terrence, "but perhaps you all aren't as resourceful as I am. We'll find out soon, won't we—or more accurately, I'll find out. I'm afraid that neither you, nor your charming lady-friend, are going to live long enough to find out much of anything."

Zora felt her heart start to hammer in her chest. She'd known, of course, that this was a distinct possibility. Terrence Phillips had killed Milton; there was no reason to believe that he wouldn't kill again.

She looked at Sam; his expression was inscrutable. Now would be a good time, she thought, for Sam to put into use any plans of escape that he might be harboring. As for her, she was fresh out of ideas. Still, she hoped for a miracle.

"Let Zora and the others go," said Sam. "They have nothing to do with this. You've got the portrait, you can very easily disappear."

"That's very gentlemanly of you," said Terrence. "I would have expected you to beg for your own life, Sam. After all, a man like you, so successful, so powerful, has so much to live for."

"You underestimate me," said Sam, coolly.

The two men stared at each other in silence, then, from the open window, Zora heard the sound of an approaching car. Her heart rose. *Help!* She almost screamed the word, until she saw the steel glint of Terrence's gun pointing in her direction.

"Come on," said Terrence, his tone harsh. "We're going back to the sitting room downstairs. Someone has apparently decided to pay us a visit—a very foolish person."

Sam sat next to Zora on the small antique settee in the corner of the room. Across from him, Felice and her companions sat bound on a brocade sofa. Terrence Phillips stood by the closed door, his gun pointed at Sam and Zora. He'd warned them all to be silent and not to try anything, but Sam's mind raced with the different possibilities of getting away from this madman. Nothing seemed viable or practical at this point, but Sam had not given up. He hoped that whoever was outside would provide them with the means to escape.

Ma Louise, help me. The words came from somewhere inside him. *Help me, please.*

He heard the front door of the mansion open slowly, and a sense of powerlessness overcame him. Whoever this person was, he was entering a potentially deadly situation. He wanted to call out, or do something, anything, to warn this person, but the gun pointed in his direction ensured his silence for now. He cursed himself for allowing Zora to accompany him into this mess. As stubborn as the woman he loved was, he was more stubborn and more determined than she. The fact that she was here by his side meant that he'd wanted her here.

Now she was in as much danger as he was, because he'd been too weak to make her go away.

The sound of footsteps on the wooden floor pulled Sam's thoughts back to the present. He watched Terrence Phillips move away from the door and walk over to where he and Zora sat. Sam was close enough to knock the gun out of Terrence's hands, but if he failed, he would be responsible for the death of at least one person in the room.

"Don't be foolish," Terrence hissed, as if he read Sam's thoughts.

The door to their room opened suddenly and Sam's mouth dropped open in surprise.

"Shelly Wong, as I live and breathe!" Terrence's lips broadened into a smile. "I underestimated you, my dear."

Shelly Wong surveyed the scene in front of her; unlike Terrence, she did not find the situation amusing. She was dressed in a long white dress which clung to her body. Her long hair was piled on top of her head in a mass of brown curls held together by a black ribbon. She did not look like a woman who had recently been in the hospital. She had a gun in her hand.

Shutting the door behind her, she snarled, "I should have killed you when I had the chance, Terrence."

"Now, now, my dear—as you can probably tell, this isn't the time, nor is it the place to settle old scores." Terrence's voice remained calm, but Sam could see that he was no longer smiling.

"Settle old scores?!" Shelly's voice rose and cracked like a whip. "You call attempting to kill me an old score? And what about Milton? Killing him was never in the plan!"

"My dear, you knew what the end result of Milton's betrayal was—you're many things Shelly, most of them admirable, but you're not naïve."

"I don't say that Milton didn't need killing," said Shelly, her hands jerking around her for emphasis, "but if anyone should have killed Milton, it should have been me!"

"How could you?!" Zora's voice rose in indignation.

Shelly turned to face Zora. "Ah, Miss Redwood. I would think that you of all people would waste no sympathy on Milton."

"I thought you loved him," said Zora.

Shelly laughed. "Tina Turner said it best—*What's love got to do with it?* Milton was fun, but he became boring very quickly. The most exciting thing about him was his willingness to become a thief—but then he turned on everybody, including me!!! He put me directly in the line of danger—I knew that he was the cause of the shooting. You don't cross men like our friend Terrence here without any consequences—but I must say, I expected broken bones. I did not, Terrence, expect murder. I did not expect to get shot."

"Did you know where the portrait was hidden all along?" asked Terrence.

"You answer my question first," said Shelly, "then I'll think about answering yours."

"You're lucky you're beautiful," said Terrence, "or I would have finished the job that security guard was unable to finish—but go ahead, what's your question, Shelly?"

"Why did you shoot me?"

"What difference does it make, Shelly. You obviously survived, none the worse for your experience."

"After everything I've been through I deserve to know the truth," Shelly snarled.

Terrence sighed, "I suppose you have a right to know. I shot you to send Milton a message. I wanted him to understand the consequences of his actions. Now, did you know where the portrait was all along?"

"Not exactly," said Shelly, walking slowly towards Terrence. Sam thought that she was remarkably cool even if she had a gun in her hand. "I didn't know the location. Milton told me he hid it somewhere in Rose Hall Mansion, but he didn't tell me the precise place. I have to give him credit for not trusting me, it was the smartest thing he ever did."

"What the hell is going on here, and who the hell is Milton?" Pearl Forsythe's words turned everyone's attention in her direction.

"That's not your concern," replied Terrence. "If I were you, I'd be more worried about my immediate future."

"The hell with that, and the hell with you. If you're going to shoot me, go ahead. You won't get away with it!" the woman snapped. "I don't know how I could have ever mistaken you for a gentleman. You are nothing more than a common thug!"

"It seems that you just make enemies wherever you go," Shelly purred at Terrence.

Turning to look at Zora, she said, "Do you still waste your sympathy on Milton—even knowing that because of him you're going to be killed?"

"Milton's dead," replied Zora quietly. "He no longer has the ability to kill anyone."

"What a nasty person you are," Pearl said to Shelly. "Whoever this Milton person was, he was a fool to have anything to do with you!"

Shelly smiled at the tour guide. "If Terrence doesn't kill you, I will."

Sam placed his hands on his lap. Forcing his breath to remain steady despite his racing heart, he looked around the room one more time, trying to formulate a plan, an immediate plan for getting out of the room alive. He was not going to sit here and let Terrence, or the equally mad Shelly Wong, shoot him and the people in this room.

"All this talk about killing," Terrence said mildly. "How do you plan on accomplishing any killing tonight, Shelly? After all, I have a gun, too, and it's pointed in your direction."

Shelly smiled. "I have my ways, dear. Trust me."

She looked over at Sam. "I met some interesting people today. Your brother, Justin—who I may add was quite attractive—and your sister Celia, an earnest do-gooder if I ever saw one."

Sam's heart beat faster and he felt his mouth go dry. Leveling his dark eyes at Shelly, he said, his voice low and deadly, "If you harmed one hair on their heads, I'll—"

"You'll what?" said Shelly. "Kill me? I'm like a cat, darling. Nine lives and counting—but don't you worry. I didn't harm the dears—I must say that their concern for you was quite touching."

Sam breathed easier, but he wondered what his brother and sister were doing on the island. They were probably trying to find him, but if he should get out of this predicament, he would wring their necks for putting themselves in danger.

"I'm getting tired of all this conversation, Shelly," said Terrence. "What do you want? I'm not paying you anything for the picture. I found it without your assistance."

"Oh, I'm sorry to hear that." Shelly raised the gun she was holding so that it was a few inches away from Terrence's chest.

Now is the time! It was as if his grandmother was in the room with him, so clear was her voice to Sam. *"Now is the time to act, Sam!"*

"Are you completely crazy?" asked Terrence, his gun now pointing at Shelly.

"Why, yes . . ." she said. "I am crazy. Crazy as a fox!"

Her eyes gleamed as she pulled the trigger and Sam heard a deafening noise as Terrence fell to the floor.

"He who hesitates is lost," crooned Shelly, as she stood still pointing the gun at Terrence. "You should have shot me as soon as I walked in the door."

She walked over to where Terrence lay, and pulled the trigger again. She turned to pick up the portrait which Terrence had carried with him to the sitting room.

"Now, Sam, now!" His grandmother's voice pushed him to action.

As Shelly examined the portrait, her eyes shining as she stared at the Black Madonna, Sam sprang from his seat and with all of his force knocked Shelly over, sending both the gun and the portrait flying in the air.

Pinned to the ground, Shelly cursed at Sam, her beautiful mouth screaming words that would make a hard-drinking sailor seem modest by comparison.

The portrait crashed to the ground and the frame broke apart. Sam's family had never changed the frame and Sam knew that after all this time it was fragile.

"Get the gun, Zora!" Sam called out.

"Holy Mother of God!" Pearl called out. "Kill that crazy woman before she kills us!"

Putting all his weight on Shelly, he pinned her arms above her head with one hand.

"Sam, oh . . ." Zora's voice faltered.

"Did you get the gun—" Sam turned to look at Zora and for a moment lost his voice as his eyes stared at diamonds, seemingly hundreds of white diamonds, which lay scattered on the floor.

"Your ancestor's diamonds," said Zora. "You found them."

"Shoot him!" Shelley yelled at Zora, her eyes wild. "Shoot him! Shoot them all! We can split the diamonds! We'll be rich!"

Zora stared at Shelly as if she'd suddenly grown three heads.

"If you don't kill him, you won't get anything!" screamed Shelly. "At least, with me, you have a chance at being rich—rich beyond your dreams, Zora! Think of it! Shoot him before he betrays you, just like Milton did—"

Zora shook her head slowly. When she spoke, her voice was loud, clear, and firm. "My Sam is nothing like Milton."

Sam felt his lips curve into a smile. She'd called him *my Sam*—and she'd defended him.

"You can be rich!" Shelly called out.

"I don't want to be rich," said Zora. "I want Sam."

Sam felt Shelly's body beneath him sag in defeat. Not loosening his grip on her arms, Sam turned to face Zora, and said, "I know this is probably the most inappropriate time to say this, but nevertheless, it must be said—I love you, Zora Redwood, and when this madness is over, I would be honored if you would be my wife."

"Say yes, child!" Pearl called out. "Say yes, or I will!"

"Sam, we've known each other less than a week," said Zora. "Under the circumstances, perhaps we're rushing things, don't you think?"

"I've never been more sure of anything in my life," said Sam. "I'm not letting you go, Zora!"

"For God's sake, don't make the man beg!" Pearl Forsythe snapped.

The security guard, for his part, grunted his agreement even though he was still bound and gagged.

"What about a long engagement?" Zora asked. "So we can actually get to know each other . . . under normal circumstances?"

"I'll wait as long as it takes, Zora Redwood . . . just say yes," said Sam.

"If I didn't have a gun in my hand, I'd kiss you, Sam Trahan," said Zora. "But yes, I'll marry you."

"You stupid little fool!" said Shelly. "Even if you marry him, you'll never have control of his money—"

"Shelly, the way I see it, of all the fools in this room, you're the fool heading to jail for murder, so I guess that means that you're the biggest fool in here!"

Sam smiled at Zora. "Well said, Miss Redwood."

Zora beamed at him.

"We come to rescue you and we find you romancing a beautiful woman!"

Sam turned to find himself facing Justin and Celia, who were standing in the entrance of the room.

"What the hell are you two doing here?!" Sam said sharply.

"Rescuing you!" said Celia, smiling at her big brother. "But it looks like you've done a pretty good job of that yourself."

"We followed Shelly by car until she turned into the entrance for this place. We parked halfway down the road and made the rest of the way by foot. We didn't want to alert her to our arrival," said Justin.

Sam turned to Justin. "How could you bring Celia into this, she could have been hurt!"

"We came to help you, Sam—and there was nothing Justin could do to stop me from coming with him," said Celia.

"Help me?"

"Yes, help you," replied Justin. "We thought that you might need some help—especially after our visit with Shelly Wong."

Sam felt a sense of peace wash over him. It was as if different parts of him had all suddenly come together. Justin had come to help him, despite their differences, despite their history, despite everything, he was here with him. *Family first* said a voice which Sam knew belonged to his grandmother.

Thank you, Sam said silently. *Wherever you are, Ma Louise—thank you.*

Sam looked over at his brother. "Thanks for watching my back."

Justin smiled. "Someone's got to do it, it might as well be me."

"Sam," said Celia, "I hate to interrupt this family togetherness since it doesn't happen too often, but who are all these people, why are they tied up, and why are there diamonds all over the floor?"

Pulling himself away from his brother, Sam said, "It's a long story, sis."

"What about this lady with the gun in her hand?" asked Celia. "Is this the Zora Redwood that I've heard so much about?"

"This," said Sam, staring down at Zora, "is my future wife."

Handing the gun to Justin, Zora said, "Keep it pointed at the woman on the floor." Then Zora turned to face Celia, her future sister-in-law. "Nice to meet you," she smiled.

Sam pulled her close. He wanted to kiss her thoroughly. He wanted to lose himself in her forever, but forever would have to wait a little while longer. There were three hostages to get freed, and there was one murderess, the body of one thief and a briefcase full of money that had to be delivered to the police. Instead, he kissed her lightly on her lips.

"I'll make you happy, Zora," he promised in a whisper.

"You already have," replied Zora. "You already have."

Somewhere, Sam heard his grandmother's laughter.

One year later

Zora stared in the mirror and did not recognize the woman in the long white dress smiling back at her. It was her wedding day. She'd dreamed of this day, but her dreams in no way foretold the joy she felt. She'd thought that she'd be nervous, but as she stood in her parents' bedroom surrounded by her mother, Aunt Essie, Celia and her future mother-in-law, she knew that she was where she was always meant to be . . . on her way to joining Sam. Her mother wiped away a stray tear and Zora squeezed her hand. There still needed to be healing in her relationship with her parents, but this year had brought them closer and Zora knew in her heart that things would work out for them. They had love, and that was a necessary ingredient for reconciliation.

A knock on the bedroom door distracted her for a moment. Then she heard Sam's voice call out, "Where is my bride?"

"You can't see her!" his sister called out. "It's bad luck!"

"What is it, Sam?" Zora asked.

"I just wanted to tell you that I love you," he said through the closed door.

She heard Aunt Essie giggle. It did Zora's heart good to see that Aunt Essie was learning to let laughter back into her life.

"I love you too, Sam," Zora replied.

"And I also wanted to tell you to hurry up, woman! Twelve months, three days, and ten hours is enough time for any man to wait to get married!"

Zora shook her head and said, "What am I going to do with you, Sam?"

She heard a deep chuckle come from behind the door. Then, he replied, "Marry me, and we'll both find out!"

ACKNOWLEDGMENTS

All blessings, great and small, come from the Lord, and so I first give my thanks to the Lord for the blessing of this novel that represents a new venture and a new road for me.

As always, I thank the men in my life for standing firmly in my corner and giving me love and support; thank you Ken and Jamaal for inspiring me daily, and for unselfishly allowing me to pursue my dreams. To little Michael, who wants to write books with me, thanks for letting me in your life.

For the rest of my family: Mummy, Mark, Paul, Barbara, Khadijah, Michelle, Micah, and the littlest McCarthy who will make his or her presence known by the time this book is published, I may not say it often enough but "one love."

To Kathi, Joyce, Lessie, Vonda, Robyn, Angie, Stephanie, Charmaine, Guilene, Dianne, where would I be without my sistergirl support group? Big Ups to you, ladies! Thanks to the Louards for their constant encouragement and thanks to Marla and Frank—I hope you enjoy the novel on our next trip together. Thanks to Tina Majkut for coming up with a great title for my novel! To my editor, Karen Thomas, for her guidance, expertise and support through this exciting process and to my wonderful agent, Manie Barron, for guiding me to Karen, many, many thanks! To Jessica McLean, much appreciation for your encouragement!

I'm sure I've left out many names of folks who have given their love and support to my writing, and I apologize for that, but I would be remiss if I did not thank my sister Jacquelin Thomas, for her constant support and advice; thank you and God bless!

For the beautiful island of Jamaica, my first home and the wonderful people who inhabit that slice of paradise—forward, Jamaica! Thanks to my Jamaican family members: the Coores, the Daleys, the Clarkes, the Christies, and Pitters and the Myers family.

To every reader who picks up my novel, thank you for sharing your time with me.

Finally, I want to thank my beloved Daddy, who even now is encouraging me from his seat in heaven. Love you, always and forever!

ABOUT THE AUTHOR

Janette McCarthy Louard was born in Jamaica, West Indies, and grew up in Harlem, New York. She started writing short stories as a child in Jamaica and further pursued her dream of writing novels at Wellesley College, where she graduated cum laude. After graduating from Columbia law school, Janette practiced law until she gave in to the lure of her first love, writing. She has published two previous novels, *Mama's Girls* and *Sisterhood Situation*. *Portrait of Deception* is her first romance.

Check Out These Other
Dafina Novels

Sister Got Game
0-7582-0856-1

by Leslie Esdaile
$6.99US/**$9.99**CAN

Say Yes
0-7582-0853-7

by Donna Hill
$6.99US/**$9.99**CAN

In My Dreams
0-7582-0868-5

by Monica Jackson
$6.99US/**$9.99**CAN

True Lies
0-7582-0027-7

by Margaret Johnson-Hodge
$6.99US/**$9.99**CAN

Testimony
0-7582-0637-2

by Felicia Mason
$6.99US/**$9.99**CAN

Emotions
0-7582-0636-4

by Timmothy McCann
$6.99US/**$9.99**CAN

The Upper Room
0-7582-0889-8

by Mary Monroe
$6.99US/**$9.99**CAN

Got A Man
0-7582-0242-3

by Daaimah S. Poole
$6.99US/**$8.99**CAN

Available Wherever Books Are Sold!

Check out our website at www.kensingtonbooks.com.

Look For These Other
Dafina Novels

If I Could
0-7582-0131-1

by Donna Hill
$6.99US/**$9.99**CAN

Thunderland
0-7582-0247-4

by Brandon Massey
$6.99US/**$9.99**CAN

June In Winter
0-7582-0375-6

by Pat Phillips
$6.99US/**$9.99**CAN

Yo Yo Love
0-7582-0239-3

by Daaimah S. Poole
$6.99US/**$9.99**CAN

When Twilight Comes
0-7582-0033-1

by Gwynne Forster
$6.99US/**$9.99**CAN

It's A Thin Line
0-7582-0354-3

by Kimberla Lawson Roby
$6.99US/**$9.99**CAN

Perfect Timing
0-7582-0029-3

by Brenda Jackson
$6.99US/**$9.99**CAN

Never Again Once More
0-7582-0021-8

by Mary B. Morrison
$6.99US/**$8.99**CAN

Available Wherever Books Are Sold!

Check out our website at www.kensingtonbooks.com.

Grab These Other
Dafina Novels
(trade paperback editions)

Grab These Other
Thought Provoking Books

Adam by Adam
0-7582-0195-8

by Adam Clayton Powell, Jr.
$15.00US/$21.00CAN

African American Firsts
0-7582-0243-1

by Joan Potter
$15.00US/$21.00CAN

African-American Pride
0-8065-2498-7

by Lakisha Martin
$15.95US/$21.95CAN

The African-American Soldier
0-8065-2049-3

by Michael Lee Lanning
$16.95US/$24.95CAN

African Proverbs and Wisdom
0-7582-0298-9

by Julia Stewart
$12.00US/$17.00CAN

Al on America
0-7582-0351-9

by Rev. Al Sharpton
with Karen Hunter
$16.00US/$23.00CAN

Available Wherever Books Are Sold!

Visit our website at **www.kensingtonbooks.com**